"We do not have to get married," Vivian whispered, clasping his coat.

Everleigh put his arm around her waist. "We must."

"I don't care if I'm ruined," she said. "I'm almost anticipating it. It's not bad compared to what I've been through."

"It isn't fair to you," he muttered. "You deserve to be respected. A place among the *ton*. Vivian, will you marry me?" he asked.

Something concerned him. He should feel sad that Vivian was ruined. He should feel sorry for his culpability in all this. But he didn't. He just wondered why he'd not kissed her more in the carriage.

LIZ TYNER

—

Compromised into Marriage

HARLEQUIN
HISTORICAL

ISBN-13: 978-1-335-50541-5

Compromised into Marriage

Copyright © 2020 by Elizabeth Tyner

Recycling programs for this product may not exist in your area.

This edition published by arrangement with Harlequin Books S.A.

For questions and comments about the quality of this book, please contact us at CustomerService@Harlequin.com.

Harlequin Enterprises ULC
22 Adelaide St. West, 40th Floor
Toronto, Ontario M5H 4E3, Canada
www.Harlequin.com

Printed in U.S.A.

Liz Tyner lives with her husband on an Oklahoma acreage she imagines is similar to the ones in the children's book *Where the Wild Things Are*. Her lifestyle is a blend of old and new, and is sometimes comparable to the way people lived long ago. Liz is a member of various writing groups and has been writing since childhood. For more about her visit liztyner.com.

Books by Liz Tyner

Harlequin Historical

The Notorious Countess
The Runaway Governess
The Wallflower Duchess
Redeeming the Roguish Rake
Saying I Do to the Scoundrel
To Win a Wallflower
It's Marriage or Ruin
Compromised into Marriage

English Rogues and Grecian Goddesses

Safe in the Earl's Arms
A Captain and a Rogue
Forbidden to the Duke

Visit the Author Profile page
at Harlequin.com.

Chapter One

~~~~~

She ached to stay alive.

Vivian put one foot in front of the other, her arm linked in her older companion's for support. The morning's rain still lingered in puddles and Vivian knew she would mark her half-boots with mud. She'd not left her home in three months and she was going to take a stroll with Mavis, or else.

She wished to be wearing her new dancing slippers, but that had been a frivolous purchase. Another pair to wear when she was alone, then hide away so no one would know how much she wished to attend soirées.

Her former governess gave her a sideways glance and Vivian smiled. They could do it. She could do it.

They walked down Park Lane, then turned so they could stroll past the town houses and return to their own home.

Vivian's heart pounded. Perhaps the words the physician had told her mother had been correct. Perhaps she should accept that she would not live to see another birthday.

She didn't really notice the town coach slowing at the

side of the street. Two liveried men guided the horses to a stop. Drivers and horses were routinely going about their work. One of the coachmen dismounted as Vivian and Mavis walked alongside the carriage.

Mavis stepped close to the vehicle, avoiding a deposit from a horse.

The door swung open—there were no steps beneath it. Before Vivian could react, the door crashed into Mavis's head.

Thwack.

Mavis's bonnet bounced from her head as silver hair splayed out and she slumped to the ground, unconscious.

Life blasted through Vivian's limbs. She called out her companion's name.

Mavis stirred.

'My pardon.' The man who'd opened the carriage door rushed the words, while his clasp on both of Vivian's arms lifted her aside as effortlessly as a chess piece.

He knelt over Mavis, assessing her injuries. Mavis moaned.

Fear clutched at Vivian, freezing her movements.

'Jasper. Go for the physician,' he shouted to the coachman. Then he lifted the older woman up, his movements swift, minimal and controlled. The shoulders of his coat tightened, but no strain showed on his face.

The servant slapped the ribands and the horses galloped away.

The stranger carried Mavis and, in only a few long strides, he was over the threshold of one of the town houses.

Vivian stood, still grasping what had just happened.

She clasped her bonnet strings, staring after the man who'd dashed away with her dearest friend in his arms.

She'd not thought someone with such long legs could have changed direction, crouched, stopped, then raced into action again. She'd watched, confusion flittering through her mind at what was happening in front of her.

She pulled her thoughts together and gathered all her resources. Then she rushed as fast as she could to the doorway without having any idea whose house it was. Nothing mattered but that she help Mavis.

Once inside the entrance, she noticed everything about the home gleamed, which somehow eased her fears.

A butler, mouth open, stared at her as she stopped in the entry. He didn't seem to know whether to run after his employer, or attend to her.

'Where's Mavis?' she asked.

He pointed to the stairway. 'Door on the right.'

She grasped her skirt in both hands and ignored all the things Mavis had taught her about being a proper lady. She ran up the stairs, her breaths coming quickly from the effort, reticule bouncing.

At the top, she shot through the open door, the butler following in her wake.

Mavis was on a sofa. The tall man stood over her, knees bent, and his shoulders obscuring Mavis.

Vivian moved to the left, reassured to see her companion awake.

'Just a bump. A bump.' Mavis reached up, her gloved hand touching her nose. When she pulled back her hand, she saw the blood, wavered, and slumped against the cushions.

The black-coated man whirled to the butler. 'Wain-cott. Fetch Mrs Rush.'

The servant retreated, following the order.

The man saw Vivian. He moved forward, his touch skimming Vivian's arm, reassuring her. 'My house-keeper will help. She'll know what to do until the physician gets here.'

His attention returned to Mavis as she stirred again.

Moments later, an older female rushed past Vivian. 'Let me see to her.' She carried a bowl of water. 'Stand back, Everleigh.'

She put the container on a table and bent over Mavis, who was mumbling about the pain.

'What day is it?' The housekeeper sloshed the cloth in the basin.

'The day I got whacked on the head.'

'Yes.' The housekeeper touched Mavis's chin, moving it a bit so she could examine her closely. 'Your nose has already stopped bleeding. You're going to have the biggest black shiner I ever saw. Let me wipe away the blood to see the damage. Next, we'll work on a good tale for you to tell about getting thumped by a jealous debutante.'

Mavis laughed.

The housekeeper directed a comment to Vivian. 'Leave it to me. She's got a drop of blood on her clothes. I want to get it out before it sets.'

'Will she be fine?' Vivian asked, her clasp tight at her chest.

'Most certainly I will,' Mavis answered, her voice gaining strength. 'Give me an instant to catch my breath, Vivian, and we'll take our leave.'

The man in the black frock coat fixed his ice-blue

gaze on Vivian. In seconds, she felt he'd beheld her so closely that she could have left the room and, had he been an artist, he could have sketched a complete likeness of her.

Then he spoke to Mavis. 'You'll not be leaving until the carriage is back, the physician has seen you and my coachmen can escort you home. And only then if the physician is convinced it is safe.'

The lady who'd rushed to Mavis's side wrung out a rag, splashing water in the bowl. 'I'll be the judge of when she's able to move.' She stretched the cloth wide. 'Us vixens got to stick together.'

Mavis chuckled.

When she realised her friend could laugh, Vivian's strength waned as quickly as a marionette with its strings removed.

'I need to sit, sir.' She gazed up at him.

She felt his fingers clamp on both her arms again as he pulled her to him, keeping her aloft by the power in his hands and his gaze. 'Were you injured?'

'No,' she whispered. 'Not until you grasped my arms.'

She almost stumbled he released her so fast. Her breathing took all her strength.

She saw a force in front of her that she'd never bet against and her knees weakened again. Then his eyes warmed, consoling her.

His arm caught her waist and his broad shoulders were no longer imposing, but bolstering. He guided her into a library smelling faintly of tobacco. Leading her to a chair big enough for her to curl up and sleep in, he released her, moving slowly so he would be ready should she fall. She could feel his touch in a different way than she'd felt anyone else's.

'You're shaken from seeing your companion's blood,' he stated.

She shook her head, and let herself slide into the chair. 'No. I'm just...' She smiled and shrugged. 'I'm dying. I saw the letter my mother wrote my aunt before she sealed it. It's a secret. Mustn't let anyone find out.' She settled and held an extended index finger to her lips in a mock command to shush him. 'There's no hope. Nothing can be done.'

For all the weakness she felt in her bones, she could see the opposite in him.

He stood solid—a man who could make Almack's patronesses fluster. He had more strength in his voice than she could ever remember having in her whole body. But at this moment, his gaze told her he would use all his resources for her comfort and the knowledge rushed through her with intensity.

'I overtired myself.' She sat straighter. 'We would be pleased to allow your carriage to see us home later. We'd much appreciate it.' She emphasised, '*I* would much appreciate it.'

'Would you like water or...' he observed her expression '...or brandy?'

She waved away the drink. 'I'm worried about my companion.'

'She is in good care. My housekeeper, Mrs Rush—well...' he shrugged, smiling '...you'd have to know her. And I much regret the accident.'

'As long as Mavis recovers, I'll forgive you.' She met his deep blue examination. She saw his knowledge that he'd already been forgiven.

'Then we must see she recovers.' He walked to a decanter, touched the stopper, then looked over his shoulder at her. 'You're sure?'

She nodded. 'I need to rest. Being ill is tiresome.'

'What illness do you have?'

She reached to pull up the shoulder of her gown. Her clothes all seemed to fall from her body.

'I had an accident involving a horse where my sides were bruised and I've never got over it. I take more and more medicines and I get weaker and weaker. The physician said my bile is building. He claims my humours are in severe disorder... Hope is diminished. He doesn't expect me to recover.' She forced a smile. 'That is what my mother wrote my aunt. The doctor tells me, "These things take time. We'll have you dancing soon."'

'I can have my physician speak with you after he sees to your friend.'

The idea tempted her. A chance. 'Who is the physician?'

'Gavin Hamilton.'

She waved the idea away, trying not to show emotion. 'I've seen him already. Not long after Mother's doctor became concerned. Hamilton could find nothing wrong with me. He said I should recover completely. My mother's physician was furious that we had consulted someone else. He said the man was insensible to not see the obvious. He increased the dosage of my medicinals and hot plasters. I have enough Fowler's solution to begin my own apothecary shop.'

'You must speak with Hamilton again. He's the best physician in London. It should hurt nothing. Give the man something pleasant to do, to have a patient as charming as you.'

She laughed and let her eyelids fall while shaking her head. 'Mother's doctor has been treating the family since before she was born. She trusts him.'

He crossed to her.

'You will let Hamilton be the judge of that,' his words commanded softly.

'He cannot help me.'

He reached up, brushing back a lock of her hair and she knew he felt dampness on her skin.

His touch soothed her.

'This chair is so comfortable.' She grasped the leather. 'It has the scent of a new pair of riding boots. I could fall asleep here.'

'I don't know about the scent of a chair.' She noticed his hand brushing her forehead again. 'But the lady sitting in it smells of roses and is quite lovely enough to be the entire garden.'

She let her lips turn up in acknowledgment of his compliment. 'I do not mind being ill so much.' Biting her lip, she hid her expression from him. 'I just wish I had more time to live. I'm never allowed to attend any soirées now, as my mother fears the exertion will make me worse and refuses all invitations.'

He reached behind him and pulled up a foot rest, sitting on it.

He clasped her hand. Even through her doeskin gloves, his touch transferred strength into her body.

'You should dance. You should live each second,' he spoke, the same timbre in his words a father might use in speaking with a favoured child.

'After the accident, my mother has seen me guarded and fussed over more than any newborn infant. She cries if she sees me dancing, afraid I am overtiring myself and preventing my recovery. Mother is napping now, or I would not have been allowed to leave the house.'

'She loves you dearly. I have not had an occasion where I could be treated so.'

'Oh, you wouldn't like it.' She shuddered. 'Although it's easy to fall into the trap of having lemonade brought to you before you raise your arm, or a shawl before the air has a chill. After my accident, Mother hired two maids more for me.' Vivian laughed.

'Can you imagine, trying to rest while having a maid staring at your every movement so she might give you a handkerchief or anything you want? One day, I said I must have a pair of new gloves. I sent one servant to Bond Street and I sent the other to purchase confectioneries.' She let out a satisfied breath. 'I had an afternoon to myself. Then when they returned, we admired the gloves and ate the treats.'

'Your mother wants the best for you.' His voice rumbled and she relaxed, wishing she could sit and listen to the roughened softness for hours.

He still held her hand and she realised she felt closer to him than she'd ever felt to another person—even Mavis. This was the first time being ill had had a benefit.

Vivian decided she had earned some licence because of the accident and her trials. She stowed propriety away. He sat much too near, she supposed, for only just meeting her. And she *was* ill. And he did have an interesting appearance, although not precisely handsome. His chin, maybe it was a bit too wide, or maybe his hair fell too straight, but, no—it suited him. She liked what she saw, especially since she'd seen him dash Mavis up in his arms.

She could not even let herself think about his legs— she'd not seen oak timbers that lean and strong.

'I wish... I just wish I could be like the others who go to soirées and waltz and flirt with kind gentlemen.' She heard the wistfulness in her voice.

'How do you feel,' he whispered to her, leaning so near she could smell ambergris, 'about flirting with an unkind gentleman?'

He moved close, closer than she'd ever been to a male other than her father.

'I suppose if that is what's available, I will take what I can get.' She savoured his proximity. 'Do you know any such men?'

'Only one present,' he whispered, standing and grasping her hands. He pulled her upright. 'May I have this waltz?'

He lifted her right hand high and his flattened at her back.

'I fear I'm too tired to dance.' She let an apology sound in her words and she drew away, but he didn't release her.

'I'm heartbroken.' His sincerity gave the words truth, whether they were true or not.

She reached to his shoulder, planning to push him back, but rested her fingers instead, feeling the firmness beneath. 'So am I. To have such a partner, and not be able to enjoy a waltz. But I—' His compassion touched her. 'I don't feel I am missing it so much now. To have been asked is as good as the dance, I believe.'

He stood, holding her as if he might whisk her into the steps. 'I'm pleased to assist you.'

The room was silent, even though she could hear street callers from outside the window.

'I realise we've had no introduction.'

'Maybe it is best.' She touched the lapel of his coat. 'Then we can pretend this didn't happen.'

She felt his hands slide to her waist. She didn't wear a firm corset—she had so little to be pulled tight. She could feel his touch pulse into her whole body. Strength blasted into her limbs.

'I won't pretend this didn't happen, although I see no reason to mention it to anyone.' He kept her close. 'A memory such as this is to be savoured.'

'I will enjoy the recollection as well.' She brushed at his chest, amazed at how solid he felt and that he didn't step away. She knew she could run her palm the full length or breadth of his waistcoat and he wouldn't move, or complain. But she stilled. She'd transgressed on his good nature too far already.

'I suppose you've decided I must escort you to your chaperon. Wise of you, I admit.'

Yes, it was wise of her. But she didn't want to be wise. She wanted to live life like the other women. She missed the soirées and the music, and the sight of something other than the walls of her house.

This was an opportunity, much like seeing a rainbow. When rain clouds disappeared and the colours suddenly appeared in the sky, she wanted to keep them in her sight for ever. But, they only lingered in the memory after fading away. Vivid colours strengthening in the sky, then vanishing. A memory to clasp before she slept.

A prospect that might never arrive again.

Like the man in front of her.

It was as if the same good fortune that created the

rainbows now worked to give her one last chance for something she had missed out on. She'd matured expecting that she would some day have a beloved and they would spend long evenings together, holding hands, whispering and, perhaps, sharing a kiss. That he would be the one she'd waited for.

But the time to wait had expired. She had to count the minutes left, not the days.

Sympathy flourished in his expression and nothing else in the world seemed to matter to him but her.

She gathered her courage, but she didn't really need it when she considered his expression. His gaze told her she could say anything in the world to him. Anything, and he would not have censured her or disapproved.

'You know I've never been kissed.' She gazed at him, knowing that this would be her last opportunity. She'd never been so bold with her former sweetheart and she'd regretted it after he'd left.

Particularly after she'd discovered she might never again have another prospect.

'Never?' His brows rose.

'Well, my gloves. But it wasn't impressive. I once saw a maid creep away with the stable boy and he kissed her, and she didn't appear to mind at all. They seemed amazed.'

He stepped back and moved to the door, still holding her hand. At the door, he shut it, then twirled her around so that her back rested against it. An arm's width separated them. He softly grasped her waist and his gaze made her feel cherished.

'But something for you to consider.' Seriousness tinged his words. 'To wonder about a kiss is to wonder.

But if you have one and like it, and can't have another, you might not be as happy as before. I'm certain of that.'

'You have a point.' She sighed. 'I suppose I must do the proper thing. As I have always done what is proper, I shouldn't change now.'

'Always?'

She tilted her head. 'Until just now. Then, I guess I felt a little sorry for myself and decided I might not have many more chances to be improper.'

She debated asking for a kiss again. Instead of speaking, she watched him move minutely, taking his time, and he pulled her into his arms. His body blended against hers and his hands secured her. Warm sensations rushed so fast she couldn't decipher them. She'd entered a dream of fairy dust.

'I might feel a little guilt,' he said as he watched her. 'But I can handle it. Can you?'

'I'd like to find out.'

His lips feathered hers, the briefest instant, the tiniest twinkling.

Her body warmed and new strength flourished.

When he released her, it almost felt as if she had stepped into a different world. He studied her.

Now she knew what a kiss was, and she could be satisfied, step away and be happy with the memory. Her heart fluttered. She didn't really want to step away. She wanted another kiss.

Disappointment overpowered her. Only one kiss. It had been rather like that first glimmer of a rainbow fading away before the colours brightened.

Her throat choked on all the words she could use to describe it.

She could not tell him how wonderful it was. How

much it had meant to her and how she would carry it inside her the rest of her life. Words would never tell him the truth of it and she could not put it into sentences. He had answered her question. But if she told him how it felt, it would seem as if she were asking for more and being truly improper. She must maintain what dignity she had left. 'It was adequate.'

'Adequate?' he asked, chin lowered as both brows rose.

She caught herself frowning, at a loss. How could she tell him he'd been correct when he'd said that she would want more?

'Thank you. That was kind of you.' She patted his upper arm and smiled her appreciation.

He deliberated. Then he took her cheeks in his hands and his eyelids lowered. He moved forward and his lips found hers, and this time they brought the promise of the full rainbow with them.

His fingertips slid down, down, until he clasped her waist and held her. The intensity behind his lips fused itself into her body. She sparkled into starlight.

His mouth kept touching, exploring and feeling her with a bursting sweetness, but also with the charge of a sip of brandy she shouldn't have taken. If not for his arms around her and the door at her back, she would have toppled to the floor.

To be held upright, aloft, by this man tingled her to her toes.

He backed away, still holding her upright. 'So, your first true kiss? Adequate?'

She found her voice. 'Exceedingly so. You taste of what I would think gunpowder should taste like if a female created it. All smoky and sparkly and a few more things for good measure.'

His lips curved and he brushed a kiss on her nose.

He ducked again, his lips taking her back to the place they'd been, only this time going deeper, further into the feelings. Further against her.

His mouth, tongue and body pressed, igniting and stealing breath.

He moved away from the kiss, his gaze darkened in a way she'd never seen.

After a few heartbeats, he said, 'I suppose we should see how your friend is faring.'

She put a palm on his coat, unable to feel him for the thickness of the fabric. 'We should.'

He rested his forehead against hers and still captured her. His voice spoke gentler than any man's she'd ever heard. 'Sweet, I tell you true when I say I would savour letting you learn all you wish to know about kisses, about a man's body, a man's desires and your own feelings. It would be a wonder.'

His lips almost touched hers. 'But it's not my place to teach you such things and I don't wish to think of you lying awake, alone, regretting our time together, or regretting that we cannot still be exploring each other.'

He stepped away. 'I could not be happy having a little of you and watching you go. I fear you are someone I might stay awake thinking of and not be satisfied because I couldn't hold you. You should return to your companion. If for no other reason, then for the sake of my sleep and my dreams.'

'I think I picked well for my first kiss.' She brushed the gloved tip of her finger across his chin and heard a quiet chuckle.

She didn't want to leave, but knew she must. Turning her head, she reached for the doorknob, but his hand was on it, reaching between her and the opening. He immediately moved aside, ushering her into the hallway.

The open door to the room where Mavis rested loomed in front of her.

'The carriage is at your disposal for as long as you need it,' he said. His footsteps sounded as he left, moving deeper into the house.

He didn't follow her and the disappointment gouged, but she knew he mustn't remain.

Vivian didn't interrupt the conversation between Mrs Rush and Mavis.

Inside the room, Mavis sat, her arms crossed and her mouth grim. 'I don't need a physician.'

'I'll send someone to tell him we don't need him,' the housekeeper said.

Mavis agreed.

'You've got a bump on the back of your head and some nice bruises. And a scratch on your nose.' The housekeeper inspected Mavis. 'You don't need being poked at. When my Jimmy was a lad, he had worse bumps and could still get two switchings by the end of the day.'

'I'm feeling much better,' Mavis said.

'A lady's ills are best treated by us.' The housekeeper dropped the cloth in the bowl of water. 'When I was young, we didn't go runnin' to physicians when we had a nose bleed. We learned quick how to manage for ourselves.'

'I have never needed a physician in my life.' Mavis

straightened her shoulders. 'And that's why I'm so healthy.'

'Are you ready to return home?' Vivian asked Mavis, concerned they might be missed.

Mavis shook her head. 'Soon, dear. I'm really dashed, right now.' She perused the housekeeper. 'The tea you've sent the maid for—did you say lemon balm with chamomile?'

The housekeeper nodded. 'A secret blend I learned from my aunt.'

Vivian saw another of the big chairs—she supposed an advantage of a household with a man such as she'd seen. She couldn't help herself. She moved to the chair, curled into it and relaxed.

'And I know the absolute best mixture for youthful skin, too,' the housekeeper whispered.

'Oh.' Mavis raised herself up. 'You must share. You must.'

'Well…' The housekeeper pushed at an errant curl slipping from her mob cap. 'I really do not tell just anyone, but the master did bump you about.'

Vivian felt herself droop and leaned back into the chair, dozing, dreaming of butterflies with attractive shoulders. Fluttering long eyelashes on them as well. And beautifully soft lips covering a masculine firmness. And they inspected her, their eyes so clear and so blue and so deep they were like staring into softly tinted glass that she could fall into and be surrounded by the shades, enveloping her into an azure-tinted world of sparkling sunshine.

She slid from her dream, surprised to discover butterflies could be so attractive. Then she tensed, realising she was being stared at.

Both women—Mavis, bedraggled, and the house-keeper—stood over her, staring down.

'You think it will work?' Mavis asked the house-keeper.

'Nothing to lose,' the other woman said, observing Vivian.

'What?' Vivian asked, body tensing.

'Now, dear, have I ever let you down?' Mavis purred, a black and yellowish cast above her cheeks.

Chapter Two

Five days later, Vivian sat in a hackney carriage with her arms crossed. She inspected the profane word carved into the side of the equipage near her elbow.

'If Mother finds out about this, she will lock me in my room.' Vivian brushed a strand of hair back into place.

Mavis slumped in the seat across from her, her bonnet sliding down over her ear. 'I assure you I'm not enjoying this either. If we'd not convinced your mother you were a bit better, she would never have gone with your father to visit her sister.' Mavis shook her head. 'Your mother trusts me.'

Vivian saw a cluster of briars and gorse beyond the window. 'We're going away from London. Down a country track, clouds in the sky—dark ones—and if it rains, we could be stuck here for days.'

'If we get stuck...' Mavis moved forward in her seat. 'Both your parents will find out and toss me into the street.'

'Convincing Mother I was feeling better was difficult. Without your help, I couldn't have managed.'

'We had no choice.' Mavis tapped her reticule against Vivian's knee. 'You're trembling even more, and weaker, I can tell. Maybe this woman can help. That housekeeper swears she can. Says she travels all about, studying remedies others use.'

'That doesn't mean they'll work.'

'Doesn't mean they won't. We had to leave while your mother is visiting your aunt because you know as well as I, she'd refuse to let you take such a journey. If you weren't so ill, I'd never let the vagrant near you. She claims to be a woman of remedies and fortunes, and will likely state she can cobble a pair of boots should she think she can get a coin from it. But the housekeeper said she trusts her like no other. It seems she works without charge for the poorest and claims to let the rich pay her double.'

'I cannot imagine how she will make me pay. My father is rich enough, but if he found out what I'm doing he would most likely send the magistrate for her.'

'The housekeeper affirms the woman, Ella Etta, saved her son once.' Mavis ducked her head, and her voice fell to a whisper. 'Vivian, we have to try. The physician hasn't helped you and it's been years. They've had their chance. *Chances.*'

'All my pin money went to hire this carriage.'

Mavis tapped her again with the reticule. 'And the silver vase in your room. I'm not sure how I'll explain that to your mother.'

'Oh, Lady Darius,' Vivian spoke in a mock-sweet voice, 'the vase? We hardly ever use it and I needed some coin to take your daughter deep into the woods and toss her to a vagabond who lives there. Your daughter… um… Vivian. No, haven't seen her since.'

Vivian dusted her gloves together and continued in the false tone. 'Fussy little thing. She wore holes in my ears with all her complaining when the carriage went over a bump, as if I had anything to do with putting the road there.'

Mavis opened her reticule and took out a handkerchief, then dotted her forehead. 'You are bearing up well. Just keep thinking things will work out for the best. Don't imagine us disappearing into the woods and never being seen of again. Our carcasses turning to weathered bones,' she muttered to herself. 'My bones will be weathered. They're already halfway there.'

Vivian let herself slide sideways in the seat and propped herself in the corner. 'Mavis. Mavis. Mavis. You've led me astray.' She brushed a glove over the window pane. 'Miles astray.'

The carriage listed to its side and lumbered along.

'We are slowing,' Mavis spoke, her voice toneless. 'I hope we are at our destination. Otherwise…'

Vivian couldn't keep herself from turning to the window. She saw two wagons, a donkey cart and a hut which might have been patched together from debris.

'The housekeeper said they would be here.' Mavis had a gloved hand at the window.

The door opened and the carriage steps were pulled down.

'Out,' Mavis commanded.

Vivian grimaced. 'You pretend to be the rich, ill daughter of the baron. I'll watch and see what happens.'

Mavis slapped at Vivian's leg. 'Out. Act like a diamond of the first water. These are common folk. They will expect it.'

Vivian stepped to the ground, thankful her legs held her upright.

The driver appeared ready to leave them without a backward glance. She hoped he remembered how upset she'd told him her father would be if anything happened to his precious, and only, daughter. She'd neglected to tell the driver her father might be so far in his cups he wouldn't remember having a child.

She examined the encampment.

A man walked around the wagon parked under a sycamore tree and gave a brief nod to them before he retraced his steps. She heard a shout and he called out to someone, but Vivian couldn't understand the name.

The man, hair streaked with white, remained far enough away he could hear them if they spoke, but not close enough to invite conversation. He sat on the ground, propping his back against a tree, his knees up to rest his arms, and watched them.

Mavis kept her voice low and barely moved her lips. 'He acts as though he thinks we might steal something.'

Then Ella Etta appeared, wearing what might have been a man's coat and boots, with a torn yellow skirt hem hanging over the footwear. The red scarf around her hair fluttered in the wind.

Vivian held herself firm and took a few steps forward, nervous to be walking under the canopy of dark trees, concerned about the forest closing in around her and the sentry who studied the ground in front of him, but knew their every move.

The tramp had nearly swaddled herself in clothes and her fingers reminded Vivian of dried-chicken leg bones, covered in rings.

'I hear…' Vivian quaked inside, but she stared down

the old woman and ignored the curious scrutiny that circled her '…tales of your skills.'

Ella Etta smirked, showing teeth so healthy they could put a bear to shame.

Vivian's strength all but disappeared. If not for Mavis, she would have pretended to be lost, asked directions to the nearest village and fled.

The hag's countenance—every day of her life was shown there—held a confidence that Vivian preferred to back away from. But she'd nowhere to go for safety. The accident had changed that.

Ella Etta touched the loop dangling from her ear, partially hidden by the scarf. 'It's said stars ask my permission before they change places. Idle talk.' She sniffed. 'People should speak of the bigger things I do. Last morning, I wanted to rise before the sun, but also wanted to sleep more, so I delayed the sunrise until I wanted it. Naught is said of it.'

Vivian gave a soft click of her tongue and tilted her head. 'That was you? Well, I cannot complain as I wished to rest longer as well. My thanks.'

Ella Etta gave a nod. 'The first gift I give you. The second will cost more. And who might you be?'

'Vivian Darius.'

The hag's head jolted forward and she examined Vivian. 'A baron's daughter. Lord Darius.'

Vivian nodded. 'I'm impressed.'

Ella Etta placed her booted feet flat on the ground and gave a shrug. 'I may not read *The Times*, but I read palms. All the same.' She frowned.

'I need your medicine,' Vivian spoke.

The older woman shrugged. 'You were hurt in a…'

she waved an arm and the people watching lost interest, turning to resume their day '…by a horse.'

'Yes. I was knocked about by one. Years ago. I've not recovered no matter how many remedies I take. They've given me enough treatments to make me well a thousand times over, but none of them has worked.'

Ella Etta gave a bare nod to the camp and stepped towards a fire pit. 'Treatments,' she said. 'Little bottles?'

'All sizes.'

The air briefly fanned the flames, stirring embers, then a stillness returned. 'Come with me,' she said.

Around the cooking area, several stumps had been turned into seats.

The woman led Vivian and Mavis to the fire pit.

Three poles joined to hold a chain and a bubbling pot over the embers. Vivian smelled stewing meat, as tempting as any from Cook's kitchen.

Vivian absently pulled at her skirt so she could sit without wrinkling it.

'No,' Ella Etta rasped, pointing a finger to a seat near her. Vivian moved where instructed, so close their hems touched.

'It's warm sitting near the coals.' Ella Etta used the end of the scarf to give herself a fan. 'But the breeze is cool and the cooking rabbit smells good.'

Vivian heard Mavis settle almost behind her.

'I've heard you may have medicine which can cure me,' Vivian spoke, trying to keep the hope from sounding in her words.

Ella Etta held out a hand. 'Give me your palm.'

Vivian slipped her glove away, dropped the doeskin in her lap and forced herself to remain unmoved when she felt the roughened skin touch her hand, pulling her fingers closer.

Ella Etta peered at the palm. Then she examined Vivian's fingernails before she pressed at the skin over Vivian's cheeks, causing her to clamp her teeth together.

'You're supposed to be examining my palm,' Vivian muttered. 'I thought you were part-fortune teller, part-matchmaker and part a mixer of herbs for treatments.'

'I fix problems.' A gleam appeared in her eye and she again pinched near Vivian's jaw.

Vivian pulled away. 'I am not a horse.'

She inspected Vivian's skin. 'I treat them also. They never complain.'

Ella Etta leaned forward. She smelled the same as Cook, but with more spice.

'The price is high.' She laughed, more to herself than anyone else. 'But I may save you and, if I don't, you will not return for your funds back.'

Vivian recoiled. 'You are evil.'

'No, I'm Ella Etta. Evil Etta was my mother.'

'This is nonsense and I am tired.' Vivian rose.

The old woman shook her head. 'I cannot let you go without my medicinal.' She waved a hand. A man stepped from the woods, holding what appeared to be a bundle of thorns that he gave to Ella Etta.

She held the bramble nest with both hands and moved the bundle forward so Vivian could examine it.

A stopper rested at the top. The thorns surrounded a bottle.

'You follow my words without fail if you wish to live.'

'First I must hear what you say, then decide,' Vivian answered, keeping her words firm.

The woman chortled, her teeth showing, then glowered. 'You bargain. But I do not change price.'

Vivian put all her haughtiness into one tilt of her head. 'Well, tell me. I don't wish to keep you from your business any longer.'

Ella Etta nodded. 'Your cost is marriage to the son of the Earl who lives in the big house you just passed on your journey here.'

Vivian searched her mind. She'd been unaware of a mansion. And to marry the son of the house? Rot.

'Thank you. No.' Vivian stood and her glove tumbled from her lap to the ground. She swooped, picking up the doeskin. 'I'll not marry some man I've not met, or even say I would, just to get a parcel of thorns.'

'You've met him.' Mavis's voice interrupted her thoughts.

Vivian veered towards her friend. 'I can't have. I've not been here before and I don't get out much, even in London.'

'Lord Everleigh. His housekeeper sent us here,' Mavis whispered. She touched the spot above her cheekbones.

Vivian didn't move. Images of him. Memories of his lips returned to her mind. 'Him?' She barely let out the word.

Ella Etta cackled. 'I say he sticks in a woman's memory. Even an old widow like me notices. Legs like a steed. Shoulders like a draught horse.' She grinned. 'I'm sure the rest of him's as strong as a stallion.'

Vivian dropped to the stump again, jarring her bottom. 'Well, you might be able to get me to toss in some gold as well.' She leaned forward. 'Does he know you talk of him like this?'

'No. I've watched him grow since he learned to escape his governess.' She sighed. 'He came here, on the day his mother died, and said his father and grandfather were fighting over what dress she was to wear last. I told him it didn't matter to her, so it shouldn't matter to them.'

Ella Etta patted Vivian's knee. 'He was... What is it said? All knees and elbows?' She lowered her voice. 'And feet. Wagon big. He grew to fit them.'

'Assuming I agree,' Vivian lowered her voice, muttering, 'though it is hard to believe I should... Assuming I agree,' she continued, 'just what does he have to say of such a thing?'

Ella Etta groaned. 'You expect me to do everything?' She thrust out her arm, waving in the air. 'I save your life—you take care of getting the marriage promise.'

Vivian laughed. 'I dare say he has no wish to marry me.'

Ella Etta held her palms out flat, her hands and sneer mocking Vivian's words. 'He does not. He has no wish to tie himself to a wife or he would have married long ago. It's not difficult for a man to find a mate when a lady's vision cannot ignore him.' She shrugged. 'You aren't able to birth a strong babe now, but with my medicine, you will be. Do not complain that I send you to a man without *love*.' She said the word as if it poisoned her lips. 'Nonsense. His heart was destroyed long ago.' Her rings shone as she waved them about. 'But it left behind a good casing.'

The words lodged in Vivian's mind. She wouldn't have said Everleigh had no heart. He had treated Mavis with consideration and Vivian had no issue with how he'd treated her. Ella Etta was daft, but still...

'How would I convince him of his marriage?' Vivian tried to read the answer in Ella Etta's expression.

The hag gaped at Vivian. 'Not my worry. That would be your cost. I give you the healing potion. Tell you the way it must be administered. If you agree. Fine. Or, you don't agree and we part.' She leaned forward again and her voice rumbled from inside her ribs. 'We are about to part, either way.'

Vivian felt the first bubble of laughter inside herself that she'd experienced in a long time.

Sure, she could be betrothed, if that was what the woman wanted to hear. Vivian could convince the hag of a secret imaginary betrothal to please her. No one would even need to tell Everleigh. And if Vivian didn't get well she could spend her last days smiling, thinking of the imaginary bond she had with Everleigh and pretending it real.

'Very well. I agree.'

Mavis's sputtering cough caused both to turn her direction.

'Smoke in her eyes,' the vagabond muttered. 'Happens to many of my visitors.'

'I will marry him.' Vivian held out her hands for the thorns. 'But it will be a quiet wedding. Few guests. You can read about it in the visitors' palms.'

'Not so rushed.' The woman put her nose almost to Vivian's. She gasped in a breath while the hag commanded, 'There are rules and you must not fail. You must stop any other curatives. Take my mixture with theirs—you may die before you've time to spit. Not a soft, sweet death. One like clawing demons tearing your entrails from your body.' She sneered, 'Saw it once. Purple lips. Drooling. He pulled out his own tongue. Gave it to me for a memento. Ugly tongue, but cooked up well.'

'We're leaving.' Mavis jumped to her feet, forcing out the words, and grabbed Vivian's arm.

The vagabond put a hand to her chest and whimpered. 'I merely say truth because I don't want the young one to suffer.'

'Wait,' Vivian said, holding back. 'It's my only chance.'

'What have you got to lose?' Ella Etta asked. 'Take a small amount of my potion each day. No more than you might cup in something no bigger than a small fingernail. Just don't forget that you must also convince the Earl's son to marry you. He's at his father's house now.'

'I must take my medicinals.' Letting her hands drop, Vivian backed away. 'I must.'

'No.' A drop flew out of Ella Etta's mouth. Vivian wasn't sure if it was spit or venom.

'My observations tell me when mixtures work—and it's not those other potions. Pay attention to yourself, Child. What you are taking now is not helping you. You were injured years ago.'

Vivian pulled at the shoulder of her gown. 'Well, the physician has given me his verdict.' Vivian held out both hands for the bundle. 'I accept it and a bundle of thorns would make a good tale to tell to...' she almost laughed '...mine and Everleigh's children.'

Ella Etta moved to her feet with a tiny huff, still holding the thorns, and her voice flowed around them with the thickness of a wetted cloth. 'You will be well. But you must not forget the bargain.'

'What if I get well and Everleigh has no wish to marry me?'

'You must make him wish.' She waved her arm. 'But what do I know? I'm just an old traveller who lives in a hut some days and some days I live nowhere. People travel far for me to help them. And I do.' She scowled. 'Now, go away.'

One of the thorns pricked her when Vivian tightened her grasp on the parcel. She put the injured finger to her lips and she remembered Everleigh's kiss.

Chapter Three

The carriage rolled from the camp and Vivian felt the brambles when the wheels jolted. She held the potion with both hands. 'Shouldn't you congratulate me on my forthcoming betrothal, Mavis?'

'I suppose,' Mavis grumbled. 'I cannot believe Mrs Rush sent me here. I cannot believe that bedraggled swindler spoke so. And then to say the Everleigh lad has no heart. Though I don't know if it matters much. If he's going to be missing something, might as well be something a man doesn't use.' She counted on her fingers. 'He could be missing a heart and a brain, and I wouldn't hold it against him.'

'Mavis,' Vivian chastised her, sitting the potion at the corner of the seat across from her. 'I'm sure he is kind. He was caring of you when your head was knocked.' Vivian peered out of the window, searching for Earl Rothwilde's estate.

Mavis put her handkerchief away. 'Ought to have been. He nearly put my nose on the back of my head.' She prodded the yellowish skin around her cheeks. 'It's still tender.'

'I am going to tell the driver we need respite. I'll promise him extra payment to take us home in the morning if we are offered a chance to stay the night.'

'You aren't serious?' Mavis frowned.

Vivian took a coin from inside her bag. 'We will see if the mansion ahead can help poor travellers, particularly one who is ill.'

Mavis shook her head and grabbed for the coin. 'No. I forbid it. Absolutely forbid.'

Vivian quickly moved aside, keeping the funds from her friend. 'I must, Mavis. I must.'

'Fine,' Mavis said, reaching out a palm for the money. 'Do what you wish. Best let me speak with the driver. I'll be able to convince him to stay until tomorrow if needed. But you're going to be in dire straits if your parents return from their visit a few days early. And so will I. We'll likely both be looking for employment.'

After Vivian gave her the money, Mavis settled into her seat, pointing to the window. A copse of trees hugged the road, one limb so close it brushed the side of the vehicle. Mavis jerked away as if the limb could grab her. 'That mansion appeared perfect for a body snatcher to reside in. A snatcher would feel he could just sit around waiting for business to come his way.'

Vivian forced a smile. 'No matter. I can meet his family. Might as well begin the courtship by cosying up to his relations.'

How foolish, she decided, to entertain any hope of recovery based on the words of a vagrant in the forest who peddled nonsense and notions. Then to stick the vial in a nest of brambles? She had to be daft.

And to accept such a potion? Vivian cringed at what

she'd done. She'd sunk to putting her hope in a jumble of balderdash.

She wanted to rip it apart, but she couldn't without hurting herself.

Suddenly, she didn't feel she could wait any longer. She reached for the stopper, tugged it out, touched the golden liquid to her fingertip and tasted. 'Mavis. This is much sweeter than the physician's remedies. It tastes like honey.'

'Don't let yourself get fooled by sweetness. You're about to open a box you can't close.' She put her hand to her head. 'It is all my fault.'

'I've had my fill of illness. I can hardly remember what it feels like to be well. If I'm going to die, I should live *now*.'

'Apparently, you wish to take me with you.'

Vivian thumped the carriage top, opened the small window and gave the driver instructions. When he stopped at the mansion, Mavis gave him the coin as Vivian walked forward, examining the house while Mavis followed behind.

When the butler let them into the house, Vivian took Mavis's arm for support. The carriage ride, the illness, the dropping temperature—all had taken her strength. She wasn't certain she could have made it back to London.

Vivian felt Mavis's nudge. They both inspected the vaulted ceiling and even though the stairway went upwards, the landing above closed in around it, the dark, ornate wood of the walls arching over. An entrance to intimidate rather than impress.

The butler viewed their hesitation, a superior glimmer of humour in his face. 'Please go forward,' he said.

He led them to a drawing room decorated with the same dark panelling as the hallway. Even the thick rug in the drawing room—she couldn't tell if it was Aubusson, although she knew the flower design woven around the edge must have cost dearly—had faded roses on it clustered among brown leaves.

An older man, cane in hand, stepped in later, head held high by a stiff collar. As he got closer, Vivian realised the clothing he wore, while elegant, had faded into hints of the black it had once been. His bearing suggested privilege, but his dress said he would not attend a tailor until he felt like it and his expression said praise from him would cost more than the rug.

'My butler says you're seeking refuge as you fear the roads may become impassable if the rain arrives. Clouds are gathering and the sky is ominous.' The older man lifted the cane from the floor, pointing the tip to the outdoors. 'You are welcome to stay the night. I have business to see to with the tenants and you can have shelter here.'

Vivian nodded, feeling the thump as her reticule bounced against her. The potion made the bag too portly to close. She didn't have to act to show her frailty. 'The journey today has worn me out. I have a wasting disease, contracted after an accident.' Her voice fell to a whisper. 'I was told nearby would be an old woman with medicinals to cure me. I've just been to see her. But the weather is threatening and I fear travelling as the night is closing in.'

The man waved his hand. 'My dear lady, that old beggar often makes a nuisance of herself and, I can assure you, she will only take your funds and give you nothing more than false hopes in return. I let her live on my property out of foolish generosity. Besides, she was once the mistress of my gamekeeper and she lived with him at the edge of my property. I've never complained when she returns to visit as she is penniless and had nowhere else to go when he died. I built a new home for the next gamekeeper closer to the estate.'

'It was very kind of you to let her stay on.'

'Her family has been near here for centuries, if the tales are to be believed. I could not give her a job inside the house. She'd likely end up hanged for theft if I did so. At least now she earns a few coins with her mixtures and her foolish fortune telling. She's the only person some of the servants trust for their ills, so I don't have the notion to send her away. Besides, she never stays long. She goes to the Bartholomew Fair, tells fortunes, sells herbs and makes her way. My wife believed in her nonsense and those curatives Ella Etta mixes, but nothing could save the Countess. She took ill so quickly. I assure you, Ella Etta is like a spider spinning webs of lies to catch people. Beware of her. She would likely poison you as not. And charge for it.'

Vivian took in a halted breath. Ella Etta was her last hope.

Her legs gave way and she fell into Mavis. The older woman stumbled to hold her and, for an instant, Vivian thought they'd both land in a heap. Then the fear faded and determination took its place. Vivian's strength returned, but she didn't let it show. She didn't want to go back into that conveyance until she'd rested. The ruts mixed with the lack of good springs, and the seats with the flattened padding, were brutal.

The man stepped beside them and clamped his fingers around Vivian's arm, causing pain.

'Burton. Burton…' he shouted. 'Help us.'

'I have her,' Mavis said, shaking his grasp loose and holding Vivian. 'She's better now. We don't need help. Just a place for her to rest.'

Mavis half-lifted her up the stairs, her voice guiding Vivian.

'The light chamber,' the older man called out.

Vivian knew she could hardly walk a few steps more, but she didn't care. At least if she died here, it would be a change of scenery.

Once they got to the room, Mavis took Vivian's pelisse and reticule, and helped her get comfortable in a chair. Then, she pinched Vivian.

Vivian jerked away. 'Mavis, if you pinch me one more time, I'm going to cut the ties off all your bonnets.'

'Fine, Miss Vivian. You've got us shelter in the last place I'd want to shelter. This'll take some coin to keep the servants quiet to your mother when she returns. If your father discovers this, he will toss me out on my ear and no one will be able to stop him. We should never stay overnight.' She crossed her arms. 'You must take a deep breath, gather your last vestiges of strength and we must go.'

Vivian pulled her arm back. 'So, I am not even to choose where I am to die.'

'Not unless you choose your family home.' Mavis tapped her arm. 'Don't speak nonsense about dying. I will not hear of it. You heard the Earl—that man must have been the Earl. He said the servants trust the hag's treatments. But then, so did his wife and she is no longer with us.'

Vivian drew in a deep breath. 'I can imagine whispers of this getting about. You know I would not be here if I weren't ill. Besides, you should be able to convince the other servants to keep silent about this trip. Give them a bottle of Father's wine. He'll not notice it because he'll think he drank it.'

'He's trying to keep himself from the wine. That is the reason he agreed to go with your mother. To get a fresh start. He knows he tipples too much.'

Vivian surveyed her reticule. Her father had never been foxed so much until she became ill. Then, the drink seemed to take over.

Her illness wasn't just destroying her. It had captured her family.

She scrambled for the reticule ties, jerking them open, and removed the thorns, unable to feel the pricks on her skin now.

'Vivian…' Mavis's voice was hesitant, but when she saw what Vivian was doing, she lurched forward, trying to pull the thorns from Vivian's grasp. 'I didn't realise how tattered Ella Etta would appear. I cannot trust her.'

Vivian stepped back. 'She surely felt sorry for my frailty and planned to soothe my mind, trying to give me a pleasant tale to think of before I slept—a handsome man to marry. Hope is a pleasant thing to give someone. Better than a curse.'

'That could be poison.'

'Then I will die quicker and the question of whether I will recover will be solved.'

'That is nonsense.' Mavis reached for the thorns again, but Vivian kept them from her reach.

'It is my last chance for life. I will take it.' Vivian retained the bundle.

Mavis backed away. 'I am pleased you still wish to

live. After the accident, when you were struggling, I feared you didn't want to get well.'

Vivian didn't hide the wistfulness in her voice. 'I do want to dance a waltz at a ball and wear a silk gown. I do want to live. I am tired of waiting until I am better, or of waiting until I die. I am tired of *waiting*.'

Mavis sniffled. 'You cannot talk of death, Vivian. You are your parents' life. It will kill us all if anything happens to you.'

A knock sounded at the door. Vivian called out, 'Enter.'

A servant marched in, mob cap crisp on her head while her silver hair hung limp. Her apron covered her dark dress and lingering smells of the kitchen surrounded her. 'I see to the house for the Earl. Tonight, would you prefer a tray or to eat...' her voice lowered and she rushed her words '...in the dining room?'

'My companion and I would prefer the dining room, of course.' Vivian knew her chin tilted up as well as any royal's.

The housekeeper ignored the movement. 'I heard the Earl's voice when you arrived. Be glad he warned you away from that thieving, scrabbling vagrant and her family which scuffles around the countryside like vultures, but without the same goodness in 'em. Rothwilde has the kindness of the saints to let them live on his property.'

'I can't believe they're murderous,' Vivian said. 'They'd be hanged.'

'Who's to say a few haven't been led to the gallows from time to time? You'll stay far away from 'em if you know what's good.' The housekeeper got caught up in her tale. 'It's said Ella Etta even gets mixtures from the apothecary and stirs them into something else. I think she plans to poison us all. I know the other servants trust her, but I don't. Whenever her troop is in the area, half the fruit from the orchard disappears. Sometimes even the root crops go missing and not because of a rabbit.'

'Why isn't she brought to a Court of Petty Sessions by the Earl, or held for the Assizes?' Vivian asked.

The housekeeper nodded. 'If the Earl runs them vagabonds away or brings one to justice, they'd probably burn the house while we sleep or curse us all. They're like a nest of bees and we don't stir 'em up.'

'Makes me long for London and the friendly cutpurses,' Vivian said.

The housekeeper nodded. 'The city's far safer, I'd expect.' She moved to the mirror, took out a cloth and wiped the glass as if wiping away the reflection of anyone she might not wish to see.

Then she went to the door, still holding the cleaning cloth, and put her empty hand on the wood. She paused and with no subservience in her gaze, said, 'Then it will be the three of you for dinner. The Earl's estate work will be keeping him busy tonight and he won't be joining you.'

'Three?'

'The eldest son is here.' She watched Vivian. 'I suppose he returned because it gets tiresome being unmarried, happy in that state, and finding oneself the object of pursuit.'

'Goodness…' Vivian widened her eyes. 'How fortunate for me to be able to meet an unmarried son of an earl. I am indeed blessed.'

The housekeeper gave a swift perusal of Vivian, then

snapped her cloth before she tucked it back in her apron. 'I'll send someone to fetch you when it's time to eat.'

The housekeeper walked out and Mavis lowered her voice, muttering to Vivian, 'She believes you're in pursuit of a husband, not health.' She gave a nod to the door after the housekeeper closed it. 'I don't like her. She's above herself. Acts like the lady of the house.'

'She is uppity and not in a nice way as you are.'

'I might have stretched the truth to get my job as your governess. I realised my good fortune at landing such a post and did the best I could to please your mother and do right by you.'

Mavis absently straightened the tablecloth. 'It touched my heart when your mother wanted me to stay on as your companion when you'd blossomed into a young woman and I wasn't needed as a governess. Best home I've ever been in and I'm not only referring to the quality of the wall coverings. I don't want to talk to you about all I've seen before I joined your family. Let you stay innocent. Life is hard enough. Those references your mother saw for me... She didn't check them as close as she should have.'

Vivian studied her companion.

'That old beggar...there but for the grace of forgery go I.'

'You could be sacked, Mavis.'

'I likely will be by your father—if he finds out about this. I shouldn't have listened to Mrs Rush.' She saw Vivian's expression and Mavis softened her tone. 'But, it's said the old drifter is as good as any physician. Mrs Rush told me the old woman's fee would be based on what she thought we could afford.'

'Ella Etta didn't ask for funds...'

'No. Just a marriage to an earl's son.' She waved a hand in the air. 'Ella Etta likely has more tricks in her head than she has brains, but that doesn't mean she doesn't know her remedies.'

Vivian studied the thorns. 'That potion is my last hope.'

But if Everleigh kissed her a few more times, she wouldn't mind so badly if the potion was worthless.

Chapter Four

When she walked into the dining room, the first thing Vivian saw was Everleigh. He rose when she and Mavis entered.

Candles were set on a table which would seat ten people.

The aroma of baked lamb wafting in the air didn't dispel the darkness created by the heavy curtains, and the walls were bare except for unlit sconces.

His lips stopped before he formed his first word of greeting, then he gave a slight inclination of his head. 'I believe we have met before, ladies,' he said as Mavis walked in behind Vivian.

'I didn't realise the travellers might be dear friends.' He bowed briefly, giving both a kiss of the hand as greeting.

Mavis laughed. 'Keep your distance, Lord Everleigh. I've just recovered from our first meeting.'

'Please, both of you, my friends call me Everleigh,' he said. 'The day we first spoke was too eventful for us to remain formal.'

Everleigh touched Vivian's elbow and he guided her

to the first chair to the right of the head of the table. 'My father has asked me to be host tonight. He's at a meeting with his tenants. They're discussing agricultural changes to increase crop yields and he wanted to get their views.'

He helped her sit and she felt the brush of his knuckles as he slid the chair forward. Even if the medicinal didn't make her better, being close to Everleigh made her feel stronger.

Then he helped Mavis to her chair, and next he summoned a servant.

He left the host's position empty and sat beside Mavis.

Vivian assessed him and he caught the question in her perusal. He answered, softly. 'I never sit in his chair, at this house. He is Rothwilde and that is where he sits.'

Vivian nodded, accepting his words.

Everleigh's lips had a tiny bracket on each side.

'To what act of good fortune might I owe your presence?' His voice, perfect, soft warmness and, underneath, strength.

'Your housekeeper told us about the medicinals of the woman who lives nearby.' Vivian moved slightly as a footman placed a large, filled platter on the table. 'I'd hoped her herbs could provide some assistance in my illness.' She placed her hand at the side of her plate. 'What trust do you put in her?'

He lifted his glass, and took a sip before answering. 'As a child, I used to anticipate her returning to the property with excitement. I have no difficulty with her. The tenants trust her mixtures and stay in her good graces. To me, she has been almost like an aunt, but not an aunt my family would ever accept into the household. It's not possible for her to keep from speaking her mind.'

'Might she put a curse on someone?'

A glimmer of humour passed across his face, but fell away. 'She would claim to.' He shrugged. 'She has her own set of rules...like most people I assume. A capable, travelling sort, who would get a young boy to steal fruit for her and enjoy it as an adventure. The servants, for the most part, have no problem with her presence. She provides them with herbals, teas, advice and fortune telling for no charge but a blind eye to the rabbits and birds she and her group take. My father tolerates the clan. They don't pilfer anything but food. If some extra hands are needed for a short time, the men and women at the camp are quick to accept the work.'

Then he regarded Mavis and said, 'In case you are wondering, my driver is careful now not to pull up near anyone on the street.'

Mavis laughed and they began to discuss the confusion they'd experienced after the vehicle door crashed open.

While the conversation continued around her, Vivian's thoughts kept returning to the kiss. He hardly seemed the same person, but he still drew her contemplation.

She'd kissed him and all thoughts of any part of him but his lips fled. Just thinking of it caused a warmth in her chest. She examined the food in front of her so he could not observe her face—just in case her feelings showed.

She'd not known how much she would dwell on the kiss. Yet he seemed unaffected by it and unaware of how much it had touched her. She supposed she should be thankful for that—but she wasn't.

Everleigh stood when the meal ended. He offered his arm to Vivian. 'I should show you the library, although it's picked over. You might find a book you'd like.'

When they got to the room, she noticed it didn't have a comforting old book smell, but an aroma of tobacco. An open box sat on a table and several cheroots lay inside it.

A large portrait of the most arresting beauty Vivian had ever seen hung over the fireplace. She had Everleigh's blue eyes, although they didn't seem to fit her somehow. Something about them almost jarred her. His mother had a stare exactly like Everleigh's and it showed in the painting. On him, the expression blended into who he was and added to his attraction. On her, it overpowered her loveliness.

'My mother,' he said, almost making two sentences from the words.

'She's lovely.' The perfection couldn't have all been the work of a complimentary brush stroke.

Everleigh swept his view past Vivian. 'I believe she was only seventeen—or somewhere around that age—when the portrait was painted. It was finished a week before her wedding.'

'She does appear angelic.'

'I've heard several say they've never seen anyone before or since who had her beauty. My grandfather adored her. His beloved daughter. She could do nothing wrong as far as he was concerned. He was a broken man when she died. She contracted a cough and, within hours, she was gone. We didn't have time to find a physician or the herbalist. It was that quick.'

Everleigh returned to a discussion of the artwork. 'But to her child—I suppose a mother could be unattractive and still a goddess. She died when she was still young. I'm pleased to have the painting as a reminder. Now, I'm a decade older than she was when she sat for the artist.'

'A tragedy.' Vivian examined the portrait. 'When you observe the painting, you almost feel you know her.'

Everleigh had some similarity in his other features to the painting, but not a great deal. His mother's were feminine and, if the portrait had been closer, an observer might have reached out to touch it, to see if it were real, or to see if her loveliness could be absorbed from the canvas.

Then Everleigh changed the subject, asking about the condition of the roads on the way, showing concern that Vivian's family might worry and offering to send a rider to let them know she was well.

Vivian shook her head, telling Everleigh that neither her mother nor her father were at home. It would not go well if a servant contacted her father and informed him that she was gone.

She and Mavis had given the maids their leisure for the evening. Since Vivian had expected to be late, she'd told the servants not to attend to them in the morning unless they were summoned.

'The time has flown,' Everleigh said. 'Please let me send someone to the stables to tell your driver that you will be staying the night. In darkness, it's hard for a carriage driver to see the road as well and the horses will be better for the rest.'

'That sounds wonderful,' Vivian said.

Mavis squinted at her. 'Such a surprising offer. We should hate to impose on you so much.'

'No imposition at all.'

'Vivian is still tired from the trip,' Mavis said, standing near one of the large overstuffed chairs.

'Nonsense. I'm refreshed.' Vivian stood nearer the portrait, but turned her back to it. 'I want to continue my good fortune of having the most interesting day I've had in some time.'

'You've not had any days of note recently?' Everleigh asked and Vivian saw the imp in him as he appraised her, giving a small challenge.

Mavis spoke quickly, her voice stern, and lips in a straight line. 'I would say the day of my fall was eventful. You have mused over that more than once.'

'That is exactly the day I was referring to as well.' Laughter hid behind Everleigh's words. His brows rose in silent comment and innocence flashed.

Vivian refused to think of the incident, because she knew if she did, her cheeks would truly ignite. Instead, she nodded. 'I'm so thankful it was not worse.'

Everleigh put a hand to his chest and, with the slightest movement, acted as if an arrow had pierced him. 'Mrs Mavis and Miss Darius, for both of you, I'm certainly pleased it was not...' he appraised Vivian '...worse.'

'I suppose I should stay as your chaperon, but this day has been a thorny one.' Mavis patted back the strand of hair that had escaped from her bun. 'I am too old to stay awake much longer, but you two can sit and read.'

'Mavis,' Vivian cautioned.

Everleigh understood Vivian's view. Propriety demanded a chaperon.

Mavis stared at the Earl's son. 'You leave the door open, Everleigh.' She tipped her head back.

Vivian watched Mavis. 'If you're concerned—stay. You are my companion.'

Mavis gave a long blink. 'Don't be ridiculous. If I were a sensible companion, I would never have let you stop here on the way home.' She fixed a glower on Everleigh. 'You will mind your behaviour with Vivian, Everleigh, or I will put a curse of my own on you.' She waved a finger. 'That concept is beyond frightening.'

'You have my word that I will be a gentleman,' Everleigh reassured her.

'You have my word that I will be sleeping softly, listening,' Mavis said, leaving.

Everleigh had kissed Vivian when they were alone before and that was a request he'd been honoured to fulfil. But he would take pains not to do anything that would give her the impression there would be more between them.

Besides, an evening with Vivian would make the solitude of the estate less stifling and she'd be on her way in the morning.

He wouldn't have returned to his father's house, except he'd broken up with Alexandria, and she'd not taken it well. She'd seen herself as a future countess and becoming a true member of the peerage. He'd had trouble convincing her it wasn't to be. He'd distanced himself from her for months, but she didn't want to let him go.

She'd taken to searching him out and he'd been polite to her, but insisted that they were not more than friends.

Her father hadn't dissuaded her and Everleigh knew

he'd wanted his daughter to be a countess, the same as his grandfather had wanted.

Everleigh had overlooked that at first, but then he'd realised that wasn't the problem. The difficulty had been his lack of feelings.

The kiss with Vivian had sealed the end of his relationship with Alexandria. What had begun as a perfunctory moment with Vivian had instantly blossomed into something deeper.

He'd realised how superficial he'd been with Alexandria and she with him.

It made him ill at ease to see how he'd made the motions of courting, yet neither he nor Alexandria had much of a rapport.

He'd still considered marriage, but something inside him had rebelled at the notion, infusing a reluctance so deep he could not propose. When he'd realised that, he'd been firm in his final goodbye to Alexandria, even as she'd asked him to reconsider. He'd insisted it was not a possibility and said it would not be fair for either of them to entertain the notion.

Now, he understood his reluctance better.

Vivian was altogether different from Alexandria. He liked having Vivian close. It seemed to take away the suffocating feel of the estate. The only pleasant memories he had of the house were with his brother, Daniel, and his grandfather. When one of them hadn't been available, he'd often visited Ella Etta if she were on the estate.

All had been well, until after university. His grandfather had died of an apoplexy. The tension had momentarily lessened between him and his father, although he'd sensed his father was dancing on the inside to have the older man gone. The peace had been brief.

He'd never stayed long at the estate after that.

Vivian paused when Everleigh touched her arm.

'I will call a maid if you wish,' he said. 'But I promise you I will act as if your companion is still sitting in the room.'

Vivian hid her disappointment.

'Why don't I read to you?' he suggested, lighting the branch of candles.

She raised her brows. 'This library only has about ten books in it. I would assume you're not overly fond of reading.'

'My father's absconded with most of the volumes. If you were to see his chambers, you'd see the library. No servant is allowed to move a book and he has them stacked along the walls. Though most of them are truly mine—passed to me from my mother's father. He considered this his home.'

He held out his arm, letting Vivian precede him to the books. 'Grandfather had a way of showing up unannounced, with baggage, for all my school holidays.'

'It is good that he could be close to you.'

'Father would usually leave or stay out of the main rooms, which overjoyed my grandfather.' He shrugged. 'Grandfather had other grandchildren, but Daniel and I were his favourites and he and I got along best of all.'

'Perhaps he saw his daughter in you and that kept you close.'

'Doubtful.' The word dismissed her suggestion as a blatant miscalculation. 'He saw himself in me, if anyone. I looked up to him, even though I could see his overbearing nature. He regarded me differently from everyone else. He valued the title I'm expected to inherit, even though it wasn't from his lineage.'

Vivian understood. Her father was a baron and the title, even though it wasn't as elevated as an earl's, meant something to him, her mother and her. Some day it would go to her father's nephew, but that couldn't be helped.

She noticed the books in front of her. 'Please choose whichever book you've been reading. I am curious to see what you might select from those, oh, ten books.'

He laughed when he moved to them, touching one of his long fingers to the spines as he peered at the titles. 'I assure you these are not the best, but the opposite.' He took a book from the widest shelf, grasping it with both hands. '*The Book of Martyrs* by John Foxe. This is the last thing I'd choose for the fairer sex to read. Grim tales.'

She examined him. The weighty book would work as well as a chaperon, she supposed. For just a second longer their eyes held. She wondered if he tested her.

She sat, relaxing into the large chair. She would show him her mettle. 'Well, I've never read it. Have always been fascinated by martyrs. Don't worry about reading around the most unpleasant parts.' Although she supposed his voice could make even a tale of being drawn and quartered less hideous.

'Are you certain?' he asked.

'I'll stop you if it is beyond me.' She would not complain at even the ghastliest section that he could choose.

She heard his movements as he sat on the plump sofa and thumbed through the book, and a few words as he read.

But when she blinked, things blurred softly around her, and she dozed.

* * *

Awakening, she was aware the candles had burned down considerably. She'd fallen asleep for some time.

His head rested, propped by his arms. The book at his side, forgotten.

He switched his attention away from her, grasping the volume he'd placed on the chair. 'You don't wake quietly.'

'What?'

'You wriggle and make small animal noises.'

She stared across at him, letting her affront show with a touch of hurt in her words. 'I do not. Mavis would have told me, I'm sure.'

'You squeaked.'

'I did not.'

He made a mouse sound and challenged her a tiny peep.

'I was dreaming of a particularly gruesome martyr. And butterflies.' She sat up, still pulling her mind back from the fog.

'I never finished the first page before you were slumbering away.'

'I can't help it. I get so sleepy since I've been ill. I never seem to get enough rest.'

'Do you feel refreshed now?' he asked.

'Yes. It is an adventure for me to be out of my room and even the jostling carriage ride was a treat. If my mother and father hadn't been visiting my aunt, I would never have been able to steal away.'

'I suspected that your parents wouldn't let you journey so far without them.'

'My mother might have if I were well. My father would have forbidden it.'

'You should follow your father's instructions.'

She could tell by his expression that he was pleased she hadn't.

Sitting across from her, in his father's house, made the room feel like a home—which it rarely did. The waves of bitterness and anger and grief that had kept the house afloat now seemed to have receded like flood waters when the rains stopped.

He hoped she wouldn't rise and decide to go to her room, but she didn't seem inclined to move. He settled back in his chair, more relaxed than he could remember being in a long time.

She moved back into her chair and tucked her hands at her side, palms flat.

'You're watching me rather intently…' She let her words flow away.

'I'm just waiting to see if you'd ask for another kiss.'

'I'm not sure about that because you said you'd act as if a chaperon were in the room. I'd hate it if you refused me a kiss.' She slanted her head. 'Didn't you already tell me no? Once? At the time of the kiss, I seem to remember you saying I should return to Mavis.'

'Entanglements can be difficult. They can cause too much upheaval.'

'I would think…a female who is not likely to live much longer would be a perfect companion for a male who doesn't like entanglements.'

'Don't spout such nonsense, Vivian. The physicians don't know everything. You must live as if you are going to remain among us for ever.'

'When you kissed me, it was the first time I had any good fortune because of my sickness. I rather liked that.' Her lips curved up at the memory.

He stood, walked to the fireplace and picked up a small figurine, rubbing a thumb over it as if it were a talisman.

'Are you fond of a particular lady?' she asked.

He challenged her curiosity with a frown.

'I'm sure you shouldn't tell me, then.' She dipped her chin. 'But I'm all ears.'

He reached to the branch of candles and let his finger flit and flirt with the flames. 'I had a friend. A lovely woman. A darling of society. Well entrenched in the *ton*, through her mother's relatives among the peerage. You could not ignore her. On the surface, her loveliness is everything, but nothing attractive is inside her. We have talked. She wishes to marry and believes we should. I considered it, but I noticed a side of her that made me uneasy. I've told her that we wouldn't suit, but she still sees herself as my bride.'

'She's brave to be so bold.' Vivian almost felt scandalised herself.

Everleigh pulled his finger from the flame and his lips turned up. 'You're a fine one to talk. You had no trouble asking for a kiss. A kiss is simple enough…as long as it stops there.'

'So your heart is taken by her, but you find her unsuitable?'

He shook his head. 'This friend and I—we had spent hours together.' He kept his attention on her. 'Talked very frankly. I'd considered her for a wife, but then I realised it would never do. I told her I would never marry. She seemed fine with it, but—'

Ella Etta's words bounced back into her consciousness. 'Why do you think never to marry?'

'You certainly ask what you wish.'

Vivian's chin went out. 'I see no reason to waste time with demure fishing for what I would like to know.'

'You are of definite opinions.'

'As are you.'

His lips firmed and his sharp nod was a statement of confirmation. 'I'm staying here because I am hoping to give Alexandria a chance to find someone else and forget me.'

In a fluid movement, he tapped his finger to one of the candle flames, drowning it in its own wax. 'I felt that she passed the bounds of friendship by refusing to understand my reluctance to go further with our courtship.'

'I am certainly glad you didn't think I passed the bounds of just meeting someone by suggesting a kiss.'

In little more time than it would have taken her to count to five, he extinguished all but one candle, using his fingers. 'That kiss.' He leaned back now into his chair, lost in memories. His face was towards the ceiling and his arms were lax, and his legs sprawled. If she'd just entered the room, she might have thought him dozing. 'It was a perfect kiss to me. Sweetness. You. I knew then that I had been correct in ending the courtship with Alexandria. I had seen the gaiety in Alexandria and thought it enough. That's not fair to her.'

The azure glimpse took in all of her, evaluating. 'I cared for Alexandria. But love?' He shook his head.

'Have you loved anyone at all. Ever?' The dim light in the room, the circumstances of her health, the tiredness gave her freedom to ask. And the wine at dinner hadn't hurt.

'Is there no question you won't ask?'

'You have the freedom not to answer.'

'And I have the strength not to answer. Sometimes, ignoring gives one the appearance of responding. If I refuse to answer, it's as if I'm agreeing. I don't appreciate that.' He pulled at the cravat tied at his throat, loosening it, then stood. With one stride, he closed the distance between them. 'But, no. I've not been in love, nor do I believe in it. It is a fleeting lie people tell themselves and others for various reasons. Much like the tales Ella Etta told me over the years.'

He leaned his upper body towards her. 'More questions, Miss Vivian?'

'Everleigh, I have been ill two years.' She had to look up at him and she raised her fingers to emphasise her words. 'Two years of reading, embroidery and trying to get the strength to read more and embroider more.' She dropped her hand. 'I have had some time to think and found I have little to think about. You are a man with much more experience in life than I have and you've all sorts of answers to questions I don't even have enough awareness to know what to ask.'

'Ask me,' he offered and let the silence build.

She waited. 'Ask what?'

'Whatever thought is burning into you with such intensity that you cannot let the subject drop.' He moved closer, lessening the air between them. 'I know what you want to know.'

She shrugged. 'I don't know… I… I don't really have a question, other than what I asked.'

His chin tilted down. 'Don't be a coward.'

'If I asked for another kiss, would you give it?' She asked the question, not as an offer, but curious.

He reached out, taking her hand and pulling her to her feet. His fingers warmed her hand, but slid up her arms to hold her shoulders. The sensation of her skin touched him, but he ignored it, reminded of how easily a female could capture a male's attention.

Vivian could just do so more easily than others, but it didn't matter. He spoke carefully, not wanting to hurt her, aware of the tenderness and innocence she held. 'No, Vivian. That was a fleeting instant. We both had just seen Mavis injured and our emotions were high. You probably wanted to be distracted.'

He looked into the distance. 'Vivian, you should have been married long ago. You have too much curiosity for your own good. And now it is time we both said goodnight.'

'I'm most curious to know what is behind the curtain of your thoughts. I want to know more of you than I ever expected.'

Now he moved closer, so near he could not breathe without taking in the warmth of her.

'Vivian.' He took her chin, and she couldn't move. He'd made her motionless with his touch, but he'd not been able to stop himself. 'There is little to interest you in my thoughts. I put them from myself.'

'You cannot.'

'Yes.' He shook his head, moving away. Standing within arm's reach could lead to another kiss and she probably would not refuse him. And he would have stepped past a layer of caution that they needed between them. He had been around long enough to know when the warnings sounded in his body. Long enough to listen.

He took a step closer to the bookshelves.

Vivian watched him. A sheltered, naive innocent. Unaware of the catastrophic consequences that could be unleashed by simple kisses, soft touches and too much trust and naivety. He couldn't bring her into his world of solitude.

'You really shouldn't have stopped at the estate. Have you never heard tales of princesses wandering deep into the woods and needing to be rescued? There are no knights to rescue you if your heart should get involved.'

'My heart?' she asked. 'I doubt that I have any strength in it. My strength is used to simply stay alive. I feel stronger around you. That's all it is and I like it.'

'That is so very dangerous. Because then when I leave, you will have used your health and have even less than you had before.'

He returned to his chair again and lowered himself into it.

He'd never expected to find a visitor at the estate.

When he'd returned, he'd searched out Ella Etta and told her about Alexandria. He'd even told her about Vivian's unexpected visit in town—but not the kiss—and how he'd felt concern for the innocent woman, asking Ella Etta to search out Vivian to see if she could help her.

Ella Etta had told him that Alexandria was not in his heart. Not in his mind. Nor even in his words. She'd claimed his voice sounded dead when he talked of Alexandria and that it would destroy both of them to be married to each other. She'd grimaced, claiming the sad part was that their children might have forked tails.

Now he had Vivian sitting in front of him—the opposite of Alexandria.

Vivian's sweetness surrounded him and he realised the trap of falling into another friendship and hurting Vivian. That, he could not risk.

Standing now, he turned away. He could not observe her reaction to what he was about to say.

His words were low, harsh, designed to send Vivian out of the room. 'I thought I needed a wife. But I don't. I have a housekeeper. I have clubs for entertainment. Solitude suits me. I gave you a kiss and I enjoyed it. But it was not anything to remember. Just an interlude to satisfy a question you had when I thought I would never see you again.'

She stood. The lighting in the room increased and he knew she'd taken the single candle, using it to light a fresh brace of candles. Her footsteps were hesitant.

'I think I should beg your pardon as well.' She spoke from behind him. 'I asked for what you thought and you told me. If it upsets me, I shouldn't blame you.'

Heartbeats passed between them, then he turned and studied her. 'Vivian. If I see you when others are present, I assure you, I will say all the proper words. We will never again be able to speak so plainly. And, if our words have offended the other, so be it. At least we spoke as we thought. I bear you no ill will at all for your questions and I appreciate your honesty. Please accept mine.'

She moved to the door, then hesitated. 'You've given me moments of peace. Almost of seeing into the future and what I could have. I will thank you for that for ever.'

She studied him, but he didn't want to dwell on what she found. He might feel something for her, and it would do neither of them any good. Then he took the relaxed knot of his cravat, releasing it more. Taking the length of it, he pulled the fabric through his hands, then he repeated the movement, sliding the cloth back and forth.

'I also came here, to sort out why I cannot love. Why

I would consider marrying someone who did not even particularly appeal to me.'

'Did you work it out?'

'Yes. I had no capability to care for Alexandria. I told her. Yet she still wished to marry me and I thought she had accepted the solitude I offered. But I realised she wanted more and I could never give it to her. She would be happy at first, but it would be the novelty of marriage and the situation. In time she would grow to hate me and I would likely do the same with her.'

'Mutual hatred would be a good reason to reconsider marriage.'

'Yes. I suppose, I have loved my mother, grandfather, my brother and my father…and the first two are gone and my father and I can't particularly agree. My brother and I do not even write to each other.'

'What of your mother?'

'I accepted that she died and I didn't grieve overmuch. I suppose I spent more time with everyone else around me than I spent with her. Each time I saw my grandfather, the man I cared most for, he reminded me that I was the keeper of the legacy. I keep the finances for my brother and my father, and my brother is sure to marry. I may marry as well, but it will be to someone who understands that my time must be spent working. I have an ability few are trusted with. London needs me. It is my lot in life and I can't let down those less fortunate than myself.'

He stood, rotated and tossed the cravat into the chair. 'It was so easy to kiss you, Vivian. A kiss that reached deeper into me than I could have imagined. A kiss that seared my soul. Too bad it could not touch my heart.'

'Ella Etta said you had no heart. I may have made a

mistake in wanting to know your thoughts.' She took one step back, pausing before she left.

'You did. At this moment, all my thoughts centre around you. All of them. It is just that that is not enough.'

Chapter Five

Everleigh watched the clock on the mantel. Vivian was still abed and it was early morning. He'd heard a maid take a tray to the room, but he thought Mavis had received the food.

The night before, when he'd realised Vivian had fallen asleep while he read, he'd stood over her, intending to speak her name and awaken her.

But he hadn't been able to. She reminded him of a tale of a sleeping princess. Shadows flickered over her, and her lashes feathered against her delicate skin. He watched, expecting her to wake and ask why he stared. An overwhelming urge to take care of her rushed over him.

He'd had trouble breathing and returned to his chair, calming himself with brandy and shutting his mind against thoughts of Vivian.

He regretted the truths he had told her. Vivian deserved soft-scented lies that caressed. Words he didn't know how to give and ones that dried up before they left his mouth.

He must ask Ella Etta what cures she had given Vivian and what she'd determined about Vivian's health.

In his room, he donned his heavy coat and noticed the quietness of the house. The home was never filled with noise, but he'd not heard anyone stirring. He wondered if the house was a tomb and none of them had realised it yet.

He hurried out of the doorway, preferring the clouded skies to the sombre walls.

He didn't have to think of the path, or fight any overgrowth. Animals, or people, kept the path travelled and his strides quickly covered the distance.

At the edge of the camp, he smelled the smoke and heard voices before he could see the inhabitants.

Ella Etta sat at her stump, plucking a chicken, saving the downy fluff in a bag. The other feathers fluttered around her, but she kept them from the fire. He knew why—the aroma of burning feathers had a stench that stuck in a person's nostrils.

He saw her brighten when he came into view. 'Ah, you finally remember where your spirit lies and visit your old friend.'

'Some friends do not have to see each other often to stay in the thoughts.'

'No matter how hard we try to forget.' She laughed to take the bitterness from the words. 'Sit. Let me tell you why you are here.'

'I know you are aware that a carriage stopped at my house yesterday. The children would carry the news.'

She shrugged, and threw some feathers in his direction, but they scattered as they left her fingers. 'Nonsense. I see it in the stars.'

'It's cloudy and the stars hide from you even at night.'

'Makes my sight more impressive.' Her voice dropped, became frail. 'But do you truly think of your old friend when you are living away?'

He nodded his head towards the chicken. 'Why do you think I have my servants raise so many fowl, leave fruit in the orchard, and not notice what disappears—because I forget you? Do not tell me you are unaware. You always return.'

She raised a finger, pointing, downy wet fluffs sticking to her fingertips. 'We return because I miss my memories of you and your brother as children. I miss him. He was lightness and you are...not lightness.'

'I miss him, too.'

He frowned, thinking of Vivian. 'What herbs did you give Vivian Darius? She's very ill.'

'Again you come to me, when you need me.'

Then he took a step closer and softened his tone. 'I truly do need some healing tonic. For Miss Darius. She's at my father's estate—I cannot believe she will live much longer. I saw her some days ago and she is much more delicate now than she was then.'

Ella Etta spoke as if the words were delivered to her by way of a righteous chariot, not merely stars. 'Baron's daughter. The girl you mentioned.'

He nodded. 'She's ill.'

Her shoulders dropped and her words lost pretence.

'Everleigh.' She held the chicken in both hands, but studied him. 'The girl stopped here yesterday. I have already given her all that I have and now we will have to see if it is enough. I have given her a potion and a promise, and now we must wait.'

'What did you give her?'

She pursed her lips. 'Honey.'

'Honey?' he gasped. 'No herbs?'

She scratched her ear. 'Honey. It might work. It does about half the time.' She kicked a few feathers away that had fallen at her boots.

He almost whispered, 'She was so frail last night. You must give her some of your medicinals.'

'You know nothing about curatives.' She glared at him. 'I do.'

'She's too thin.' Her frailness bothered him, causing a tremor of worry within him. Vivian had had no chance to experience life. Had only been kissed once and his arms could have folded twice around her. She was more delicate than a candle flame in a draught and he wanted her to stay alive. To dance the waltz she'd dreamed of and do more than collapse after a kiss.

'If she lives, she will fatten.' Ella Etta beamed. 'She has long length, fine bones and too much expression for her own good. She will be able to bear a large man's children.' She tilted her head and studied him. 'Everleigh.'

He stared back, censuring her words with his frown.

'You need the babies.' She snapped her chin up. 'Alexandria is a leech and has taken what remnants of affection you had and stomped them. She was not right for you. I told you.'

He didn't speak or change his stance.

She dropped the chicken into a water-filled bucket at her side and pulled the remaining wisps away from her ringed fingers. 'You must.'

'I won't.'

She took a breath. 'I know what is in your thoughts, but you must regain the heart that died inside you.' She reached for a knife from her sash and assessed the carcase. 'Although this bird's heart is more alive than yours.'

'I have no wish to hurt anyone, or be hurt.'

She grimaced, pulling the chicken from the bucket. 'One day this old hen ran in the woods. It preened with the others. It gave us eggs, then clucked in pride when leaving the nest. It had more knowledge of how to live than you do.'

Then she spoke again. 'Marry. Or you will live as Rothwilde does. You will be cursed. Just as he is. Perhaps he did not deserve such a fate. Perhaps he did.'

He would not abide such nonsense. 'You know I am not scared of your words, your threats or your curses. You and Grandfather taught me not to be easily gulled.'

'I am not scared of your words or threats or any curses, and…' She showed her teeth and then she raised her hand, giving him a gesture that would have shocked most women.

'Now you see why I do not visit.'

'I do not care. Just keep the orchards and gardens plentiful, and the fowl fat.'

He waited. 'As long as we understand each other.'

She examined the chicken carcase, then pulled away one last pin feather. 'We do. I am telling you as a mother would have told you…a mother not like yours, but one with more than a dollop of perfume in her head. You need to get married.'

He paused. 'Should I send more food your way?'

'No, but tell your servants to put out another rose bush like the one that died. Picking the roses was nice.'

He gave her a deep bow, preparing to leave.

'Everleigh.' Her words halted him.

He waited.

'You need a wife. You are doing yourself no favours by not marrying. You'll just grow older. Not better.'

Giving a sharp nod, he strode back to his house, making quick work of the path, especially after he heard a carriage—a carriage going to his father's house. Not away.

When he got to the front of Wildewood and saw the second vehicle, he increased his stride. He had not expected this.

Alexandria.

The words he had told her had left no room for doubt. He heard her scream of rage as his hand touched the door. Pulling the latch open, he saw Alexandria, the tip of her fan at Burton's neck.

Burton stood, board like, his glare locked on the guest, speaking. 'Miss, you will be removed if you do not take yourself away.'

Everleigh tensed and didn't flinch from the anger.

Alexandria snapped around. Her blonde hair pulled up on her head in perfect order. Her day dress no worse for the travel. She glared.

'I was told you were not at home,' she snarled out the words. Evidence of tears glistened, but he assumed they were indications of rage more than distress. Her maid stood near the wall, almost flattened into it, staring.

'I wasn't. But now I've returned. However, I am not here for you. Never again.' He wished he'd ignored the first post she'd sent him and wished he'd known her true nature.

She whispered, glowering, 'I do love you.' Her lips shook on the words.

He didn't know if he should shout or whisper, so he kept his tone emotionless. 'The more you've pressed your love for me, the more I have realised I have no wish to marry. I told you the first time I took you for a carriage ride that I was uncertain about marriage and I have never said anything to change that. In fact, the opposite is true.'

Burton—and the maid—and probably every servant in the house—listened, but Everleigh didn't care. He knew, from the contempt Burton exhibited, that the butler would gladly sweep Alexandria into a rubbish heap and even the maid would applaud.

Then Alexandria stalked forward and slapped him. The sound cracked into the room. He didn't flinch.

'You told me you cared for me.' She flashed rage.

'I said I cared for you. I do. I wish you the best. But I will not marry you, nor continue to visit.'

'You have to.' Her words were quiet. 'You have to. I love you. I cannot live without you. I'll tell everyone you led me on.'

'Say what you wish, if you don't mind being ruined in society. But nothing will make me marry you. Nothing. It would be a mistake for you to marry me, you just don't realise it.'

Her back straightened. She raised her arm, ready to strike again. 'I haven't told anyone yet that you have done this to me. But don't think this is over.'

He didn't speak.

She lowered her arm. Her tears had faded, but her stance hadn't changed. 'I have nothing to lose.'

'You're not ruined by my connection to you and you do not have to be, if you don't go shouting your love from the rooftops. That would ruin you. Loving someone who doesn't love you is a mistake. Changing the course of your life because of it is to truly be ruined.'

'Oh, I am not hiding this.' Her voice grew stronger. 'If I cannot have you, then it doesn't really matter that I can't marry.' She took a step backwards. 'You will not toss me aside and march on without a backwards glance.'

She whirled around, jerked open the door and left, her maid following. Burton took a step, grabbed a key ring and locked the door, muttering under his breath.

Everleigh noticed his father watching him from the top of the stairs.

'If she wants you that badly, wed her. She'll come to her senses then.' Then he relaxed. He moved his hand over his chin, checking to see if the valet had missed a whisker when shaving him. 'And do try to keep your pets from following you home. They're taking over the house.'

Vivian heard muffled shouting and sat up in bed. Her head felt stuffed with handkerchiefs being trampled by horses.

She noticed the dark walls and the overpowering wardrobe.

Mavis stood at the door, opened just a little, with her ear at the crack.

They both listened to the female screeches, but at this distance, the male responses were no more than a mumble.

'Your sweetheart has a problem,' Mavis said when they heard the visitor was leaving. Mavis shut the door.

'I have no empathy for her. I fear I'm following in her footsteps. I don't have a choice in the matter. Ella Etta's orders. Curse and all. But I won't scream at him in front of servants.'

Mavis snorted. 'You say that now. But you've not married him yet.'

'Mother never raises her voice at Father. She shouts at his valet and tells him to give Father the message.'

'And how did your night with the young man go? The young man who has just thrown a female out of his house because she thinks to marry him.' Mavis tapped her forefinger to her cheek.

Vivian stretched. 'I fell asleep.'

Mavis put a hand over her mouth. 'You need new courting methods.'

'May not matter anyway.'

'You're worse without your medicinals.' Mavis clasped her hands in front of herself, then crossed her arms. 'I should never have brought you to the area.'

Vivian let out a deep breath and realised Mavis wouldn't let her rest. 'Get me the thorns.'

'Very well.' Mavis's lips firmed over the words. 'You're worse—and only one day without the curatives.'

'No. I didn't take them the last few nights either.' She challenged Mavis with a stare. Vivian pulled up her elbows to push herself from the bed, but found no strength. 'Mavis. Get me the thorns. I've been sick for long enough now. I refuse to take any more of the physician's cures. It makes me feel as if my head is wobbling on my neck. My hands shake constantly and sometimes I can hardly feel my fingers. I refuse to drink any more of the apothecary mixtures that smell like the insides of a chamber pot. At least the old woman's potion has an interesting appearance. I'm tired of being treated with blistering ointments and mixtures that I can barely swallow.'

Mavis pulled the bottle from the reticule, turning the

thorns, examining the points and tied bits. 'I will never forgive Mrs Rush if this ends up hurting you.'

'Pull out the stopper. If I'm going to die, I'm sick of waiting for it.'

Mavis picked up the mixture and sat it on the bedside table. 'I'll get a spoon—though how I'll pour around this mess is anyone's guess.'

'No.' Vivian lay back on the pillow. 'Drop a bit of it on my lips.'

Mavis shook the potion, then twisted the stopper and held her hand under the coated glass to keep a drip from escaping to the floor. She raised it over Vivian's lips and a drop settled on Vivian's tongue. She tasted it.

'Really not bad, Mavis.' She licked her lips. 'Pleasant, actually.'

'It could be poisoning you. We've got to get you home.' Mavis put the stopper in the bottle, and tucked it back into Vivian's reticule. She rubbed one of her fingers, frowning. 'The points are sharp. I suspect Ella Etta fancies the world to be her Drury Lane.'

'I'm in no hurry to get home.' Vivian assessed the room. 'At least the surroundings are different here. More like a dungeon designed with all the bars hidden.'

'We've got to go. The driver is waiting and I've a bundle of food given to me by the cook so we can feast on our way. Your mother will have the physician called for her own needs if she discovers what you've been up to. She'll not be able to handle the shock.' Mavis looked at Vivian. 'I might marry Everleigh if you don't. Just to keep you from sacrificing yourself. Surely the old witch won't mind the change. To think, he held me in his arms and I don't even remember it.'

'He's just a man, Mavis.'

But he wasn't, to her. The way his voice rushed over her when he spoke to her—when it was unguarded—she'd never heard a man speak so. He had a tone she'd never before listened to. It wasn't just what he said, but the way the words moved around her, like air trying to brush her from all directions and touch her all over. She felt a surge of envy that anyone else might hear that sound and a small measure of pride that he'd talked to her of his feelings.

But it wasn't just his words. The huskiness of his voice, especially when he talked quietly, was almost more than she could bear.

Mavis snorted. 'That old trickster. I bet she saw him a few times, felt pity on you and decided to give you something to dream about.'

'You're so kind, Mavis.'

'How are you feeling?' She squinted and examined Vivian.

'No better.' She pushed her hair from her forehead, fingers threaded in the locks.

Mavis opened her reticule and pulled out a length of cloth. 'His cravat. He left it in the library after you both came out.'

Vivian stared, garbled her words as she spoke, then gasped. 'You took his cravat? You were spying?'

'I found it in the library this morning.' Mavis examined it, then quirked a brow. 'Are you sure nothing happened.'

'Nothing.'

'This does smell good. Very nice shaving soap.' She handed it to Vivian.

Vivian held the cloth to her nose and breathed in. The scent of a man's strength.

She heard the rustle of Mavis's skirts and saw a grin as she darted out the door. 'I'll tell the servants we need the carriage.'

Vivian went to the library. She tried to remember where he had left the cravat, but decided anywhere would suffice.

She dropped the cravat when she heard footsteps. Everleigh walked into the room. He had none of the openness she'd seen the night before. His hair didn't hang straight and perfect as it might have had a valet been at his shoulder. Instead the ends hung with a dash of an unkempt air which gave him the manner of a man who didn't care much about his appearance—at least not as much as nature did. Nature must have taken extra care and precision when sorting him into a form.

In that instant she understood he was bidding her farewell—she could see the goodbye in his expression and a certain finality.

She asked, rushing the words, 'Might I borrow the martyr book?'

He examined her and she forced herself not to babble. She needed an excuse to see him again. Returning the book was the best she could think of.

'Of course.' He walked to the bookcase, lifting the weighty volume. 'I'll take it to the carriage for you.'

She knew he didn't think her strong enough to carry the large volume and she wasn't sure she could manage.

He let her precede him and she thought he kept himself ready in case she might fall.

When they stepped into the sunshine, she looked up at him, ignoring the carriage as it pulled to the front, wheels creaking.

'At the risk of speaking what is on my mind—will

you be returning to London soon, or has your last visitor made the thought unpleasant to you?' she asked.

'I must return. I have some architect friends whom I help further their projects in London. The city needs to move forward and, with patronage and introductions, these men can change our world.'

She pulled her head back. 'That sounds ambitious.'

'Merely practical. Much of the most important works they do is not with the façades which impress people, but with the small, and sometimes large, things to improve lives. In the past people did not want their kitchens attached to the house because of fire. Now we feel comfortable with our chimneys and our food is delivered to our tables warm. Some day, gas lights will be commonplace in homes.'

'I cannot imagine.'

'You do not have to. Architects and engineers imagine for us.'

She paused and he almost bumped into her. Her reticule bounced against him.

'What is—? Is that a parcel of thorns?' He shifted so he could peer into the bag.

'Mementos.' She spoke quickly.

'You often collect thorns?' Curiosity sounded in his voice. Then his brows narrowed. She could have sworn she saw distrust in him.

She kept her chin high and used her hand to cover the top of the brambles. 'As you are not of a mood to speak with frankness and I am not willing to be the only one doing so, I suggest we do not discuss my collections.'

'Did you find the thorns near here?' he asked, raising a brow. 'Near a person called Ella Etta?'

'Possibly.'

'Thorns?' he asked. 'She must be——'

Vivian carefully lifted the bag so he could see inside. 'They're wrapped around a bottle, with a medicinal inside.'

He shook his head. 'I cannot believe she would give you thorns.'

'Do you not think I should take it?'

He put his hand over hers. The touch spiked through her body, reaching deeper than even the thorns could have pierced. 'If she told you to take the liquid, you should. Do exactly as she says. She's wise.'

'Oh. My.'

They stopped at the door of the carriage and he tucked the book under his left arm, easily balancing the large tome there. A breeze ruffled his hair, bringing more coolness to the air and a contrast to the rays of sunshine warming her. She shivered, though she wasn't sure if it was from the air, or his regard.

She dreaded the journey home, fearing what she was returning to.

The driver had already arranged the steps and now had the door open.

Mavis bustled from the house and moved to the carriage door. She gave a long glance at Vivian, then a brief peek at Everleigh before moving inside.

Everleigh waited for Vivian to step into the vehicle.

'It has been an eventful trip,' Vivian said. 'The most eventful of my life.'

He took her glove in the same way he might if he were intent on pulling her hand to his lips for a kiss, but only raised it chest high. 'I must apologise for your awareness of the disastrous visit from Alexandria earlier. The frankness I had with you. Please forget this happened.'

'I suspect I won't easily forget these past few days.' She pulled her hand from his and put her fingertips to her temple. 'You do tend to linger in a woman's notions.' She tapped her forehead, but her upturned lips took the seriousness from the words.

'You may keep the book.' He again took her hand to guide her on to the steps. 'I hope that while you are reading it, you do not feel that our time together has been more of a trial for you than the misfortunes mentioned in the pages.'

She contemplated his serious manner. Then she moved into the carriage. He stepped inside enough to place the volume in her hands before exiting and shutting the door with a quiet snap.

She stared at the tome and the carriage lurched forward. He'd ended the one excuse she'd had to see him again by giving her the book. And the regard he gave her said he understood what he did.

She hoped he did not regret telling her to follow Ella Etta's instructions—because if she lived he would have to marry her.

Chapter Six

Vivian stared into the mirror. Every day her mother commented that Vivian appeared so much healthier. She could see it and she could feel the strength growing each day.

A stranger's reflection stared at her. The countenance in the looking glass, while thin, had gained strength. Now, she had been corseted, plumped, lightly coloured with cosmetics and adorned from her toes to well beyond her temples.

The day before her maid had practised three different coiffures on Vivian, until they found one which met with her mother's approval. She'd insisted Vivian should appear perfect for what she called a modest gathering. Just a few friends of her father's for an evening of music, dance and boring discussions about lumber. Her mother's words.

Vivian knew full well what pursuit stood foremost in her mother's plans and Vivian had contributed.

She herself had crafted the guest list with more precision than Wellington would have given to the War Office missives.

Twenty-four days had passed since she'd taken the first drop of the sweet mixture. Even under the cosmetics she wore, her skin glowed more vibrantly than she would have believed possible.

As far as she was concerned, though, her journey to recovery had started when she'd kissed Everleigh and if she was wrong, she didn't want to know it.

And, at night, if she didn't dream of Everleigh's kiss, she dreamed of the promise.

The door opened, and Vivian expected to be summoned to help with the event, but instead her mother bustled into the room, a maid following.

'We've brought more Fowler's solution for you, dear.' Her mother touched a glove near her lips and blew a kiss Vivian's way. 'And also the extra apothecary mixtures.'

The maid moved more slowly, a small crate of jostling bottles in her hands.

Vivian hid her scowl. She didn't want to upset her mother. 'Wonderful.'

'But you must let me send for the physician. I'm so thankful the cures we've tried are finally working. You must be sure to continue the Fowler's solution.'

The maid moved to the dressing table and began placing the bottles about.

Mavis stepped inside the open door. She scowled at the curatives.

'Mother, I'm sure the last time the physician saw me before you visited your sister was all the curative I needed. He doubled his mixtures before that. After you returned, I was so much better.'

'I suppose. But you should see him again, just in case.' Her mother rushed to Vivian, took her daughter's face in her hands, examined her, and the older woman's chin trembled. 'You are much improved.' Then she rotated, advising Mavis, 'You'll see she takes her remedies.'

'Miss Vivian's health is my foremost concern.' Mavis bounced to alertness. She moved to the bedside table and lifted the spoon, holding it as if she were about to rap a child's hand. 'I watch over her with all the care of a—a gaoler.'

Her mother took a step to leave and the maid, holding the empty crate, opened the door. The sound of violins wafted in. 'After you take a dose of the Fowler's, then come and join our guests.'

'Thank you for taking care of me, Mother.'

Her mother fluttered away and the maid darted out behind her.

Mavis moved to take the stopper from the bottle of Fowler's solution. She sniffed it. 'I've been pouring this into the bowl that Mrs Cuddie uses to feed the stray cat and mixing it with his food. I thought it might help fatten up the puss…but now he's wasting away.' She eyed Vivian and sniffed the bottle again. 'I think I'll put it in the chamber pot from now on. I will not even let that stray cat near it.'

Mavis stared at Vivian. 'I would not be surprised if that Fowler's solution was part of the problem. Mrs Rush thinks it is a disastrous mixture.'

'I'm not taking it ever again.' Vivian held up the glass vial that the old woman had given her, staring at the light that filtered through the bottle. 'Besides, this tastes better—not at all bitter.'

Then Vivian took out the novel she'd hidden behind the mirror when she'd heard her mother's footsteps. 'Have you finished the martyr book?'

Mavis grumbled, 'No. I've not enjoyed it.'

Vivian tucked her novel inside the wardrobe press. 'I let Everleigh read a few pages to me because he didn't think it suitable for females. I wanted to show him how tough I could be. But I dozed off. Then, when I got home and viewed a few pages, I couldn't tolerate it at all. I tried and it would give me nightmares if I finished the stories. It reminded me of how precarious my own health has been.'

'If Everleigh asks if you've read it, just mention that people died most inelegantly and agree that it's not for ladies—not because we're too weak, just because we're above that sort of thing. Your mother didn't train you to be an improper daughter.'

Vivian stood and smoothed out her skirt. 'Mavis, who actually guided me?'

'I will take responsibility for a few tiny errors in that regard.' Mavis took the bottle and placed it on the table. 'But you're old enough to think for yourself now. You must get to this gathering you and your mother have planned so carefully. Your guests await,' Mavis muttered. 'Architects.' She grimaced. 'Architects and musty old men. Do they even know how to dance?'

'There is one way to find out.' Vivian felt something spark inside her body. If all went well, she intended to waltz with a certain friend of architects. His hand would be at her back and he would glide her around the floor, and her feet would move like petals on a cloud. Or at least she would remain upright.

She had practised and could manage the waltz better than any other dance.

He'd given her her first kiss and now she wanted her first real waltz to be in his arms. She felt her heart thump stronger at the thought. Maybe it wasn't Ella Etta's potion which spurred her to health, but the promise of Everleigh's touch.

She hurried to the ballroom, the strains of music becoming louder with each step and increasing her anticipation.

When she walked through the doorway, she shivered inside. She imagined herself in the waltz with Everleigh, and her heart pounded. She could hardly wait until the dance. The musicians had been instructed to change the order of their musical numbers depending on when she stopped next to a tall blue-eyed man—assuming the maid had passed the message along.

In the ballroom, feathers bobbed from the heads of silver-haired matrons. Many of the males had waistcoat buttons burdened by the tension of holding fabric together.

One group of three older women talked in one corner. A cluster of four mixed at the edge. Many of the husbands had made their way to the smoking room where they could be comfortable with more boisterous talk.

Her father raised his glass to her when she entered and immediately started her way. In only a few strides, he stood at her side.

But she didn't see Everleigh.

'What are you up to?' her father asked when he stopped beside her. 'When your mother told me the men you wished invited, I thought you must be planning a construction project. Are you? Are you planning on building some sort of nest? If so, I must say I am pleased.'

She couldn't smell wine on his breath. She noticed his glass and wasn't sure what it contained.

Blast it, she hoped he did not get foxed.

She pulled the top of the long glove taut. 'I like the smell of sawdust.'

He took an exaggerated sniff of the air. 'On the right man, I'm sure. All but one of the ones you suggested is stodgy and smells of eau de camphor as much as wood shavings. Everleigh would make a good match, but...'

He took a sip of his drink, downing a good portion.

She followed her father's stare to find Everleigh, who stood with his back her direction.

'I see there's method in your madness. Though your mother might be bored, the men are clustering together like bees working a hive. And, since I know their interests...' he spotted a group wearing coats behind the fashion '... I can only suppose they're buzzing about timbers or some form of waste water.'

'Important topics for men.'

'I must warn you...' his voice lowered '... I think the particular bee you're watching is not marriage-minded. Not long ago Alexandria Abernathy was pursuing him and she couldn't get him to wed.'

She waited, hardly breathing while she wondered what her father would say next.

'He's standoffish, but not rude. Hardly ever at the clubs, though I know he belongs to Boodle's. Never jests much. Solitary much of the time. Never been connected with any particular woman long, except Miss Abernathy.'

'Anything else bad of him?'

'Vivie, most women only wish to hear good of the men they are interested in pursuing.'

'I suppose I could find that out on my own. But the bad—that is often concealed more.'

'But spoken of more hastily sometimes,' he said.

Her father observed Everleigh. 'Vivie, he's just...' He grimaced. 'I don't see the two of you making a match. I've known of his father for a very long time. He was a few years above me at Oxford.'

He took his empty glass and retrieved fresh drinks, returning in seconds to hand her a glass of lemonade. She took it, relieved he wasn't slurring his speech and was taking care what he put in his glass. He wasn't foxed.

Vivian took a drink, and pretended she was more interested in her own glass. 'Thank you, Father. Now tell me all you know about Everleigh that might give me pause. Not the soft things I might hear from Mother about the way his grandmother embarrassed herself or his father beheaded a rose bush.'

'Apparently, he gets his reserve from his father, who left London and moved to his country home. He rarely graces events. The man never considers his duties. Barely attended his studies, though he was smart enough. Makes it all the sadder how he has wasted his life. For all I know Everleigh could have inherited the title now.'

'No, his father is very much alive.'

Her father snapped his head towards Vivian. 'How do you know this?'

'Well, as you know, unlike us, servants do talk.' She examined the glass in her hand. 'Mavis has become acquainted with Everleigh's housekeeper and you would think they are sisters. Mavis has taken to visiting with the lady on occasion and sharing titbits of family news.'

'So that is how you know of him?'

'Mavis.' Vivian took a delicate sip. 'Plus, his town house isn't far from ours, so it would be expected that I might see him about.'

'I don't trust your companion either. Never have. Your mother insisted we keep her on.'

'His housekeeper has no complaints of Everleigh,' Vivian continued, 'and she said he is amazingly reclusive even in his own home. His valet tends him with great care. Everleigh is reluctant to spend time with his father, though the Earl visits him regularly. In town, Everleigh is dedicated to improving the conditions of the city. But he's not much for socialising—as you're aware. Even with choosing the guest list carefully, I wasn't sure he'd attend. Mother worked hard. Mavis passed the news to Mrs Rush, who was to tell his butler to put in a word with his man-of-affairs to speak highly of the night.'

'Viv. I must warn you off. I don't think he is a man you should be aware of.'

'How many unmarried men of the *ton*—the ones you see at clubs—do you think are suitable for me to court?'

'You ask too many questions.' He stepped away, taking the pitcher of lemonade from a passing footman, pouring himself another drink, then swirling the liquid in the glass. 'I am so pleased to see your health returning, but I would hate to see a setback caused by a romance with him. Vivie, you are my daughter.' He frowned. 'It's my job as your father to keep the unworthy men away from you.'

'Well, put some worthy ones my way. I'm curious.'

'You certainly did not invite the right crowd for yourself. It is time you married, though.' He patted her back.

'I'm so pleased to see you taking an interest in society.' Then he walked away, humming under his breath.

Vivian stood at the refreshment table, thinking of the way Everleigh's cravat had felt in her hands.

At the beginning of the night, her father had consented to introduce her to Everleigh. Everleigh had been overly solemn, treating the meeting as if he'd never heard Vivian's name before.

Then a guest with his mind focused on sewers ambled over and motioned him away to talk of rain drainage.

Now, she noticed Everleigh's study of her. Then he gave a slight bow.

From across the room, she gave a small curtsy.

His lips pressed together, but the edges shifted upwards—almost as if prised. It took a heartbeat, but then he walked her direction.

She turned to the quartet and signalled the leader, who nodded.

They'd just started the current piece of music, but next would be a waltz. She wanted to adjust her gloves or touch her hair, but instead, she forced herself to stay still and her appearance calm.

Everleigh stopped in front of her.

'I almost didn't recognise you earlier. I'm so pleased to see your health has improved.'

The music isolated them from the rest of the room. She had to move close to hear his words and noticed he dipped his head to her. Watching his mouth to read his lips heightened her awareness.

'I've been getting well.'

'I'm pleased.'

She checked his expression carefully. He told the truth in a way that went deeper than idle speech.

'Yes, but I've still no wish to waste time. Pretend it's well into the night and continue speaking your thoughts to me. I find them enlightening.'

'No man wishes anyone to know everything he thinks. He would likely lose all his friends.'

'I would say a man doesn't even know all his own mind if the actions I've seen some of them take are any indication.'

'We're not a perfect gender. We leave perfection to the women.' His head swooped closer to hers and her mind took him in like a blast of something much stronger than lemonade. He smelled of starch and clean linen, and maleness. Better than new gloves and slippers combined. The same power his lips had wielded on her with a kiss now she felt just from his proximity.

'Your questions revealed as much as you asked and I didn't feel as if you were trying to manoeuvre me as much as know my thoughts.' His words softened. 'But don't expect such frankness again.'

'Perhaps you will miss it.'

He glimpsed the other guests before his perusal returned to her. 'I could not say otherwise. But I notice the men who've been invited here and I imagine all the preparations involved in a soirée. All the guests are solemn, content to gather in groups to discuss work. An event designed around guests which would make it necessary for me to attend.'

She didn't back away from it. 'Give me recognition for the attempt. It took careful planning and research. Mother even visited wives so husbands' arms could be twisted, pleasantly of course.' She paused. 'I wanted a waltz, I suppose.'

He lifted one brow. 'You refused it before.'

'Yes. But I'm not dying now. And to speak with you is so different from what I am used to. Do you think I could ask the same questions of any other man that I ask of you? I've never even spoken so bluntly with my father, although I do with my mother.'

'Well, I don't think it is expected of you. Particularly if you are interested in marriage. Fluff catches more notice from the male of the species than seriousness.'

She didn't let her expression falter. 'Of all the sins in life, I don't remember seeing blunt conversation on the list.' She shrugged. 'Nor is selecting a husband, although sometimes I'm not certain it shouldn't be. Depends on the husband, I suppose.'

He laughed, then shifted sideways, moving so no one in the room but she could read his expression. His words were soft.

'Your father is not happy at the sight of our standing close.'

She couldn't see her father past Everleigh's shoulder. 'In that case, he would be disgruntled if he knew we'd visited previously, I'd imagine. I don't think he'd understand that my main concern was recovering.'

Edging around Everleigh, she peered at her father. He frowned at them, then glowered at his lemonade, gripping it with white knuckles.

If he'd had a stronger libation in his glass, he wouldn't have noticed whom she danced with. His attempt at sobriety might not last past the evening.

'Your father doesn't like that I am near you.'

'Are you certain?'

'Yes,' he said.

'Don't believe that you are the sole cause of his glares. He combats his weaknesses and the fight inside him shows, but is directed at himself.'

Her father appeared distant and Everleigh more so, but she could sense his attention. She wondered how she could ever have asked someone for a kiss who appeared so confident. She would not have thought herself brave enough. She'd been so ill her mind must have been muddled, but she didn't regret it.

The first bars of music from the next dance would have covered his words, except his mouth had moved near her ear. 'A waltz is beginning. I do remember your refusal of my first request and I'm giving you a second chance to turn me down.'

'That is your error, then. I have no plans to refuse, and had asked for the waltz to be played should you stand near me. I hated to say no the first time. I wanted another opportunity.'

He swept her into the dance and kept a more-than-respectful distance, and a perfect light touch on her back, as he swirled her around the floor.

He didn't speak and neither did she. The movement of their steps joined them, but the silence changed the dance into something different. She refused to chatter on about nonsense and relished the music, the motion and the man.

In her mind, this truly signalled the rest of her life. The dancing was glorious.

This was the first time her slippers had been used and would not be the last. She'd planned that her initial return to society would be with Everleigh in a waltz she had dreamed of, and could manage with ease. Proof she had returned to a life that had been interrupted.

He had kissed her. That day had initiated her journey into a world that she could now take part in. Now she swirled through the movements with him, putting the last bit of polish on the adventure of living again. Only this time, she would not flutter at the edges. She would leap into the experience and savour her existence.

She had carefully planned this first guest list and she would plan the next one without architects.

She had tried to fulfil the promise to Ella Etta, and perhaps she would at some point, but Everleigh would have to agree and that would take time.

The music ended and Everleigh escorted her near the entrance, which had been abandoned. Both waited in a companionable silence.

Then he bowed to her. She inclined her head and strolled away to her father.

'He's not for you.' He offered the words with a mild grimace. 'You're smarter than that, Vivian. If you marry, you want a husband who adores you. One who thinks of you first. Who is over the moon for you. Much like the man I was when your mother and I married and I intend to become again.'

'Would you mind too terribly if I didn't wed?' Vivian asked.

Her father ducked his head. 'I would feel I'd failed you.'

'Nonsense.' She tucked her hand around his arm. 'You have encouraged me and cherished me.'

'I appreciate your saying that. But you must have a husband. It is the way of things.'

Then a guest called to him. He patted Vivian's hand

and extricated himself, but Vivian squeezed his arm, signalling him to wait.

Vivian clenched her jaw. Marriage would have been the way of things for her had she not stared at the walls around her. Before, she had known she would some day marry and, if her parents' rules seemed constricting, she had always expected that soon she would have her own household.

When she came out in society, all the world had glittered in front of her. But before she could immerse herself in it, her body trapped her into a world of solitude and immobility. She'd been crushed inside as well as out.

Her parents adored her and they were celebrating her return and understanding of her wish to experience life.

Everleigh's form flashed in her line of vision. He talked with someone—another of the architects. She noticed the way he held himself. The way he towered above the others. His dark hair. Imagined his devilish stare, but she'd experienced his kindness.

Her voice remained calm, but she didn't raise it more than enough to reach past her father. 'I think I might almost be, thereabouts, in fondness with him.'

She did like Everleigh, and she had made the promise.

Her father faltered in his steps, waving the other man away, and his mouth opened.

'A young girl's fancy.' His voice, the same one he would have used to calm her if she'd seen a snake. 'Vivie. You've been sick. You've missed the chance to be courted properly.' His posture stiffened and his hand tensed at her waist. 'You need to reconsider. To be courted. To be pursued by someone who cares enough to seek you out.'

'He's been kind to me.'

She knew her father evaluated her words. Watched her. Suspected she'd seen more of Everleigh than he knew.

'Vivie.' He shook his head. 'No.'

'So, he's ice. I don't need love. I have plenty of it from you and Mother.'

His voice was a harsh whisper, so close she could smell the lemonade he'd been drinking. 'He'll ruin you. He'll leave you. Don't think to marry him. He won't propose. But I should be thankful he won't wed you—at least you'll have an escape.' He paused. 'Where have you seen him and how has he fascinated you?'

'Father, those are good questions. I have no answers to give you.'

'There will be no more events like this. He will not be invited again to my house. A man is to pursue you. Not the other way around. I will not have it. You deserve all the fripperies of a romance.'

He stalked away, the forced pleasantness he emitted not reaching far.

Vivian joined the edge of a conversation held by women twice her age. They spoke of how to keep one's cook abreast of new menus, comparing cookery books and meals they'd served their guests. She pretended interest and surreptitiously watched Everleigh.

Even from across the room she saw the movement of his mouth, and remembered it touching hers. Surely she imagined…? No. Her body warmed. She imagined nothing. She'd noticed his strong legs when she first saw them and recognised the compassion when he'd carried Mavis.

Even if she didn't love him, even if he had no heart, the man had other assets. Assets she could see and she was sure she could enjoy completely if he'd a mind to show her how.

But she might fall in love with him and that would be painful when he moved on to his own interests. Besides, she had been held prisoner by her illness for far too long. Even getting her mother to accept when Vivian left the house had taken promises of taking care, of not overtiring herself, of not staying away longer than planned, of not leaving sight of her companion. The rules had stifled her and almost made death seem like a release.

She had escaped a gaol. She would waltz, but not right back into another walled world where someone else controlled the drawbridge.

But Everleigh fascinated her. And the length of him, so still while he talked. A human animal of stored strength—power at rest.

Her mind tried to commit him to a place in her imagination that she could retrieve at any time. She'd made the promise and she didn't regret it. But her father had a point.

Vivian blinked twice. She felt a hunger inside herself she didn't know was possible or had existed. Everleigh bent his head. Something sparked, flint and steel in him, capable of lighting even more fire in her.

His head jerked, as if a sound had caught his attention. An animal scenting a change. If she'd not been watching him closely, she would have missed the altering of his features. His expression didn't falter—

instead it locked into place. Darker. Something at the door had affected him.

Gone was his affable nature. His kindness. She now knew why Ella Etta had said he had no heart. This man might not have tender feelings. The softness he showed her might have been actions learned so he could relate well to others. The innate charm of the surface could hide coldness deep within him.

Her mother had once told her that a man's heart worked differently from a woman's. A man could speak tender sentiments, but they meant no more to him than singing the words to a pretty song. A man liked the sound of his own voice and the results. Then he could turn to a different companion, or a hand of cards, or a bottle of brandy, and sing the same song again. A man lived to sing, a woman to hear.

Now Everleigh was staring at the doorway, even though he wasn't facing it directly.

Alexandria and her father stood at the entrance. Alexandria wore a pale yellow gown, simple, with gold bows at the tiny sleeves. She didn't have the appearance of a princess, or a Roman goddess. Instead, she dressed to be the virginal sacrifice. A determined one.

A man almost drowning in his own whiskers stepped up to talk with Alexandria's father and, after a second, both men chuckled.

But Alexandria was unaware of anything in the room, except Everleigh. She wasn't smiling.

Alexandria?

He and Alexandria assessed each other, her scrutiny the one of a gladiator in the ring.

She moved, slipping away from her father, walking around the edge of the dancers. She stopped in front of

Everleigh. Vivian could only see her profile. Alexandria reached out her gloved hand and let it touch the sleeve of his coat. He stepped aside. She followed. This time, he didn't increase the distance. Everleigh spoke, but his lips hardly moved. Alexandria's head jerked closer to him so he bent forward. He gave a tight, negative shake of his head.

When Alexandria raised her hand again his glare stopped her. Vivian couldn't see his face well enough to read his expression. He spoke to Alexandria, words clipped, straightforward. Then Alexandria wove through the crowd, pretending not to see anyone, and searched out the wine.

As Everleigh walked away, a casual observer would have noticed nothing out of the ordinary, but Vivian saw the irritation. He spoke to an older man, laughed, and the man slapped Everleigh's back, chuckling as well. They moved to the billiards room.

The musicians increased the volume and she felt she had to escape. Too many people around her and she'd not completely regained her strength.

Seeing Everleigh with Alexandria had taken the breath from her body.

Alexandria.

Vivian had not expected Everleigh to notice Alexandria so quickly. But he'd had anger in the tightness of his jaw.

Chapter Seven

Vivian stared at the wine in her glass and could not force her thoughts from Everleigh. She'd believed him finished with Miss Abernathy.

A voice interrupted her thoughts, its bell-like tone ringing in her ears. Alexandria spoke. 'Did you see where Everleigh vanished to?'

Vivian flinched at the voice. She'd heard it so strident when Alexandria had shouted at Everleigh at his father's house.

Alexandria's blonde hair, more perfect than anything her lady's maid could ever create, was upswept and circled with a strand of pearls. She wasn't frail of form, but something about her made her the kind of exquisiteness men wanted to save from raindrops. Brown lashes flicked gently and her red mouth needed nothing to brighten it.

Vivian didn't answer the question. 'You're lovely tonight, Alexandria. The dress is magnificent.'

The blonde grasped the skirt lightly and gave a tiny twirl. 'I ordered another in blue.'

'I'm surprised you came,' Vivian said, knowing she'd

not put Alexandria's name on the invitation list. 'This is a gathering of my father's architectural friends. Rather stuffy.'

Alexandria laughed. 'Then you must be glad I'm here so you'll have someone to talk to. Your mother didn't invite me. But when your father and mine were talking Father realised his friends would be here, so of course your father invited us, and *of course* I knew you would want someone to break the monotony. Although…' she gave another twirl '… I'm not finding it as dull as I thought. Especially since Everleigh is here. He's delectable.' Alexandria linked her arm through Vivian's.

'How are you acquainted?' Alexandria purred, but the tightness in her grip gave Vivian the feel of being prodded with a stick.

'I've had occasion to meet most of the men my father knows.'

'Is your father matchmaking for you?' Alexandria's eyebrows rose. 'You're barely on the shelf. Not a true, true spinster. He might be thinking it's past time for you to marry.'

'I'm perfectly happy being unmarried.'

'That's what all women say who haven't been asked. Just don't have designs on Everleigh.' Alexandria pulled back, unlinking their arms. 'He doesn't plan to wed, or he would have married me.' She held her gloved hand in front of her, as if examining where a wedding ring would go. 'I will miss him.'

Any semblance of friendship left Alexandria. 'I know you were at his house. I saw the carriage, and I waited to see who was visiting him. You followed him to the country. I saw you and your companion leaving. You stole him away from me and I don't take that lightly. Watch your step.'

'I always watch my step,' Vivian said, 'so I will know where to put my foot. I wouldn't want it in my mouth. I would not want anyone to know I had been rejected.'

'It doesn't matter to me.' Alexandria moved closer and lowered her voice, tapping her fan on Vivian's arm. 'I've a vengeful spirit and I assure you that I will remember that you tried to turn Everleigh's attention to you—what I simply do not fathom is why you thought he might fancy you.'

'It shouldn't matter to you at all. If his wishes are considered, by the time he marries he may be so doddery that he can't remember you.' Vivian could still feel where the fan had tapped her arm.

'No. He's going to marry soon. I'll see to that.' Alexandria flicked open the fan.

'You should be careful, Alexandria. You might appear desperate.'

'Desperate? And, what were you doing at Everleigh's house?'

'What makes you think it was me?'

Alexandria threw back her head. 'I saw you leaving with my own eyes.'

'I assure you, I don't care. The important thing is whether Everleigh wants to marry and we both know he does not. There is nothing either of us can do about it and I'm thankful it doesn't matter…much to me.'

Alexandria grinned when she caught the hesitation in Vivian's words.

It did matter. She had promised the old crone she would marry. She hoped Ella Etta was simply jesting and hadn't taken that seriously.

Alexandria said, 'Watch yourself, Vivian, you could so easily be ruined and it would not break my heart to see you in a heap of misery.'

Just as Alexandria tapped her fan at Vivian again, she moved away. 'Lovely accessory, Alexandria. Please take care with it. No one need be scared of a fan.'

Alexandria fluttered the ornament open. 'I will remember you said that.'

Everleigh watched the billiards game, making a wager because it was expected, without caring about the outcome. The men talked loudly enough to cover the sounds of the music in the ballroom, which pleased him. He let the jesting fade into a buzz of noise, drowned out by his own thoughts.

He'd not had a complete night's sleep since Vivian had visited with him at his father's. He'd known she was ill and the anger he'd felt at not being able to mend things had almost consumed him.

He'd accepted the invitation expecting—if she attended—to see frailty. Instead, he'd almost not recognised her. She'd gained weight and the weakness had vanished from her frame. He'd caught himself as he'd taken a step to her side, but then he'd stopped.

He wanted to lift her from the floor, swirl her around and make her laugh with the joy of being alive.

Euphoria floated inside him. More happiness than he'd ever felt and it wasn't because of anything except the life he'd seen in Vivian. She'd blossomed.

Something jarred his shoulder. A gruff voice jabbed into his ears. 'You just lost your wager.' Vivian's father stood at his side.

Everleigh left his reverie. The game was over. Men

laughed. The winner blew a puff of air over the tip of his cue stick. Everleigh didn't even remember which man he'd bet on.

'I saw you…watching…earlier.' Lord Darius acted ready to dash his drink over Everleigh.

Everleigh looked at the glass in Darius's hands, half-expecting to be wearing it soon. One couldn't throttle the host in his own house, particularly as he understood Darius's anger. 'I enjoy watching a good game.'

Darius's brows shot up. 'This isn't the only game in London. Some have higher stakes. Some have less to lose. At my house, the wagering is done with me.'

'Just pay up, Everleigh, so Darius will not have his feathers ruffled,' one of the older architects, a man whose white whiskers were in need of a shave, interrupted. He clapped a hand on Everleigh's shoulder. 'That was such a small wager, I'll cover you if you'd like.'

Everleigh reached into his purse for a coin and, with it trapped between two fingers, he held it out to Darius.

Darius didn't move. Everyone in the room watched.

Everleigh adjusted his stance slightly, so he and Darius were not side by side, but facing each other. Everleigh put the coin away.

'I say that, if you wish to continue,' Everleigh challenged, 'we finish this discussion somewhere private.'

'If you do not take care—' Darius raised his glass to Everleigh '—you can count on it,' he said, walking from the room.

'Imagine how upset he would have been if you'd won the bet,' one of the older men said. 'He's been a bear since he cut out the brandy. I tried to tell him, but he wouldn't listen. Probably had something to do with your waltz with his daughter.'

'That was a most proper moment. We hardly exchanged a word.'

The man laughed. 'I saw it. Everyone did. The two of you were so obviously, and perfectly, avoiding each other while you danced that I would have guessed a quarrel was underway. Only married people are that put out while with each other, or ones who have a few secrets tucked away. Darius might have reason to be upset.'

Vivian awoke to the sound of a maid's quick knock. The door opened before the sound had faded. She'd slept raggedly the previous night and the refrains of the waltz had resounded in her head long after the musicians had left the house. She'd dreamed of waltzing with a blasted butterfly in a sea of rainbows.

When she'd awakened the violins had faded and the room was silent, chilled, empty and dreary.

The gathering had been disastrous, she feared. Her father had left the billiards room and put his glass down on a tabletop, glared at her and stalked over to some of his cohorts. Everleigh had walked out soon after, avoided everyone, then walked to her father, put a coin on the table beside him and left.

Several men appeared to have followed Everleigh out of the billiards room and they'd hidden laughter.

The wives had been puzzled about their husbands' behaviour and whatever had occurred would likely have been shared on the carriage ride home.

Now the bedroom door opened and the servant rushed in so fast her skirt whirled around her. The girl held a silver salver, but it trembled in her hands. On the plate sat another bundle of thorns tied around a bottle.

'A person—a beggar, I expect—is at the servants' entrance. She said you must have this,' the maid apologised. 'I did not want to bring them to you, but she said she would put a curse on the whole house if I didn't.' She shuddered, glancing at the wardrobe where the first packet of thorns sat. 'I've seen that one. I know you are aware of her. I put her at the servants' table and gave her tea and biscuits.' She crept closer to Vivian. 'I didn't want your father aware. He'd be upset.'

Vivian rose from the bed. 'I understand.' She pointed. 'And, yes. Put it in the wardrobe.'

'She insists she must speak with you.'

Vivian touched the ties of her chemise and a shiver of concern formed in her stomach. 'Does Mother know?'

The maid's head quivered in denial. 'She'd get us all cursed.' The maid opened the wardrobe with one hand and sat the bottle inside. 'Not 'a purpose, of course. Not that I believe the beggar. But, miss, the hag's stare is pure evil. She frightened me.'

Vivian considered her choices. She had only one. She couldn't let her father find out what was going on. 'I'll see her.'

The silver salver scraped where the maid placed it on the table before reaching to pull out a day dress. 'Beware of upsettin' her. Your sickness could return.'

Whether her illness came back or not, her father could not learn what had happened.

The maid worked quickly, then stood at Vivian's back, fussing over the chignon she had crafted from Vivian's brunette locks, commenting on how her hair texture had regained its former glory.

Vivian had felt stronger each day—except today. Today she felt drained. Tired. When she'd awoken, she'd detected smudges when she checked the mirror. But the exhaustion thrilled her. It was from a night of dancing.

She'd never expected to see the old woman again, but a bargain had been made. Vivian felt a pang of guilt. Everleigh hadn't had a say in the transaction. But surely he'd not want her dead. If the situation were reversed, she'd marry him to save his life.

He'd thought he needed a wife, but Alexandria had convinced him that was a bad idea. But if Vivian could change his mind… If she could convince Everleigh that marriage didn't have to be more than a few words on paper.

She stood. She was a baron's daughter. Suitable to marry. She'd bring him a dowry. Children hopefully. And, if he wanted her to live in one house while he lived in another, she'd agree. The marriage wouldn't be morally binding, just legally. She would be happy to become whatever kind of wife he needed. A small sacrifice for life. Deep within herself, she knew she would have died without the woman's remedy. The thorns… those were just nonsense.

'There, miss.' Her maid put the brush down on the dressing table. 'You're radiant this morning.'

Vivian contemplated the maid. 'I don't seem pale to you?'

Her maid hesitated. 'Well, miss, you had a late evening. It's normal to be tired after all that dancing and lateness. Especially when you're not used to it.'

'Of course,' Vivian answered and stood, taking the stairs to learn what waited for her.

Vivian wanted to slide quietly into the room, but, instead, she strolled nonchalantly into the servants' dining room, straight into Ella Etta's line of sight.

The vagabond sat at the table, her clothing still the same vibrant shades as before. A teacup and empty plate sat in front of her. Ella Etta stood, yawned and scratched her belly. Vivian knew the gesture didn't show boredom, but a belief in superiority. She was staking her right to be in the house.

Ella Etta moved around the table, trailing her fingers across the wood, tapping as she meandered. Her boots, possibly a man's cast offs, clumped on the floor. Vivian realised one boot had a yellow ribbon holding the eyelets closed.

Ella Etta didn't stop until she stood directly in front of Vivian and she glared at her with the same respect a bear might give its baiters.

'Your payment, Miss Baron's Daughter?' Her chin gave an extra wiggle with each word.

'Of course.' Vivian tensed her shoulders, not moving far from the door. 'I have coin. I'll pay.'

Ella Etta tilted her head and stared into the wall. 'I believe I hear wrong, I do. You can't have said what my ears tell me.' Dark eyes swivelled to Vivian and her voice softened. 'Gold? No. I mentioned no gold. Though I should have it for being kind enough to bring you another potion to keep you alive.' She pulled the edges of her shawl together and folded one side over the other. 'Alive. Not mouldering in the dirt. Alive.' She reached to Vivian, but she dodged. Ella Etta grinned like a demented hangman anxious to begin his task. 'Alive. How does it feel to breathe? Or—even more important—how would it feel not to breathe?'

'I am grateful.'

Ella Etta pulled at the fraying fringe at the end of her shawl, frowning over the wayward thread. 'Your mother has never even sent a flowery note around, thanking me for saving her girl's life. Why would that be?'

'I...' Vivian let out a puff of breath. 'We shouldn't spar. I doubt I'd win.' She kept her voice soft, making sure no ears outside the door could hear. 'To marry Everleigh is no curse. It's a boon.' She held her hands wide. 'His shoulders alone... And they're not the best part of him. They might be his worst feature.'

Vivian raised her palms. 'What I see isn't going to get a complaint. He's...pleasant. I am working to see if he might wish to court me. I had a soirée and he attended. Just last night.'

'Words you say mean nothing.' She waved her hand, rings snapping against each other. 'You agreed to marry. I hear of no marriage banns.'

'I shall marry him if he asks me. But he might have a say in the outcome.' Vivian stumbled through the words. 'I'll marry him, if he'll just show up and say the proper words.'

'My love potion would not mix with the medicine I gave you. Of course I'd use it—but then you'd turn back into a bag of bones and I'd be wasting a potion. It's harder than owl's ears to get,' Ella Etta grumbled. 'Matchmaking wears on a body so. The lucky woman or man wants to escape. Sometimes both try.' She kicked at the floor and gave a soft groan. 'But it's my calling.'

'I'm not opposed to Everleigh.'

Ella Etta worked a crumb free from her teeth, then arranged the scarf at her temple with the care a queen would give a tiara. 'You'd be daft in the head not to want him. But you are too careful. I cannot do everything.' She rapped her knuckles on a bowl someone had left on the table. She lifted the vessel and thumped its bottom. Her teeth showed when she smiled.

'I'll take this present—not much to it—in exchange for giving you more time to marry. I would say my patience grows thin—but then I'm not known for tolerance. If truth be known, I've no patience. Threw it in front of a galloping horse and haven't missed it.' She contemplated the ceiling. 'Wait. Memory fails me. That might not have been my patience, it might have been my husband.' She chuckled.

Ella Etta held the bowl up to the window light and squinted, examining the crockery. Then, she tucked the cookware under her arm. 'You have until the potion I brought today is used. If you've not married by then, you'll not get another.' She gave another tap to the vessel. 'You'll either be a lovely bride or a fetchin' corpse. No matter to me.'

Ella Etta walked to the door, then twisted around. 'If you choose the path of bein' dead, don't worry about your mother mourning you. I'll take her health as well so she doesn't suffer your loss.' She touched her shawl. 'I'm just inclined that way.'

She left the room, the basin tucked tightly under her arm.

Vivian felt her strength wane. All she had left in her bag of seduction was a book of martyrs.

That afternoon, Vivian tried to think of how best to approach Everleigh and she remembered the only excuse she had.

She gathered Mavis and dressed for an outing, offering to go to the lending library to select a book her mother might like to read. Her mother was so pleased to see Vivian active that she beamed over the suggestion.

Vivian took the brimmed bonnet which would sit back on her head and arranged it not to cover the careful curls the maid had fashioned. She checked the placement, pleased that the pink ribbons matched her dress.

The door to her chamber opened and Mavis stuck her silvery head around. 'Carriage is at the front, ready for us.'

'Is the book too heavy for you?' Vivian asked.

Mavis smirked, grunted as she raised it with both hands and spoke. 'I'll tell you the good parts on the way down the stairs. That's all the time it will take. If the conveyance is slow, I'll tell you the unpleasant bits on the ride. I am now, too, officially a martyr and have been punished for all the embellishments I made in order to get this job.'

Vivian bustled Mavis from the house, shushing her.

When the coachman moved to help Mavis up the steps, she grabbed the side, gave a startled pause, gripped the volume close and squirmed her way inside.

Vivian didn't see inside the carriage until she was halfway in the door. She stopped. Her father sat, staring forward, arms crossed, mouth in a straight line. His cravat wasn't the normal showy burst at his neck she was used to seeing on him, but a flat, drooping twist, and his brows were narrowed.

'Do you…want to visit the library?' she asked him. 'I will be pleased to select something for you.'

Mavis raised the tome. 'Builds your constitution, reading. If you've not heard about all these saintly folks, you could enjoy this one.'

'I'll travel with you. Wouldn't want the two of you to get lost. Who knows where you'd end up?'

'You don't enjoy the lending library,' Vivian insisted, one hand clutching the door frame.

'Much more enjoyable than an outing to the dressmaker or a shop to get hair ribbons I'd never wear.' He thumped his hat. 'Get in. You're holding up our departure.'

She settled herself beside him, arranging her skirts to keep wrinkles away.

Mavis held the book for him to see the title.

He pointed to the word martyr. 'Is it about fatherhood?' He reclined fully against the seat.

'No,' Vivian grumbled. 'This is a ladies' outing. To return that book and then search for one for Mother. And a detour to select fripperies. Ribbons. Reticules. Pelisses. Perfumes. Scented soaps. Things I like.'

He let out his breath slowly. 'I am sure that this is a ladies' trip and I'm certain you're searching for something. Am I disrupting your plans?'

'We are also going to discuss *The Book of Martyrs*.' Vivian nodded to Mavis and the companion raised the volume again.

'Read every word of the first chapter.' Pride coated Mavis's words. 'Near killed me. They need to add a section about the many companions who have left this earth in dedicated service to the family.'

Lord Darius reached out, taking the book, thumbing through it, before sitting it casually in his lap, and, reaching up with a free hand, thumped the top of the carriage to alert the driver to begin. 'I'll see that your name gets added in the next edition.'

The wheels rolled with a forceful creak. 'Odd,' he

mused, gazing again at the book, and flipping briefly through the pages. 'Watson said he'd been requested to take my daughter to a certain town house before you went to Piccadilly.' He squinted. 'If memory serves me right, I believe I might know who resides there.'

'My dear friend Mrs Rush lives there,' Mavis inserted.

'Is that all?' The last word lingered on her father's lips, accusing.

'And we are to return the book to Everleigh,' Mavis continued.

Vivian speared Mavis with a look.

Mavis raised both hands, palms out. 'I'm no martyr.'

Vivian spun towards her father.

He patted his pocket. 'I pay wages. With everyone but Mavis that does earn some loyalty. They may not volunteer information easily, but will answer when asked directly. I discovered that, when your mother and I visited her sister, the two of you disappeared one afternoon.' He glared at Mavis. 'You are sacked.'

Vivian's spirits plummeted. She could not be the cause of Mavis losing employment.

'Father, you can't toss her out. She went to protect me. I had heard of a medicinal and I went in search of it.' She moved forward. 'My complexion. It's improved. I'm not trembling now. I'm recovered.'

'What was in the concoction you took?'

'I don't know, but it tastes like honey. I just know I was dying and I started taking that cure instead of the others and I started saying I was well so I wouldn't have to see the physicians.' Vivian pleaded for him to understand. 'I improved. Each day.'

She stared at her father. 'You know how ill I was.

I wanted to live. I would have tried anything to keep alive. The physician had said he could do no more and I didn't want him to say it again. Just seeing him at the house made me feel worse.'

'If you are better because of the search, then I can forgive it, certainly,' he said. 'I can forgive the trip, only. So, what is *this* excursion about?'

Vivian didn't speak, avoiding her father's question.

'Well, since I am sacked,' Mavis said, 'I will admit that I have been reading a book from Lord Everleigh's library. That block of a book…' she wiggled in her seat '…that could break a toe if you dropped it on your foot. It's full of hideous tales worthy of nightmares and I hated it. I wanted it out of the house as soon as I could get it out.'

'How did you get a volume from his library?' her father's voice threatened.

'Well, it all started when I became friends with his housekeeper, Mrs Rush. Now, she knows how to keep a tidy residence.' Mavis chattered faster. 'Dear friend, Mrs Rush. Helped me when I had a bump on my nose. You remember that bump… From a door. I didn't see it until it was too late.'

'The housekeeper? I remember you telling me Mavis and the housekeeper are friends.' Her father eased into the squabs. 'Is that true?' he asked Vivian.

'Yes.'

Vivian soothed Mavis. 'Since my dear companion is so devoted to me, she was studying the volume for me.'

'I am. That I am. Trust me, you wouldn't want her delving into it.'

Her father stared at the carriage roof, teeth clamped.

'We had to obtain the medicinal,' Vivian insisted.

'Everleigh's housekeeper told us where we might discover it.'

'And, you received this book of barbarous acts?' The words reverberated inside the walls of the carriage, hurting Vivian's ears.

'Yes.'

'Vivian, he is wrong for you and he is not interested in courting you. A suitor gives a treacly book of poetry. A suitor pretends fascination in your stitchery and fripperies. Not this.' He slapped a palm on to the cover. 'This is a volume a man would give a female he wishes to discourage.'

'Then we really must return it, as I am offended.' Vivian shuddered. 'I am fortunate to discover this now.'

'Good heavens. You are your mother's daughter.'

'Yes. I am fortunate to have you both.'

Her father observed her, silent at last.

When the carriage wheels stopped, the voice of the groom filtered through the vehicle while he murmured to the horses as if they were favoured children. The springs squeaked and the carriage wobbled as the driver stepped from his perch to open the door.

No one spoke until Mavis said, 'I believe I'll remain in the carriage. Surely the both of you can return those sweet tales without my help.' She peered at Lord Darius. 'Your presence will add respectability and I can ruminate about my next employment.'

'You're so right,' Lord Darius snapped when he stepped out of the carriage.

Vivian followed, examining Everleigh's town house. She'd not noticed the austere stones on the façade earlier, being too overcome by Mavis's accident.

Lord Darius gave her a prod. 'Move along. Don't

gawk at the windows. You've seen houses like this before. All along the streets.'

He gave her the volume. 'You get the privilege of returning these fascinating tales.'

She walked up the steps, gripping the book, and the door opened. She remembered the butler, Waincott, from the day Mavis had had the accident. She didn't see any recognition from him, but that was probably his training. He smelled, appropriately, of starch.

'We're here to see Lord Everleigh,' her father said, reaching into his waistcoat pocket and producing his card.

Then, Darius followed as the butler showed them into a drawing room.

When the servant left, Darius muttered, lips hardly moving, 'You are making such an error having any fascination with someone who'd lend you those narratives.'

Chapter Eight

⤜⤏⤠⤜

Everleigh glanced again at the card, then pushed his chair back from the breakfast table and stood, stopping to take a last drink of chocolate. Vivian's father.

Probably come to give Everleigh the coin back and he likely had heard of the visit, or wanted to warn Everleigh away from Vivian.

Vivian.

The kiss had been memorable. Not just for her. Pride flourished in him. Darius could grouse all he wanted. She'd relished it and her father could not be aware of it because only two people were there. Vivian wasn't the type to discuss something so private.

Vivian had merely passed by his father's house on the way to get her curative, and Darius might be dismayed over that, but it was too late to do anything about it.

Besides, Vivian was better.

Anyone would give respite to an ill person. Darius could not make much of a fuss because it would hurt Vivian's reputation.

'Who is it?' the Earl asked, fork poised over his plate of kippers.

'Lord Darius,' Everleigh answered. Those were the first words they'd spoken to each other during the entire meal and almost the first time they'd conversed since his father had followed him to London.

He'd claimed curiosity at how Everleigh would handle two women vying for his attentions.

Everleigh had ignored the barb.

He'd expected his father to gamble every night, but he hadn't. Everleigh had checked the betting books and had paid attention to his father's excursions. The man spent more time in coffee houses than he did gaming.

When Everleigh reached the formal drawing room, Vivian was perched on the edge of the sofa, clenching the martyr book. Lord Darius appeared enthralled by his boot tops.

Ah, he realised. Her father had discovered the volume and enquired about it. She'd told him the truth.

Darius gave him a brisk bow, but his scrutiny completely erased any politeness in the greeting.

Vivian stood, gave a small curtsy and held out the tome. 'Thank you for lending this. Very informative.' Her smile wavered at the edge. 'I know you said I could have it, but I thought it best to return it.'

He reclaimed the book. 'Can I offer you both tea?' Everleigh asked, blinking away the glare Darius was sending his way.

'So very kind, but, no,' Darius said. He reached to tug his daughter's hand and bring her to his side. 'My daughter... Could hardly get her to stop talking about all those martyrs. But we must be on our way to see about the purchase of some flintlocks.' He tucked Vivian's hand snug on his arm, took a step to the door, then paused. 'And, I was wondering, when did you lend the book to her?'

'Some time ago.'

'I believe,' a gravelled voice answered from the doorway, 'it could have been the night Miss Vivian took ill and was forced to spend the night at my country estate.'

Everleigh remained still. Darius rotated to view Rothwilde.

'It was *incredibly*...' the word 'incredibly' had never been so long '...kind of you to rescue my daughter.' Darius spoke softly, first acknowledging the older man, then fixing a stare on the son.

'Yes. Very. We've lots of shopping to do.' Vivian took a step forward, but her father didn't move.

'Father. Flintlocks and reticules. Remember?' She grasped his wrist. 'Mavis is waiting in the carriage. We mustn't let her catch a chill.'

'I'm pleased to see Miss Vivian doing so much better,' the older man continued. 'My son was genuinely concerned about her. Such a lovely young thing—and so ill that day.'

'I'm so much better,' Vivian agreed, bobbing on her heels.

'I hope you didn't visit the vagabond.' Everleigh's father gave a mournful groan. 'She's a trickster. She would gammon you for nothing more than a handkerchief. More poacher than anything else.'

Darius's head jerked to his daughter.

She patted her father's arm several times. 'I did visit someone with medicinals. Please thank her for me if you see her again.'

One side of Everleigh's mouth moved up. 'Trust me,

she takes gratitude easily from the estate and considers it her due.'

'Let us leave.' She tried to placate her father. 'We've imposed on the Earl. Mother will expect us back soon.'

This time Darius gave a harsh nod to Everleigh and the Earl. 'Many thanks for your hospitality to my dear daughter, who's been ill for some time. I have taken to going about with her as she is…recovering. I can only hope the past few years have not affected her good sense.'

When Darius escorted Vivian to the door, Everleigh's father stepped with her, quickly grasping her glove. He brought it to his lips, brushing a kiss above it. 'You and your family are welcome to visit any time, Miss Vivian. It does my son good to leave his ledgers and have someone so lovely to speak with.'

'Thank you,' she mumbled and Darius pulled her away.

Vivian got into the carriage, chin high, stomach the other direction.

Darius moved into the vehicle as if he expected the wood to move aside for him. She didn't think it would dare not to.

Mavis watched, but didn't speak.

Darius directed his words at Mavis. 'Last night I warned the man to stay away from Vivian when I should have had the good grace to offer him a guard for his door to keep her away from him.'

Vivian muttered, 'I am unmarried. I am chaperoned. I am of age. I have had only one short kiss from a man in the whole of my life, and I do not see any problems with my actions. Do you, Mavis?'

Mavis shook her head, then viewed Lord Darius and nodded.

Darius repeated the statement. 'She is unmarried, of age, barely kissed and has now taken on an obvious pursuit of a man who has questionable tastes in women,' he complained to Mavis. 'A man should court her, as I explained. It should not be a one-sided pursuit.'

'Well,' Mavis said, 'I can see—'

'You are sacked again, Mavis. This time it's permanent.'

'You do have a point, Lord Darius.'

'Everleigh did attend the party last night.' Vivian straightened her back.

Her father raised his forearm, one finger pointing sideways. He seemed unable to continue without his voice becoming loud. He stopped to compose himself and lowered his voice to a hiss. 'You will not leave the house again without a *trusted* servant. Or me. Or your mother.'

'Father. You cannot do such a thing.'

Mavis ducked her head. 'If I must hope to find work elsewhere...' she examined her fingernails '... I will only tell the truth. That I was with Miss Vivian when we were in search of a curative and she was ill, and we spent the night at the Earl's extremely well-staffed house instead of venturing into the cold night. We didn't want to risk our lives on country roads at night, which was, of course, wrong of us, and I was the, oh, so-vigilant chaperon. It was almost a house party, as another female guest arrived to speak with Lord Everleigh. After our return, I was sacked for not telling her father, as is the proper response.'

Darius calmed. 'You're not sacked, Mavis. Instead,

I'm promoting you to take care of the chamber pots. They all need cleaning, by the way. And polishing.'

He leaned towards his daughter's companion. 'Why, Mavis? Why could she not just attend a soirée like the other ladies and flutter a fan?'

Mavis shrugged, then opened her mouth to speak. 'Chamber pots?'

He waved the words away.

'Fans?' Vivian stared. 'I find them belittling and hideous.'

Her father coughed his derision. 'No. You merely go to a house to return a book that apparently was given to you. Can you not take a telltale sign as an indication?'

'This began when I was seeking a—' Vivian interrupted, peering sideways at her father. 'I was hoping to be cured of my illness by a woman who lives on the Earl's estate. Mavis knew it and went with me for protection. The trip was arduous. You cannot think an earl would let anyone corrupt stay on his estate.'

'Please, Mavis, tell me she did not get some elixir from some poacher. Her mother's physician has been with the family for years.'

'It saved my life,' Vivian insisted.

His voice softened. 'That explains it. You have been given some poison which has altered your mind.'

Vivian raised one hand and waved it in assent. 'There you have it.'

'Don't worry. I will get with the physician. We will find some way to clear that up. He will treat you as long as he needs.'

Vivian heard the doors clanging shut on her freedom. Her throat constricted.

'Sounds like a good idea to me,' Mavis murmured. 'I'll make sure she takes all her treatment.'

'We let your ill health destroy you.' Her father drooped.

'Well, Everleigh seemed much more irritated at you when I returned the book than at me,' she said.

'Your mother will be embarrassed to think of you straying so far from the way you were raised. You'll likely end up a spinster...chasing after a man not interested in you.'

'That's fine. I've already been one for two years... Two years of my life when I rarely left the house. I learned to dance, but hardly was allowed to walk. It's time I enjoyed my spinsterhood.'

He thumped his head with the heel of his hand and then let it bump back against the side of the carriage, dislodging his hat. He righted it. 'This must stop. You are pursuing a man, yet you say you don't particularly care whether you wed or not.'

Darius growled, thumped the carriage top and, when the driver stopped, her father stepped out. But before he left, he peered inside. 'Mavis, you are the cause of all this, I know it. Don't miss a chamber pot.'

Then he slammed away.

Vivian waited until he was gone from sight before instructing the driver to return to Everleigh's.

Mavis sighed. 'If your father finds out, and he will, you may be helping me with my new duties.'

'I hope Everleigh doesn't mistake me for Alexandria,' she muttered when the wheels stopped again.

'She is blonde. You are brunette. That is the difference at this point,' Mavis said.

'I mean to have a talk with him and you're going with me. I need a chaperon. Someone to tell Father the truth.'

'You'd better hope Mrs Rush is there.'

'I do.'

The carriage drew up to Everleigh's house. Vivian jumped out and strode forward. Determined. It didn't matter whether Everleigh wanted to pursue her or ignore her.

Her mother could not be involved in Ella Etta's wrath. Who knew what the old woman might do? She'd already found Vivian's house, and had had no compunction about making herself at home.

The driver gave both women a look between humour and horror. Vivian supposed her father would hear about this as well. She could offer the groom a bribe—which he would refuse. Her father paid better.

'I can only hope he isn't at home,' Mavis mumbled, her reticule looped near her elbow. Her bonnet obscured her face, but Vivian knew that Mavis grimaced.

When the butler opened the door, he gave them a nod, but this time, he forgot his poise and did a double glance.

'Yes, I know we're a nuisance, but the young miss would appear to have lost a jewel when she was here before,' Mavis stated. 'Lord Everleigh about?'

'I will see.' The man left.

'I should have just brought a few lengths of rope for you,' Mavis said, staring at the high ceiling, and the lamps, though unlit, glittered. 'Simpler to just tie him up and wear him away with your persistence—and you are persistent.'

'Mavis. Lower your voice,' Vivian insisted, moving nearer to her friend.

'Well, after today I'm sure the man will have us worked out.'

The butler came for them, leading them to the drawing room.

At the doorway, Mavis didn't proceed. 'I'm going to speak with Mrs Rush,' she said to the butler. 'I need to see if she saw a handkerchief I could have lost here. I know the way.'

She darted down the stairs.

Vivian entered the room and Everleigh stood, a dark warrior in a dim room.

He spoke, bemused. 'After your visit this morning, I never expected your father to allow you here again.' Everleigh strode to the window and opened the curtains to their full width, the fabric rustling. The light brightened the room, but not the man. 'Why are you here?'

The sight of him made her insides flutter.

'Everleigh. I appreciated the kiss. The dance. I truly agree that you do not want to court me and I am in total accord. But I have a solution for us both that might be beneficial.'

She saw the flicker in his regard. Shock, possibly. Disbelief for certain.

He gave a small shake of his head. He didn't seem to think the question worth a full response or explanation. 'Your father will not like this.'

Vivian held up a hand, almost in the same pose she might adopt to grasp the handle of a teacup. 'I have a plan. Just a few public outings with me would help Alexandria realise you aren't going to marry her...'

She met that sapphire stare, which sent spears of

longing to the pit of her stomach, where they fizzled away in despair. She did feel she was making a deal with a dark angel. But she didn't care. 'Just for a short time. In the meantime, I will be at soirées and having many chances to dance. I will make it obvious to everyone that we will not suit.'

'You are persistent, too…' He sat on the arm of an upholstered chair, one hand on his knee. 'I'm fond of you, but I need some time to think about this.'

'We do not ever have to kiss again. This is not about that. While it was wonderful, I am recovered now and have my mind in another direction. You would be a disguise for me. It would seem as if my heart is taken. I could dance.'

'Vivian.' His voice became gentle. So did his observation of her. 'You've been ill and you spent a pleasant hour or two with me when you began your recovery. That's all it is. You may somehow believe my presence made you well, I suppose. But it's not true in any way.'

She swallowed, choosing her words carefully. 'But you could use me to keep women like Alexandria away. I'm of passable appearance. No scandal about me.'

'I can only think you've escaped scandal because of illness,' he inserted.

She continued as if he'd not spoken. 'It would be just an arrangement between us. A game. Like billiards. Nothing personal, binding or lasting.'

'And the fairies will dance around with their songbooks and diamonds will rain from the sky. I cannot use you to keep Alexandria at bay. I would not put you in such a position. She is most persistent, although it is revenge as much as anything. She has a wicked sense of what is humorous and she is like a cat who toys with a mouse before it gets bored, and goes on to something else.'

He stood up and walked between her and the open window, causing the shadows to darken him again. 'If Mavis rushes in and says we are in a compromising position, she'll be wasting her time. The door is open and I have servants about.'

'I would never do such a thing. Never. Ever.'

'I told you I am not a man who believes in love and I have no wish to marry you.'

'I'm only asking for a pretence. We do not even have to speak. My father explained the difference between martyrs and poets, and I'm not asking you to be either one. But I completely understand you're not a poet. Never will be.'

He shut his eyes. 'It must be something in the water that addles women in this town.'

She raised her hands out. 'Everleigh, I have all the qualifications you need. You'll be hard pressed to find someone as biddable as I am for a temporary courtship, for appearances' sake only.'

'I'm certainly feeling hard pressed, and you—biddable?' He moved his head to the side. 'Are you sure of that?'

She nodded. 'You could outline the type of sweetheart you wish for. Take several days to think about it. Make a list. I could examine it and follow the requirements. If any concern me, we can then discuss it. A pretence. Just a pretence. That is all I ask for.'

'Vivian.' He walked towards her and put both hands on her shoulders. The caress silenced her.

This could not do. Must he stand so near? Because

when he did, she forgot the business part of her discussion and savoured the awareness.

She grasped the sides of her skirts and pirouetted out of his reach. 'You could never touch me, though. I must insist on that.'

He studied the ceiling, before clearing his throat. 'You have been ill. You need to fully recover before you consider any conversations without your father present. It's for your own good.'

'Blast it, Everleigh. You are heartless. You really are. And conceivably conceited. I could not make myself any clearer that I am not interested in a courtship. Yes, I did ask you for a kiss, but that was before. Not now.'

'Vivian. You are a dear. But you are not to visit me again.'

She took a breath. Ella Etta frightened her. And she claimed to be able to hurt Vivian's mother. 'You sentence me to death.'

'No. I sentence you to living.' He spoke softly. 'I am more wed to my work. I can't let anything stop me because I can make a difference in so many lives.'

He didn't understand.

'I'm asking you to make a difference in my mother's life. It means a lot.'

'I will discuss it with her, then.'

She saw the chill in him. He would tell her the curse was nonsense. He wouldn't understand.

'The butler will see you out,' he said.

Before she could close her mouth, he was gone.

Later, she would find Ella Etta and tell her that the courtship had failed. Vivian had tried. But Everleigh would not co-operate. She'd done her best, but he'd refused.

She would go home, take whatever curses were hurled her way and accept them.

But her mother could not be harmed.

She ran her fingers over the place he'd clasped her shoulders. No, he could not ever hold her. He just couldn't.

Chapter Nine

Everleigh held the small miniature of his grandfather, staring at the picture, but not seeing it. Waiting. He'd told his butler to get Mrs Rush and he'd see that she communicated to Vivian's companion that she might need the physician again.

He must keep away from her. She was too distracting.

He'd thought them in agreement.

Then she had appeared asking him for a list and a temporary courtship.

The illness had addled poor Vivian. He had inspected her, searching her eyes for a difference. But she appeared perfect.

Vivian had blossomed. He would have had to have been insensible not to have noticed how she'd changed. Her dress had probably weighed more than she had at their first meeting.

She'd reminded him of a bird he'd once found fallen from a nest—mostly skin and feathers. But she'd looked at him as if he could vanquish all the evil of the world.

Innocence. She had no idea of the mare's nest the world was in.

He'd kissed her. The kiss had been his most virtuous—in a sense. He'd concentrated strongly on bringing a response from her. He'd wanted nothing but her pleasure in it. A lady's first kiss, and maybe her last, should be memorable. He'd tried. He'd put more effort into it than he'd put into a whole term at Oxford.

And from Vivian's reaction, he'd not failed. No. Not failed.

The effort to please her had set off something in him. Something different from any kiss he'd felt before.

He didn't want to think of it and he couldn't risk repeating it.

She'd some day find a proper man and settle into a proper life, and have proper children and a proper governess.

She would become like every other wife. The thought thickened the air and made it harder to pull breath into his lungs. Vivian would be in some man's bed.

Any man in the market for a wife would see her now and the trim shape of her dress, with the hint of bosom peeping from the top and the creamy skin shouting of innocence, and would be ready to promise whatever it took to get a ring on her finger.

He pulled himself tighter when he heard a rap at the door.

The rap sounded again. 'You sent for me?' Mrs Rush spoke, entering.

'Yes.' He would have to choose his words carefully. He didn't want to hurt Vivian's reputation.

'Miss Darius… Is she well?'

Then Mrs Rush took a deep breath—too deep, too

long and full of portent. She could have shouted and Everleigh's attention would not have focused on her more.

'I thought you and Miss Vivian's housekeeper might have discussed Miss Vivian's health,' he said.

'We have.'

'She is recovered?'

'Most certainly.'

'Today, she seemed jittery. Are you certain?'

'There is the little matter of the curse concerning you.'

Everleigh scrutinised Mrs Rush's expression. 'Curse?'

Mrs Rush's nod was brief. 'I am correct in this disclosure. It is a curse directed at Miss Vivian. It seems she must marry you or die.'

Everleigh scratched his jaw. A certain vagabond had once told him how easy it was to gammon people. She'd explained it almost in the same terms Grandfather had used when he taught Everleigh how to handle business transactions and how to bluff.

'I sent Miss Vivian for a medicinal. Ella Etta charged her much more than I ever expected.' Mrs Rush wrung her hands. 'I never thought the vagrant would do such a thing.'

'Ella Etta?' Dread entered his body. He wouldn't have suspected she would mislead Vivian.

'Yes. Miss Vivian has to marry you in order to be given more medicine. If she doesn't, she will die.'

'What a choice.'

'I fear it would flummox me.'

Everleigh raised a brow and waved the servant away.

Then Everleigh left the room, taking the longest strides of his life, his hands in balled fists at his sides.

Memories flooded his thoughts, pushing his feet forward and his mind into the past.

He could toss Ella Etta from the land.

But she'd fed him and Daniel and let them sit by the fire on cold days while she told them tales of boys' bravery. Chased them with a broken stick when they'd hidden inside the woods and jumped out at her. Made their time together an adventure and a respite from the severity of his father and the loss of his mother. She'd not instructed him constantly as his grandfather had, gathering promises of how Everleigh would continue the responsibility of using the influence he had been born with. She'd provided a haven.

And now she'd told Vivian she had to marry him.

He shook his head.

Then, he felt his pride deflate. It would have been nice if Vivian had wanted to court him of her own accord. Not only because she needed him in order to continue living.

After he remembered to watch for people standing too near the carriage, Everleigh jumped from his vehicle when it arrived at Vivian's house.

Her father wasn't at home, which didn't distress Everleigh.

Vivian arrived in the drawing room, her hair swept up, with loosely flowing waves escaping the knot. She appeared elegant and proud, except for the wariness of her footsteps.

'I think you threw me out of your house.' She stared forward. 'I received the impression you never wished me to be near you again.'

'I did not throw you out.'

'Figuratively speaking, you did.' Her lips formed a line.

'My heartfelt apologies.'

'I would prefer not to accept them, but I fear I must.'

'I've been told you have a dilemma. Does the reason you would court me have to do with Ella Etta's words?'

'Why would you think otherwise?' She moved to a chair, sitting down. 'Of course I would consider you an interesting prospect for a suitor under regular circumstances…possibly. Before I got to know you. But…'

She indicated the chair near her, but when he declined, she rose.

'I did promise Ella Etta I would marry you,' she said. 'I *was* ill at the time. Near death. Could barely sit, hardly think and was getting smoke in my eyes.'

'I understand.'

'I'd seen you. You'd been gracious enough to kiss me.' Her brows furrowed. 'I had no preference in the matter since I was expected to die. My intended might as well be a man of kindness, instead of someone I'd never met.'

'So, you thought I might be gracious enough to throw in a marriage along with a kiss.' He had an urge to rail at her. Why had she not told him?

'I'd not truly met you. Nor yet been tossed from your sight.' She said the words as an accusation and her voice increased a notch. 'I consider myself someone a man should joyously accept as a wife.'

'If he was of a mind to marry.'

'I would think,' she grumbled, 'if he realised he might have the opportunity of a wife as fine as I am, he might become inclined to wed even if the idea hadn't occurred to him before. The opportunity to acquire a treasure should never be missed.' Her chin moved up.

'A treasure is a fine thing, but some men are best left in poverty.' He noted Mavis silently at the door and a glower sent her scurrying.

'I realise my recent illness might put some suitors off—but I am of good family. A baron's daughter. Who has a respectable dowry, is pleasant-natured—'

'You do not have to write me a journal,' he assured her. 'I can see enough of your attributes myself.'

'It is not obvious you do.' A twinge of hurt passed behind her expression. 'You could have pretended chagrin when sending me from your house.'

'I have not found that to work in the past. And I thought you appreciated honest speech.'

'Very well.' She paced between the chairs. 'I would have appreciated some feeling of regret from you. I had, after all…' she lowered her voice '…done the unthinkable. I had kissed you and mentioned marriage to you. Two crimes, apparently.'

'No. Not the kiss. Yours was not the first such offer I have received of late. Alexandria had also done the same. It is not such an unthinkable topic for women as you might imagine.'

'We both know she is daft,' she said. 'All this attention has made you high on the matrimonial instep.'

'While I admit you are of suitable appearance and agreeable conversation—' he said, then rapidly stopped. 'I am not high on any instep. I don't wish to marry. End of discussion.'

He stepped so close he could have kissed her again.

'Please sit. You're towering over me. I don't like it.'

She had her arms folded over her chest and regarded a space behind him.

'Nor do I.' He lowered himself into the chair.

'That's better.'

'You're welcome. Miss Darius, please sit. I will be able to solve your problem. Painlessly.'

'I will accept my fate. Mavis and I have talked. She said it is utter nonsense. But, if there are any repercussions, I will make sure the old woman knows they are to fall on me.'

He stood, walking towards her.

'I shouldn't have taken the first kiss from you. It was wrong of me. I know how much it can mean. How it awakens something within a person. I do ask forgiveness.'

'No. We are—were—friends. A friend doesn't apologise for doing a kindness.'

His shook his head the merest bit. He could see her lips in front of him and it would be no crime to kiss her again. Except it would. He could not be in her thoughts. But he was already there and would remain there, until someone else kissed her.

'Vivian. You must attend those soirées you wished for.'

Her jaw tensed.

Holding her shoulders, he touched too much thinness, but he absorbed warmth, too, and smelled her flowery scent, which reminded him of springtime fields. He commanded her attention by slightly pulling her towards him.

'Dance and laugh and find a gentle sort. You would have your pick of all the unmarried men interested in marriage.' He smiled, speaking just above a whisper.

'After all, you are worthy of love and sonnets every time the sun rises. I am not able to provide that.'

She put her hand to his chest, but didn't push. Her words burst from her. 'I don't want to die. And I don't want my mother to be under any curse.'

He stepped back, taking her hand and lifting it. Her fingers curled softly, but she opened them when he kissed her palm.

Lowering her hand, he said, 'Ella Etta will release you from the curse. She won't dare not.'

Vivian made him feel bigger somehow. His anger at her for trying to manipulate him disappeared. His old friend had tricked Vivian.

For Ella Etta to take food from the estate was one thing, but she'd overstepped her bounds.

He no longer felt angry at anyone but Ella Etta. He would discuss this with her.

He saw Vivian, imagining her through a different viewpoint. And, he could almost hear Ella Etta's mind humming. She would see nothing wrong in picking out a wife for him. She would think as other people who saw Vivian. Vivian would be a wonderful wife for the right man and the crone viewed it as her duty to tell the sun how to rise and the moon when to set.

'Let us go visit Ella Etta.' He felt himself tense at the words. He would make her tell Vivian the curse wasn't real. Vivian had been ill. She didn't need such nonsense hanging over her head.

'We'll rid you of the hag's threat,' he said. He had to be careful. If he spent more time with Vivian, he knew that when he rid Vivian of the problem with the trickster, he would be adding another one for himself.

'I doubt my father would agree easily for me to go

anywhere with you. But I will be at your house on Sunday morning. If we could travel then, it will be less likely to be noticed.'

'This curse nonsense will stop,' he reassured her. But before leaving, he took one last look at Vivian.

Chapter Ten

'Mother.' Vivian walked into her mother's bedchamber without knocking, knowing she would be surrounded by servants.

A blast of heat from the fireplace hit Vivian's cheeks.

Her mother sat on the chaise longue, one hand extended at her side, her fingernails being trimmed by a maid. Another servant stood at the back of the chair, carefully massaging her mother's temples. Vivian tried not to inhale. Her mother insisted gardenia calmed her and her room smelled of the scent.

'I've a bit of…' her mother said, wilting briefly, '…a concern on my mind. Nothing to worry yourself with. I'm almost beyond it.'

Vivian tried not to breathe too deeply. Her father was doing so much better. 'Is Father ill again?'

Her mother chuckled. 'No. Nothing like that.'

'I cannot tell him that I wish to take a carriage ride with Lord Everleigh. I don't want him more upset and I know he won't understand.'

This time her mother opened one eye, raising her head. 'Are you thinking of marriage to him?'

'We have discussed it. But, no.'

'The only young man you had me invite to the soi-rée?'

Vivian gave a sharp nod.

Her mother relaxed back against the *chaise*. 'Well, don't take Mavis. And, whatever you do, don't think to let him compromise you and expect a ring. That's romantic foolishness. I would advise against meeting him. A man wants most what he cannot have, especially if it's wrapped in as beautiful a package as you, Vivian. Remember that. Always be fierce in your heart.' Then she threw up her hands. 'But you are old enough to decide for yourself. I just don't want you hurt.'

'I don't want anyone hurt—'

Her mother shrugged and interrupted. 'Dress warm. Don't get chilled, it'll make your nose red, and there's nothing attractive about a dripping nose. And wear Mavis's Sunday bonnet.'

'That hideous one which droops so much she can barely see?' Vivian asked, shaking her head.

Her mother chuckled again. 'Dear. Why do you think I had it made for her and pay her extra each time she wears it out of the house? Any time I wish to visit somewhere without being noticed I wear it and everyone assumes it is Mavis. It embellishes her reputation and protects mine.'

'Father has asked the servants to alert him to anything I might do which is a change from my routine.'

'That man.' She relaxed again. 'Don't worry about the servants, dear. Just leave early before the house is awake on Sunday. Slip out in the darkness and send the carriage back so we can use it to go to services. Tell the carriage driver to be quiet as he readies the horses and he is to discuss it with me later, not your father. Return while we are at Sunday Services. Mavis will stay home. Your father will think the two of you are together. You must not let anyone else know you are disappearing. And, if this earl's son doesn't work out, I know the half-brother of a duke who we'll consider.'

Vivian pulled the door closed to the sound of her mother asking to be fanned.

She longed to see Everleigh again, which, in its own way, might be a completely separate curse.

The silence in Everleigh's carriage was more jarring than the ruts in the road, in Vivian's opinion. The curtains were closed. Vivian sat against the squabs, interlacing her gloved fingers.

The vehicle interior absorbed the darkness from the overcast skies. The ornate brass trim framed the gloom more than dispersing it.

Everleigh sat across from her, wearing a frock coat, his beaver hat sitting on the squab beside him. He could walk in a blizzard and, if his countenance gave insight into him, he would leave puddles of melted snow in his wake.

'By the end of the day, this will be over and soon will be forgotten. It is not your concern any more. I will see to that,' Everleigh reassured her.

'I will be so pleased when I can put this behind me and never travel this road again.' She glimpsed out of the window, pushing the hideous hat backwards on her head. 'I have no doubt that she saved my life, though.'

He moved his legs, letting them stretch to the empty space under the rear-facing seat. His arms were crossed. 'Ella Etta should share her mixtures, but keep her machinations to herself. She is not above—well, she's old and she didn't get that way by being senseless, or, in her case, sensible. She knows what she can get away with and what she can't. She's willing to try both. She had no right to scare you into thinking you had to wed.'

This time, Vivian pressed her palm to the window and didn't respond.

That, Vivian decided, was the heart of the matter. Still watching the barren trees, she asked, 'Do you truly have no intention to marry—ever?'

'My brother can easily marry and have heirs. My father could even marry again and have children. Or the title can move to my cousin. It's not as if it leaves the family. It's a legacy passed down in my family so we can continue the heritage. My father more or less abandoned his birthright.'

She checked to see if he jested, but no.

'I have a brother and I can guide his children,' Everleigh said. 'I have suggested to my father that he try for more sons.'

'You told your father to select a new wife?'

'Of course. Seems a logical way for him to have heirs if he wishes it. Add a few more sons to the lineage. A safety aspect. He's pressed me to wed. When I gave in, I almost ended up with Alexandria.'

'I'm surprised he hasn't remarried.'

'He has a mistress. He didn't choose to marry her after my mother died, when they could have had children. He felt she wasn't of suitable lineage for a society wife—not worthy of providing heirs. After all, his first wife had had beauty and funds. He has high standards.'

'But did the marriage make him happy?'

'Happier than he would have been with a poor and plain wife, I'm certain.'

'But if he cares for a mistress and now he has the money...'

'He doesn't have the money, I do. As for his sweetheart, I suspect he believes his mistress cares for him for himself, as she requires negligible attention. He married my mother for her funds and she married him for his title, and they tolerated each other like two privileged people put in the same pot with a fire heated under it.'

Everleigh reached to push back his hat from where it had jostled near the edge of the seat. 'My maternal grandfather called it a marriage of love. Grandfather loved the title and Father loved the money Mother brought.'

'Did they bicker?'

'Mother would flick her wrist, behold Father longingly across the table and say to him, *"If only you'd been a duke."* Father would smile and tell her, sadly, that her father only had enough funds to purchase an earl. The conversation was always pleasant and always aimed for the jugular. I think they enjoyed it.'

She grimaced, flicking at a piece of road dust near the window. 'It seems lonely for them. Matrimony should provide a friend. Not an enemy close at hand. That gave you a bad memory of marriage.'

'Vivian. Men can have solitude. Soldiers. Sailors. Men who cannot afford a wife and family. I would suppose I have less of it than they do and I prefer my life. Vastly. When I told Ella Etta I wasn't going to marry Alexandria, the old woman must have decided to find me a wife.'

'I wished to marry until I became ill. Then I felt so

trapped. Both by my body and my parents. I love my parents and understand their actions completely. Yet, now I know that I could be happiest unmarried. I'm alive. I'm mostly alone, because my friends tired of asking me to do things with them as I refused so many times. But I'm well.'

'It's expected of you to wed.' His voice, a low drawl, said the words as if that explained away every feeling she had.

'As it is of you, Your Lordship.' She raised her chin.

He shook his head, but it was in total agreement with her words. 'Expected, but not a requirement to be an earl.' He quickly dismissed her words.

And, she realised, it was only the curse that had aligned them together, even if it wasn't in the expected way. The curse and the kiss.

He shifted forward, covering her hand with his. 'I understand that you were ill, but you still agreed to wed me. Much like my parents agreed to marry. I don't find fault with you for it, but it does bring back the memories of my parents sparring with each other every day my mother lived.'

'Forgive me. I didn't know.'

Slowly he trailed his hand up her arm, to her elbow, then stopped at the hem of her sleeve. His grasp closed around her, creating an imprisonment she could never have expected from such a light touch. Every time her heart beat, fire inside her ignited under his hand.

'So delicate.' He let his fingers trail down a few inches. 'And yet, so much stronger than before. I believe Ella Etta saved you, too. I believe it completely. She seems to have an innate understanding of mixtures. For generations the women in her family have studied healing herbs and she even knows what apothecaries mix, and sometimes obtains their cures. I hope she meant you no ill will by cursing you with me. But that is what it would be for you. A true curse.'

His other hand reached to touch her cheek. 'I saw the mistake of a marriage with my parents' union and, when I considered it for myself, I chose someone I could hardly like. Just as they did. That wasn't an accident, I'm sure. I wanted the expected wife, but not the marriage. I'm fortunate to have discovered it before it was too late.'

She edged closer. 'If you considered Alexandria for a wife, I would say you erred. And...' she shrugged '... I did pursue you much the same as she did. Please forget that.'

His lips parted, but he didn't speak at first. Instead, he examined her. 'The first meeting... That was a surprise and had a pleasant ending.' Emotion laced his words. 'I'll not be kissing you again if you continue to wear that hat. It's daunting.'

'The strings untie. Imagine that.'

'You look chilled.'

'The morning is cooler than I expected.'

'Would you like my coat or would you prefer us to sit closer?'

'Closer.'

He moved.

'So vibrant.' His hand skimmed the spot where hers had been. His brows rose. 'You once asked for a kiss.'

'Only as a last dying wish. It meant a lot to me.'

'Well...' He touched her jaw, running a finger down one side of it and up the other. 'If I were dying, I could see my last wish as being a kiss from you. A reason to go on living.'

The distance between them lessened again.

'Is a second one ever as good as the first?' she asked. 'Not that I'm asking for another. Just curious.'

He took her chin in his hand and pulled her closer. 'You should be the judge of that.'

The carriage jostled at the same moment he moved forward, almost thrusting him against her, but he maintained his position. He reached up, balancing with one arm, and untied the bonnet, pulling it back from her face, tossing away the covering and leaning in.

His lips took hers, soft and sweet for only an instant before his body moved further forward, his mouth angling, taking her, and then his tongue dipped into her mouth.

When he pulled away, she almost moved with him and discovered her hands gripping the front of his coat.

Her fingers wouldn't loosen and he remained poised, not relaxed back in his seat, but close enough that he could move forward again in less than a second.

'I am fascinated by you.' Everleigh's voice flowed. 'I don't know if it's the depth I see in your eyes, or your mouth, or just a fascination with the way you've blossomed since we first met. I imagine, falsely, that somehow I've helped you regain your health. But I can't play with fire and I won't hurt you.'

'So far, I have enjoyed your company.' She released her hold on his coat. 'But I think it would be preferable if you spoke more fluff.'

'That's what I mean. You deserve someone who can say those tender words.'

She crossed her arms. 'I'm not sure I only want to hear them. I think I want to live them instead.'

He smiled, then folded one arm over the other and stretched out a leg to one side of her, but didn't brush her skirts. 'As you wish.'

Those were the last words he spoke until they reached the camp.

His smile captured her when he helped her from the carriage. 'I'll make sure you're confident you have no fear of anything she might do.'

They came closer to the group. Ella Etta stepped out, scratching her back, and giving a sigh. When they stopped in front of her, she said, 'Everleigh. I have missed you. And your betrothed.' She squinted at Vivian, frowning.

Next, she looked around. 'Please, pull up a stump and we'll talk.'

Everleigh used both hands, and hefted the makeshift seat back from the fire so his boots would be able to stay out of the ash. He lifted another stump, placed it and held out his arm for Vivian to sit.

She chose to sit furthest from Ella Etta.

'I hear you have told Vivian she must marry me.' He made himself comfortable on the stump, stretching his legs.

Ella Etta's head bobbed around like a twig on water. 'The idea doesn't agree with you like I hoped.'

'And you threaten her family?'

'I have never hurt a girl. Never would. You know that, Everleigh.'

He nodded. 'I know. She doesn't. Probably because you said something about a death curse to her earlier.'

'And she still sent a friend my way...' She cackled.

'That was wise of you, miss, or not, depending on how a body views it.'

'I would send no friend your way,' Vivian said.

'What are you talking about?' Everleigh asked.

'Miss Alexandria came to visit me. I read her palm.' She laughed. 'I told her she must go on a long journey. She must start it soon. A gunshot into the air above will kill the spirits that put love into her.' She kicked a boot towards Everleigh. 'Her heart will be free of you for ever. I saw no reason not to tell her a few truths and a few lies.' She glanced at Vivian. 'I mixed a bundle of thorns for her. It was an unlove potion.' She shrugged. 'I had to do something to get her to leave.'

'Why didn't you send me a message that Alexandria had been here?' Everleigh asked.

'The girl is a lovely heiress. It is ridiculous for her to form an attachment to a man who doesn't want her.'

'I suppose you do not consider me as falling into that category or you would not have asked me to pursue Everleigh.' Vivian frowned.

She scrutinised Vivian. 'Everleigh was on my mind.'

'You said I'd die if I didn't marry him.'

'Girl. We all die. Some soon. Some late. Haven't you noticed?'

'You put a curse on me.' Vivian pulled her shoulders tight.

'I will show you my magic.' Ella Etta held up both hands, made into fists, then splayed her fingers abruptly. 'Poof. You are a rabbit. I put that curse on you.' She asked Everleigh, 'Do you not think she makes a lovely rabbit?'

He didn't speak or move, but Vivian saw the humour escaping.

Ella Etta waved a hand, leaning towards Vivian. 'You are a rabbit. You just do not have a looking glass to see. Now I conjure you into a person.' She waved her hand again. 'I should ask next time what creature you want. The children love it. They hop around for hours. Everleigh always had to be a bear, though.' She groaned. 'But I did it for him. I tell the children that as soon as they leave my sight they turn back into a child.'

Lips closed, arms crossed, he gave a good imitation of a growl.

'See,' Ella Etta said. 'He liked that. Even then, he did.'

Vivian looked around her. Trees. Leaves. Sky. Earth. Normal. The woman in front of her, a slippery swindler.

'You want to be a rabbit again?' Ella Etta asked.

'You put a curse on me.' She dropped her voice. 'You said I had to marry.'

'I remember, you near tripped over your skirts leaving so you could get on with it.' She appraised Everleigh. 'Thanked me, she did. Said she'd pay me to wed a stallion such as you.'

He nodded sombrely.

'You—' Vivian wished she could manage a good curse. She glared at Ella Etta. 'You said he had no heart and I'd die if I didn't wed him.'

Ella Etta shrugged. She spoke to Everleigh. 'Couldn't wipe the smile from off her face when I told her you were the man she must marry. She almost kissed my ring. Asked to pay me as well. Said she might throw in some coin.'

'*You are evil.*'

'*No.* I told you. That was my sister, Evil Etta.' She touched a hand over her breast. 'Or did I tell you that was my mother?' She contemplated Everleigh. 'Everleigh. Do I lie?'

'Ella Etta, you try never to let truth influence your words.' He lifted a stick and used it to poke the burned firewood closer to the flames.

'I may have told a lie to get Alexandria to leave you be. But I promise you both, she wasn't using her thoughts. I had to send her on her way with a tale that will make her content to leave.'

'You put a curse on me.'

Ella Etta glared. 'I might have said words, but you wanted to hear them.' She paused. 'Everleigh, what did I tell you long ago?'

'A curse only works if the mind wants it to. A free spirit cannot be cursed.'

'I say a lot. Maybe I say my curses are like feathers to tickle the mind. Only stick to wet, puddle-headed people.' She looked at Vivian. 'I read palms, too. I taught Everleigh as well.'

'She told me I would marry a beautiful princess,' Everleigh said, smiling towards Vivian.

Ella Etta sighed, raised her hands slightly, and said, 'Sometimes, I make an error.'

'You vicious witch.' Vivian jumped to her feet. 'You came to my house and scared me to death.'

'I needed a bowl. And don't worry about a curse on your mother. I would not harm a hair on a mother's head. Children give them enough grief.'

Vivian stalked to the vehicle.

'I needed a bowl,' she heard Ella Etta say again.

Everleigh watched Vivian march to his carriage. High dudgeon sat well with her, her fists doubled and her skirt flying almost too tight for the length of her footsteps.

'She ruffles,' Ella Etta said to Everleigh when Vivian left the camp.

He nodded, keeping his voice low. 'You should not have meddled with Vivian. You should not have told her to wed me.'

'You do not sleep again, Everleigh. I see the light at night when you visit Wildewood. I send her to help with that. She'll make you sleep.'

He shook his head. 'No.'

'You need a wife.'

'But at what cost to her?'

She shook her head and her nose moved as if she'd smelled a bad odour, then she laughed. 'Give your father many heirs to distract him from his concerns about who will get his title. I want to see your children. See if they favour you. Many times, I sent you away from the camp, happy, but then fearing the wrath of your parents. Later you would return, even dragging along your brother when he was old enough.'

'Eating here was better than eating in the nursery. The food from around the fire always tasted better. At first, it was like walking to the edge of the crevasse, seeing how close I could get into your family. Then I discovered you would fluster if I knocked over the firewood, or got near the tinctures.'

'Some could have poisoned you if you tried them. The little heir would never listen.'

'You liked chasing me into the woods, flailing a stick.'

She snorted. 'When your grandfather discovered you

were visiting us, he said we were to leave. You told your father and he insisted we be left alone.'

'Father always disagreed with Grandfather. It was a manoeuvre. Father relished having something he could control in his household. So did I.'

She laughed. 'Your father cannot leave you just as he couldn't leave your mother. You are his curse. Your mother's revenge. Each time he sees your eyes the curse revisits him. You have your mother's eyes. It makes him remember the siren he disliked, but could not keep himself from wanting. The lovely one who could control him as easily as the wind controls leaves and she didn't care for him at all.'

'You never spoke with her. How could you be so certain?'

'You told me so much as a child and never knew the true meaning of your words.'

'I'm sure I always spoke well of her.'

'You described her well. If a boy didn't know a serpent was poison, he might think it a thing of beauty. That was your mother. Men could not see her venom. Even her father only saw the serpent's beauty. In death, she left behind the family she sprinkled her harm over and it still surrounds your heart.'

Chapter Eleven

When he stepped inside the carriage, Everleigh saw Vivian huddled in the seat and he lowered himself beside her instead of moving across. She was sitting so tight, like a bundled cocoon. An upset one.

He had the ridiculous urge to say *I told you so* and watch her ruffle. And, he had a more ridiculous urge to pull her into his arms and soothe her, and himself.

Holding Vivian close would make the trip back to London pass in a heartbeat, but it wouldn't help his nights pass any faster. He had to keep his distance. It wasn't fair to her to make her think he would offer her more than a passing illusion.

'Well, you must be pleased now.' He gave her a smile and resisted the urge to give a bear growl. 'No curse.' He whispered, 'But you made a nice rabbit. The whiskers not too long. And I liked the ears.' He lifted his hand over his head, shaping imaginary ears.

'I pursued you—' she bit down on the words '—for naught.'

He frowned, pretending puzzlement. 'Is that how you see it? Ella Etta thought you were pleased.'

'Ha. She has a bigger imagination than any I've ever seen.'

He laughed. 'I told you that. If you'd believed me about her curse in the first place—' He stopped. 'You were ill, Vivian. I did see the physician Gavin Hamilton yesterday. I asked him about you and told him about your illness. He thought the cures the physician mixed were making you ill.'

'I can't believe you defend Ella Etta.'

'If she is the one who helped you to recovery, then I will be grateful to her for ever.'

'I don't know whether to hate her or hug her.'

He nodded. 'I do.' He reached out, taking her hand, and only needing a slight amount of pressure to pry it from the cocoon. 'I can read palms, too.'

He pulled the fingers of the glove away.

Vivian felt his fingertip run the length of her palm, sending his touch deep into her body. She tried to make a fist, but his grip wouldn't let her.

'Vivian,' he cajoled, 'don't hide your lifeline from me. It's long, like you. Sinewy. Not so wiry as this brief line.'

'How can you truly see it in the dim light of the carriage? Open the shades.'

'Can't risk you getting seen. Besides, I can see enough. This thin line bothers me a great deal.'

He moved, so she could peer at her skin. 'There's no line there.'

'This sparse line that is so small that it's invisible… I fear it is a line for laughter.'

She tried to jerk her hand away again. He let her, then he let his throat rumble into a growl.

'You beast,' she shot back.

'Bear,' he corrected. He clutched her hand again, holding it in a light clasp. Tenderness gentled his words. 'Vivian. Are you satisfied you're not cursed?' His touch reminded her of the summer sun, warming deep past the surface.

'I suppose. But I'm so angry about the curse. All that nonsense.'

He gave Vivian's hand a squeeze. 'Sometimes Ella Etta fed two boys who would run from the house in the morning and not return until dark.'

'Your parents didn't mind. Or your governess, or tutor?'

'My mother had a temper where servants were concerned. They were always sacked quickly and replaced slowly. She and Father would be gone for weeks and weeks, searching out new staff. They would return home with boxes of new dresses and gifts for me and my brother.'

'They should have watched over you.'

'We did just fine. We found our own way.'

'That sounds sad.'

'It wasn't particularly. Roaming the lands was idyllic.' He squeezed her hand again. 'Good memories. The men taught me to strike flint to make a fire and traded me one chicken for the flint.' He shrugged. 'I didn't have to even steal the chicken. They did. It was fun to talk with them over what they might steal. Once, I had to toss a blanket from an upstairs window at midnight and later Ella Etta wrapped me in it when I visited her.'

The carriage bounced as it turned a curve. Vivian balanced against the window. 'Did your father dislike you?'

'No. My brother and I were his coins. We were

Grandfather's heirs. The reason he could have the roof over his head, and the carriages, and the gambling trips to London to enjoy his status. Grandfather would visit and Father would leave. Finally, he left for good until Grandfather died.'

He leaned across her, and pulled at the shade. 'Wildewood. The one thing my father holds with the title. But he didn't have the funds to put a roof on it. And…' he leaned back, letting the shade fall in place '…all prisons do not have bars. Some have velvet sofas.'

Everleigh didn't like the truth of his own words. 'I am a gaoler. My father has no funds of his own. Sometimes he likes to gamble and sometimes to drink the best brandy. For the money he wishes to gamble away, he has to come to me and ask. A letter will not suffice. I do not answer them. He has to present himself to me. I always give him the funds. A few years ago, the sums became vast. Now, he can gamble, but he cannot wager more than is in his pocket. When he does that the world around him narrows. So, he knows he will get what he asks for, but he has to ask.'

'You shouldn't.'

'I didn't do this. Until my mother's portrait was ruined.' He rubbed a hand over his neck. 'After she died, I walked in and two black spots had been painted where the eyes were. My father had them corrected, but it is obvious to me. It's never been the same.'

They were within an hour from her home, Vivian knew, but she left the ridiculous bonnet in her lap, rolling the ribbon ties into a curl, then unrolling and repeating. Everleigh's view flicked to the window.

He stretched his legs and looked in her direction,

the place between his brows furrowing. 'Do you believe in love?'

'Of course. My parents love each other. Even with their difficulties. Mother will eventually find the right time and she'll tell Father about this trip. He will be angry, but she will explain and it will all work out.'

'I decided I had found a proximity to it with Alexandria. All was wonderful and she was witty. Then one day, she was speaking with her father and I saw how she manipulated him into doing exactly as she wished, just as she did with me. I decided she wasn't so delightful and, the more I moved back from her presence, the less amusing she became.'

He used his thumb to trace the bottom of the window. 'I imagine that my mother and Alexandria had similar personalities. They are so friendly, so nice, so kind when they want something from you, or to manipulate you. But they turn into serpents when they believe there is no cost to them.'

'You fear letting someone so close they can use you in that way.'

'I would not say I fear it. I would say I refuse it.'

'I should understand.' She lowered her fingers and slapped the bonnet. 'When I was ill, I believed myself in love. Lord Barrow had asked me to wed him. My mother begged me to think about it, then he and my father discussed the wedding contract. My mother told me I should approve of Lord Barrow's requests and put the papers in front of me. I made sure he disappeared faster than a fog on a hot day.'

She grimaced. 'Then later, I realised I didn't ever admire him. Even though I knew I didn't care for him, it was months before I could stop myself from thinking of him. By then, he had already married someone else.'

Sighing, she arranged the ribbons around the brim on the bonnet and when the vehicle moved, the hat slid from her lap. 'Before that, I had thought myself in the deepest love. But I was too young to wed and my father flatly refused to consider us courting. I'd met the young man at my cousin's house. I thought him the one I would cherish for ever.'

'What happened?'

'He went to war. He never wrote to me and I realised he didn't care for me. Part of the attraction, at first, had been that I was simply young and I wanted to be in love.'

After he went to war, she'd accepted that he couldn't manage to write her. She'd understood. But then she'd visited her cousin again and discovered he'd written several letters to her aunt and uncle. Vivian had realised the feelings she had for him were all one-sided. He'd merely tried to keep from hurting her.

The carriage creaked.

She leaned forward, raking the bonnet from the seat and plopping it on her head. She ran her fingers along the crown, then pushed her hair into place. Next she tied the ribbon and leaned back, but this time, she let the brim shield her face. 'I like you, Everleigh. Annoying bear though you may be.'

'And I am fond of you, Vivian—you are first, second and last on my list of potential wives. It's just that the list is useless.'

'I understand.' She pushed the hat back, just enough to see him. 'I'm not an expert on matters of the heart. I'm good at choosing the wrong man.'

He laughed. 'I can see why I might appeal to you, then.'

'You actually do.'

She couldn't help being pleased Everleigh said she was the only person on his list for a bride. Even if he had no wish to marry, she liked the thought of being someone he esteemed.

He took his boot and very firmly moved her slippered foot back towards her. Leaning forward, he took her hand.

He smiled, truly smiled, and she felt it deep in her heart.

'I have enjoyed having your friendship,' he said.

'Well, feasibly that is much better than having you as a husband.' She gave his boot a tiny kick. 'One cannot have too many friends, but one can definitely have too many husbands if the women I hear conversing are to be believed.'

She would always remember their kisses and would hold the secret deep inside herself, one thing she could cherish. A memory of a kiss given just to please her.

'It's unlikely that our paths will cross many more times in our lives. But I want you to know how much I've appreciated your telling me that I'm not cursed.' She touched his hand and he clasped her fingers. 'I'm fortunate to have survived the accident and I'm fortunate to feel better every day.'

He tilted closer. 'I am displeased at the chaperon, though.' He flicked the brim of the bonnet. 'She keeps hiding you from me.'

'Apparently the hat is the perfect chaperon.' She reached up, touching the ties. 'But confining.'

Her fingers tangled in the ribbons and she pulled the wrong section, knotting it.

He touched the tangle, moving closer, the masculine scent of his soap mixing into the air around her. As he unfastened her bonnet, his touch brushed against her.

Taking his time, he slipped the hat away and put it on the seat across from himself. 'I don't think it's as effective as a chaperon as it once was. Now I can see you.'

She touched her cheek. 'It surprises me when I look in the mirror. How different I seem. So much better. So quickly.'

'You do appear a different person. Not the same one I kissed the first day.'

His lips closed over hers, enveloping her with his warmth, lips moving like liquid, bonding them close. No longer did the air around her feel chilled, but it encompassed her, turning the dreary day into perfection.

The sound. An explosion. It barely reached through the kiss to her consciousness.

Everleigh jerked back, pulling her closer into his arms, and leaned across to move aside the shade, still protecting her with his body.

A woman screamed.

The carriage lurched and would have tossed her into the other side, but Everleigh's grasp saved her. He steadied them.

The vehicle continued to swerve and the driver shouted a curse she didn't understand. Finally, the carriage stopped and the driver continued to curse.

Everleigh released her. He jumped from the carriage before it had completely stopped.

She stared out of the window. They were in front of the cathedral. Someone was shouting Everleigh's name.

'Everleigh.' The cry again.

Vivian moved the shade slightly and did her best to peer out. Alexandria stood in the middle of the street.

'I know your sweetheart is in the carriage with you.' The shout reached Vivian. 'Ella Etta told me she would be with you.'

Everleigh's sweetheart wasn't in the carriage. She was.

Everleigh stepped towards Alexandria. The carriage driver was calming the horses and not only had all the traffic stopped, but several people had stepped outside the cathedral and were watching.

Alexandria stood in the middle of the road with the discharged gun, still pointing it into the air.

'I know Vivian is in the carriage with you.'

Alexandria dropped to her knees, the empty gun falling to her side. 'You chose Vivian instead of me.'

'Alexandria.'

A crowd had gathered. Watching. People were craning their necks to see the event.

'I went to the matchmaker,' she sniffed. 'She told me…. She told me Vivian was to marry you. That I could not have you.'

All the others were gawking and their mouths gaping.

'I understand,' she said, her voice shrill and loud enough to carry to rafters three streets over. 'I want you to know that I forgive both of you. You never told me you loved me. You told me you would not marry me. I did not believe it. Even when the old beggar told me the two of you were to be married, I didn't believe it. But when I saw you leave with Vivian this morning, I knew it was true.'

Everleigh walked towards Alexandria.

'I thought I might kill myself in front of both of you,' she shouted. 'But I didn't really want to. I decided that I should wish you both happiness.' She collapsed on to the ground.

He lifted her by the arms.

She blinked and whispered, 'You said you would never marry, Everleigh. We'll see about that.'

'Thank you,' he said. 'Perhaps we should get you home.'

'Vivian!' He heard a voice from the front steps of the cathedral. Vivian's mother came running out. She screamed, 'Is she hurt? Is Vivian hurt?'

She ran to the carriage. 'Vivian?' She wrenched open the door. 'Are you shot?'

'I'm fine, Mother.' Vivian stepped out of the carriage, knocking Mavis's hat into the dirt. Her mother rushed forward, almost suffocating her with a tearful hug.

Darius parted the crowd and moved to Vivian and his wife. 'You knew?' He glowered at his wife. 'My heavens. I am going to sack Mavis for real this time. She brought Vivian into this debacle. And you'd better not give Mavis references.'

'Well, children do as they wish when they become adults.' Lady Darius's voice wavered. She wilted. 'With all the changes in our life, I decided that you, and Vivian—your actions—are not my responsibility any more. If you're both alive, that's all that matters.'

Darius caught his wife in his arms.

Alexandria blinked up at Everleigh, her lashes fluttering. Then he saw the barest hint of a smile. 'I must wish you all the best in your marriage, Everleigh, as my heart is broken. My father has agreed that I can go away to recover. He truly had hopes I might marry you and his disappointment is even stronger than my own.'

'I wish you the best as well, Alexandria.'

'Perhaps you should have answered my letters,' she said, standing, giving a quick slap to her skirt to dust herself off. 'You can keep the gun,' she said, strolling away. 'Father doesn't need it. Ghastly thing nearly knocked me unconscious.'

Everleigh watched Vivian stand beside the carriage. Her mother ran to her side long enough to hug her. The gathering crowd watched from the steps of the cathedral.

Nodding to them, he walked forward, handed the driver the weapon and strode to join Vivian. He addressed her parents. 'Would you prefer to take your carriage home, or ride with us?'

'I will get my driver,' the Baron said. Then his chin dropped and his tone tensed. 'Everleigh.'

One side of Everleigh's mouth made it into a smile. The other would not co-operate. He gave up the effort. It was easier to help Vivian into the carriage.

'I was wrong,' Everleigh said as the vehicle rolled again. 'You may be cursed.'

Chapter Twelve

'**B**ecause this rakehell—'

Lord Darius's voice rose with each word. He stood in the centre of the room, closest to the door. Everleigh stood with Vivian on one side and her mother on the other.

'He took you to some camp of thieves on his father's estate, if I understand correctly. As he was bringing you home a paramour of his took a shot in the air—oh, so discreetly...'

Even Darius's hair had an angry wildness to it.

'Nothing in the sermon topped that. Nothing ever will.'

He glared at his wife.

'You knew.' He kept his elbows close to his body, but his palms were still splayed out. 'But at least they're betrothed.'

'No,' Vivian said. 'We don't wish to marry.'

Everleigh clasped Vivian's hand. Her fingers trembled within his. Stealing a glance at her, he let his gaze connect with hers and reassured her with a light squeeze, drawing her closer to him.

'You can take a honeymoon trip while this fades away,' her father said. 'There will be a new scandal to replace this before long, and, in public, you can appear to be doing exactly as you'd planned all along. We can all just be one big happy family.'

'I'm not betrothed,' Vivian insisted.

Everleigh corrected her. 'I proposed the second we walked into the room.'

'But you didn't want to propose. And I didn't want Father to accept on my behalf.'

'You don't have a choice,' her father groused. 'A gunshot into the sky cleared the air on that question.'

'I think I have an option,' Vivian said. 'If I have to be present for a ceremony.'

'Let's all discuss this rationally.' Her mother captured Vivian's stare. 'Scotland is gorgeous. Perfect for a marriage and a honeymoon.'

Darius spoke through clenched teeth, his cheeks red. 'The marriage needs to be quick, quiet and not questioned.'

'Well,' her mother added, 'my second choice would be the special licence route and Everleigh can surely get an appointment for one quickly with his connections.'

'I'm not going to marry him.' Vivian stepped a bit behind Everleigh. 'We have discussed this and both of us don't wish to marry.'

Her mother peered around Everleigh, touching a hand over her heart. 'Oh, no, dear. That has been decided. Now, we have to make plans for the wedding breakfast.' Everleigh stepped sideways, putting a hand at Vivian's back to keep her from disappearing behind him.

'You have to marry.' Her mother sniffled. 'Living with your father like he is will be a nightmare.'

'This is beyond anything I ever expected of my family.' Darius sounded choked. He scowled at his wife. 'This is what I get for drinking so long. I let my family just do as they pleased and now we're all paying for it. Vivian is going to have to marry Everleigh and you know he couldn't care less about her.'

Everleigh stared at the man. It would not be in good form to break his future father-in-law's jaw. Then, Everleigh felt movement at his side.

'We do not have to get married,' Vivian whispered, clasping his coat.

He put his arm around her waist. 'We must.'

'I don't care if I'm ruined,' she said. 'I'm almost anticipating it. It's not bad compared to what I've been through.'

'It isn't fair to you,' he muttered. 'You deserve to be respected. A place among the *ton*.'

He repeated the first words he'd said when he'd entered the room. 'Vivian. Will you marry me?' he asked, taking in her expression.

She paused.

'Of course she will,' Lord Darius glared at her.

'She must,' Lady Darius added. 'It's well past time she married. You're not nearly as bad as that last one.' She shuddered.

Everleigh inhaled.

Then she caught what she'd said. 'I hardly know you, but I am certain you'll be kind to my daughter.'

'Now it's all settled. Except for the vows,' Darius said.

Something concerned Everleigh. He should feel sad that Vivian was ruined. He should feel sorry for his culpability in all this.

But he didn't. He just wondered why he'd not kissed her more in the carriage.

* * *

Vivian listened as her parents debated a trip to Scotland versus a special licence and a wedding breakfast.

'I beg your pardon,' she said, interrupting her parents. 'When I woke, I believed I was forced to marry him because of a promise I'd made. I was so relieved I could hardly comprehend it when I had a chance to live again. To be well and to dance. I don't want to be forced into marriage. Not with him. Not with anyone.'

'You shouldn't have taken off with him if you'd not wanted to marry him,' her father said. 'You're ruined if you don't, ruined if you do…because he is just like that grandfather of his. He's a ledger book with arms and legs. His grandfather would be so proud of him.' Vivian's father gave him one of those *I dare you to knock this smile off my face* looks.

'He was proud of me.' Everleigh fought the urge to take Darius up on the challenge. 'Unbeatable. Unstoppable. One of a kind.'

Darius snorted. 'She might as well reap the benefits of the title your grandfather worked so hard to get for his grandson.'

'You would have her marry me when you think I am heartless?' Anger boiled red in Everleigh.

'Even a love match is no guarantee for happiness,' Vivian's mother whispered, glancing at her husband.

Vivian touched her forehead. 'I've not had anything to eat or drink today and I'm feeling faint.'

'Tea,' Darius shouted. 'Bring us tea. Now.'

From somewhere in the hallway, footsteps skittered.

'Vivian,' Everleigh spoke as if they were the only two people in the room. 'You're wan. You've paled.'

'I didn't have breakfast,' she said. 'This hasn't been a smooth day.'

'You must marry me,' Everleigh insisted. 'There's no other option if you are to remain unscathed in society's opinion.'

'I've not been in society while I've been ill,' she said. 'I don't care what they are thinking.'

Vivian examined Everleigh. He appeared closer to a stone pillar than a husband. And while he did kiss rather softly, one could not live on kisses.

'I don't want to get married. To anyone. I'm alive. Nothing else matters.'

'Not even married to me?' Everleigh asked.

'No. You would be my first choice, if I were to marry now.' Her lips wavered for a half-second before she spoke. 'I suspect it's unlikely that I will get another proposal soon. But I'm fine with that. I want to dance. Not get married.'

Her future had opened in front of her. She wanted to enjoy it. Her parents had secluded her for her own good. Now she had a chance to be in society...or not. She might be ruined, but, well...the lower people on the societal ladder would find her interesting.

Each of her parents treated her well. She could not ask for better now that her father had curtailed his drinking. Mavis was a dear and she might need someone to help her find employment.

Vivian didn't feel the need to take a risk.

She'd just got her life back.

She'd been to the countryside and seen a different way of living, and someone who did not follow the rules. A dreadful, hateful crone who wore boots and probably spat into the fire, but did as she pleased.

The ne'er-do-well had probably even been to the Bartholomew Fair which was something Vivian's parents had never allowed. *'When you're older'*, they'd said. Well, now she was older, and she wanted a chance to do all the things she'd been told she would be able to do when she was 'older'. That part of life had almost passed her by.

Her parents had worried that she should not overtire herself. Something might happen. Well, it had.

They'd finally relented about the fair and they'd been right. Vivian had got hurt when a man's horse had moved sideways. Then it had kicked her.

She'd been injured and now she wanted to experience what she'd missed. No, that wasn't true. She wanted to experience more than what she'd missed.

She wanted to dance and stay too long at soirées, and visit somewhere exotic. Like Bath. She'd never even been to Bath. Everyone had been to Bath.

'I might like to go to Scotland, some day,' she said. 'Mavis and I might. I've never seen it. I've never been across the Channel. France might as well be on the moon.'

'There are wars to consider. It's not safe,' Everleigh said.

'I'm certainly not going to let you head off with Mavis,' Lord Darius shouted.

'You sacked her. She can do as she wishes and she has relatives in France.' Vivian stood firm. There was a world out there. The longest distance she had ever been away from her home had been to Rothwilde's estate.

She was certain she could find the funds. She had enough trinkets in her room to pay for several trips.

'I'm rehiring Mavis,' her father muttered. 'And you're marrying, and staying home.'

Everleigh took Vivian's arm. 'Perhaps we should talk. Can you show me where the dining room is?'

She nodded. 'Only if we do not have to discuss marriage.'

He put her hand over his arm. 'We do not.'

They walked to the dining room as her parents remained in the background.

No, she didn't want to get married and she could not understand why her parents would wish such a thing on her. They loved her. She knew that. And they loved each other, didn't they?

But she had been ill and thought she might not live. Before that, she'd thought marriage would be a grand thing and then she'd fallen in love with the worm who wouldn't write to her, and she'd fallen for the man who knew she was ill and expected funds for it, and she'd told her father it would be a snowy day in a certain place that she had heard about on Sunday before she married her suitor.

Marriage just didn't seem so grand any more. Particularly with a man who admitted he didn't believe in love and was heartless. He told her it would be dangerous to travel. Well, staying home hadn't been exactly a promise of safety.

She didn't want to be a mother like Everleigh's mother had been. She didn't want to travel and return with gifts for the children after letting them roam about on their own.

She could never do that. Her family would be first in her life, but first and foremost, she wanted a life.

And she'd never be able to see the exotic places she'd read about when she was ill.

Like Scotland and France, and Rome. And Bath.

Chapter Thirteen

Vivian stood at the window, sipping her tea.

The panes had fogged over. On the streets, horses passing by nickered. Vivian hoped for sunshine warm enough to stroll about with a parasol.

Perhaps in Rome. She imagined herself as a creature of the world. Perhaps she would wear trousers and learn to duel.

She'd once read of a female, in some high court, who got into duels because she could best the men—until the King forbade anyone to fight with her because she was bloodthirsty and killing his friends.

'Have you ever been to France?' she asked.

'Once.'

Everleigh stood at her shoulder, staring outside with her.

They'd not talked of marriage, or of food, or even of the weather, or of anything else.

'I should have stayed in today.' Vivian took another sip of the liquid.

'You really didn't like the kisses?' Everleigh asked.

She bit the inside of her lip, considering her answer. 'I liked them.'

'It's hard to believe that man you were considering marriage to didn't kiss you.' He touched a lock of hair that had fallen from her bun.

'Mavis was always scowling at him. He was scared of her. She once made a grabbing motion with her hand, clenched her fist as if she was grasping something, then twisted and gnashed her teeth together. Scared me, too.'

'I must thank her, then.'

The wind shuddered the window pane. The temperature must be changing. A few drops of rain splattered.

'Do you ever think of it? The kiss?' she asked. Her cup rattled in the saucer.

'Of course.'

The warmth in his voice convinced her he'd not just said it to please her.

She took another sip. 'It's odd, but I feel, if I were to marry you, my life would end as I know it. I want to dance. To travel. Just to live, basically, and live to the fullest.'

'We're not to discuss marriage.' He twisted the lock of her hair, fluttered it across her cheeks and tucked it closer to the bun.

She moved just a bit, so that she could feel the barest bit of him at her shoulder. 'What do you usually do on Sunday?' she asked.

He shook his head. 'Ledgers. Check my man-of-affairs's progress from the previous week. I must keep caught up so I can have time to attend the events I need to appear at. People are important to progress. I have to keep among them. No progress is ever made alone. You have to work with others.'

'Your wife would be expected to attend a lot of soi-rées and spend a lot of time with the architects' wives, her back straight and accepting many invitations.'

He shrugged. 'I've never given it any thought.'

'I did. When I was getting better. What it would be like to be married. To you. I'd promised it. There was little else to do but think about it as I waited to see if I would live.'

Mavis had been married once and her husband had squandered the household money on new plans to make them rich, or make them appear to be rich. Creditors had knocked. A mistress or two. Her companion said she had considered the best night of her marriage to be the night she'd sat with his casket. She often remi-nisced fondly about that night—*the un-wedding night*, she called it.

Vivian looked to her left, only seeing the side of Everleigh's shoulder.

Everleigh was a fancy, caused by the first kiss and circumstances. He was a tower of masculinity and stood firm, much like one of the battering rams people had once used to push in the doors of castles.

Everleigh touched the window pane, standing so close she could feel the heat of his body through her clothing.

His fingertip sketched against the moisture on the glass.

It almost squeaked when he wrote the words *Marry me?*

This was not her dream of love. His proposal hadn't been spoken again, or penned on to a note that she could hold close for ever. It could easily be wiped away, or would fade on its own.

It was rather like her father had suggested. She was of suitable lineage and so was he, and they would produce children of suitable lineage, and those children would marry other children of suitable lineage. The country would be happy. The *ton* would be happy. The households would be just as they had been for centuries before.

'Do you usually drink spirits, on those Sundays when you are doing the ledgers?' she asked.

He waited a heartbeat before answering. 'Yes. Usually. I like the routine of my Sundays. I put away the ledgers when I'm brought a glass of brandy late in the afternoon. I make my notes for the next week. The events I wish to attend and the people I need to meet with. Sometimes I have a second glass, while I strategise my week. At night, if I cannot work out how to solve a problem, I get a cheroot and step out under the stars to think about what needs to be done.'

Her father had once had two glasses as well when he drank, except sometimes he didn't notice when the second glass had been replaced with a third or fourth. He would mix his words and think it grand. The more he drank, the more he laughed, until he became angry and shut himself in his room to drink more.

'I want to dance,' she said. 'Just go to dances. I know I should have loftier ambitions, but I want to swirl around the floor as if everything is light-hearted and all that matters is the laughter, and the music, and the dance. I thought I'd never be able to do such a thing and I want to.'

She swept her hand over the words on the window pane, erasing them. 'That sounds so frivolous, but I know I wasn't meant to march in wars or pursue ambitions of such things. I'm satisfied with that. I know I was meant to marry and I'm not satisfied with that.'

'A ruined lady does not garner many invitations.'

'I'll get Father to hire musicians. I'll get a dancing teacher. Because I am going to dance. I am going to have music. Laughter will be around me. It may only be mine, but I will have laughter. I'll dance in Bath and perhaps in Scotland. I'll dance in the places I've dreamed of.'

She let out a long breath. 'I thought I was to be forced to marry. Marriage does not seem so important to me when I compare it to being alive.'

She twisted around to speak directly to him. 'Alexandria is not such an innocent and that has not kept her from dancing. She wanted me to be ruined and you to be forced into marriage. I will not have it.'

She had thought she had no choice but marriage before. Now she had an option.

She thought of the darkness of Rothwilde's estate. The coldness of Everleigh's father. *The Book of Martyrs* and the other books in the library, each one almost seeming alone in the space.

Everleigh's town house had rooms just as sombre.

To have a kiss was one thing, but she had been living in the shadows long enough. She didn't want to remain in them.

'I have a choice: to be forced into spinsterhood, or to be forced into marriage. I plan to smile, to live and to embrace life…not a husband.'

She would dance and put the last years behind her, and enjoy quadrilles and reels and life.

She would never let her heart and her spirit wither away again and she would seek out others who needed laughter. She would make certain that if someone were too frail, they would be able to count on her for a moment of joy. A respite from their pains and something other than four walls and sadness.

Her mother and Mavis, and even the maids, had provided lightness when Vivian was ill. They'd given her respite over and over again.

She would do that for others. She would find joy in life and pull people around her into the merriment.

If there was to be a time for everything under the sun, then there would be a time for everything under the stars. Laughter soothed pain better than poultices and she would distribute happiness. Only the people receiving would never know what had happened.

'I will let your parents know.' He left the room. The door remained open behind him.

Her father's oath shattered the air.

Then everything was silent as her mother murmured placating words. Her father grumbled.

The voices moved away and a door was shut. Her future was being discussed.

Everleigh's kisses—those she would miss. But a kiss was so fleeting. It made her feel alive, but didn't keep her alive.

Soft footsteps sounded behind her. Her mother came into view.

She'd not realised how close she and her mother were in size. Nor had she realised how pale her mother was. Her mother seemed different. Puffy. Wan. Momentarily Vivian was distracted. 'Are you ill?'

Her mother laughed. 'No. Not at all. I will stand with you on whatever you decide. Right now, it will only make your father feel I am goading him if I say so and

I am so trying to keep all the best parts of our marriage. But you need to know, Vivian, that I don't care whether you marry or not.' She dusted her hands together. 'I've heard tales of Everleigh's maternal grandfather. The man happily married his daughter off to get that title in the family. No one should be bartered so.'

Her mother walked out of the room. 'Unless, of course,' she mumbled, 'Everleigh might take your father in addition to you. Right now, that could cause me to change my mind.'

Vivian waited, listening for Everleigh to leave, wondering if he might come into the room to bid her goodbye.

She didn't know if it was a quarter or half an hour later when she heard footfalls on the stairs. She couldn't see him from the window as he departed. All she could see were the grey colours tinting everything beyond the window pane.

She imagined the cold hues surrounding her and being locked inside them for ever. She imagined Everleigh, never loving, but holding her heart captive.

Sitting at the table, she put her elbow on the wood, and rested her forehead in her palm. Something inside her felt lost, abandoned, and more alone than she'd ever been—yet she could change nothing of her decision not to marry him.

The seasons would change. Over and over. Spring would arrive again and it would be followed by summer, and autumn, and then winter—perhaps a winter colder than she'd ever seen before.

But never colder than the depths she'd felt inside Everleigh.

* * *

Everleigh gave his hat and gloves to the butler. Then he moved up the stairs, stopping midway.

Vivian's father wanted Everleigh as a son-in-law. They had discussed that after Everleigh had written the words of proposal on the window pane and then left Vivian alone in the room.

Darius had been angry to have his daughter ruined. Only one thing would solve that…a marriage. To Everleigh. He'd insisted that Vivian would have no choice, eventually, but to wed.

After all, Darius would not fund foolish ventures where Vivian might travel, and fall into trouble, or into the waters of Bath. He would see that she married Everleigh. The chance to marry an earl's heir did not happen every day.

Everleigh had listened and it had been rather like a negotiation, he supposed, of centuries before when one ruler wanted to make an alliance with another country. A discussion of the benefits of alliance. The heritage of the Baron aligned with the heritage Everleigh carried.

Negotiations had begun, with Vivian at the centre. He wondered if his father and grandfather had had the same conversation.

It had seemed odd having the discussion without Vivian in the room, and pointless. Talking with her father had made the idea of marriage less appealing.

Then her father had grumbled that he'd not even known Everleigh was in Vivian's mind until the soirée when she'd invited the architects. He'd been so surprised because she'd never once mentioned Everleigh to him.

Her father had told Everleigh that Vivian had never stopped speaking of the fortune hunter who had once courted her, until she found out the settlement the man had been promised for every month she lived past the wedding.

Then she refused to consider anyone.

Everleigh went to his room, shrugged off the coat, and threw it over the back of a chair.

He could not blame Vivian.

Not at all. He didn't want to marry.

Neither did Vivian.

She wanted to dance and he understood her wanting such a thing. He'd never wanted to dance. Life was too short for such nonsense. There was so much work to be done.

Everleigh had insisted the negotiations stop.

He didn't encourage projects that wasted time.

Later that night, he heard the clump of footsteps on the stairs and the tapping noise of his father's cane.

He raised his face in time to see his father step into the room, chortling. 'What is this I hear about two women fighting over you in the streets?'

Everleigh stared around the room. The stories had already started. Vivian was at the centre of them.

'A mishap. With idle chatter taking it out of proportion.'

'It's said shots were fired.'

Everleigh put his elbows on the desk and rested his face in his hands. 'Alexandria did not take well to my rejection.'

'Are you going to marry the other one?'

'We have no plans to wed.'

His father's cane crashed into the floor. 'You did not propose? The men at the club told me it is Baron Darius's daughter. She would make a fine wife for you.' The tip of the cane kept rattling against the floor.

'You also told me Alexandria would make a fine wife for me.'

'Well, she was breathing, and would have passable offspring.' Another slap of the cane on the floor.

Silence.

'I cannot fathom how I raised you. You know your duty. How long do marriage vows take? Less than an hour. A matter of hours beforehand to get the special licence. A few hours,' he sputtered. 'A few hours of your life and you cannot spare them.'

More silence.

'I cannot believe that.' He rushed down the stairs as fast as he could, shouting to a servant, 'Tell them not to unhitch the carriage.'

Everleigh raised his head and walked to the window, watching a servant run for the carriage. Thankfully, his father would go back to the estate. At least the house would be peaceful.

His father walked to the street and stood, tapping the cane.

When the carriage pulled up, the driver stepped down to help him in. His father gesticulated wildly with the cane. Realisation flashed in Everleigh's mind. His father wasn't telling the driver to return to Wildewood. He was pointing in another direction.

Chapter Fourteen

The carriage trundled along to Rothwilde's estate. Vivian noticed the vibrancy of her skin. She'd been so much thinner on her first trip into the countryside.

She glanced at her father and her mother beside him, both with backs straight, lips in a line, arms crossed. Both wore grim expressions as they alternated between observing her and sharing stern glances.

She supposed even the horses were irritated because the driver kept shouting to them.

When the vehicle stopped at Rothwilde's house, Vivian looked at the dark entrance. 'I'm not going to marry him.'

'I understand,' her mother said. 'It's unseemly for us to be out here chasing after him. If he can't come to you…'

'We are *not* chasing after him.' Darius scowled. '*We* were invited. By his father. The man was apologetic, and far more understanding than I expected. He said his son isn't even here at the moment. That he is alone here and would like visitors. He suggested we become better acquainted.'

'Did he suggest a chance for your daughter to become a countess some day?' her mother asked.

'Nothing wrong with that,' he said, descending the steps and turning to help his wife. 'As long as Vivian's future husband, whoever he may be, never has to take a long carriage ride with the two of you, I would think it might be a satisfactory marriage.'

Her mother pulled her pelisse closer with a twist of the wrist, causing it to billow out. 'I suppose it would also depend on whether she has to put up with him criticising everything she does.'

As her father mumbled a retort, her mother reassured herself by inspecting Vivian. 'Are you sure you are feeling well?'

Vivian nodded, staring at the windows and the trees surrounding the house. Their limbs stretched like arms warding off visitors. It was no more welcoming than the first time she'd seen it.

'Cheery place,' her mother commented. 'I'm sure it's nicer inside.'

'Come along.' Her father reached for her mother's arm.

They walked into the entrance hall. Rothwilde greeted them. 'Sadly, my son isn't here.' His face belied his words. 'But who knows if he may arrive later or not?'

He guided them to the drawing room.

Again, Vivian studied the portrait of the Countess of Rothwilde. The portrait dominated the room. But Vivian felt uneasy when she observed it, saddened by the knowledge someone would deface a work of art and that the woman had had a short life, and an uneasy marriage.

Rothwilde walked into the room and observed the

portrait as if he'd never seen it before. 'My late wife. Painted before we married. It would have been hard to miss her,' Rothwilde admitted. 'The painting doesn't do her justice.'

The housekeeper appeared in the doorway, scowling. Vivian wondered if she'd decorated the house. Her clothes matched it.

'Would you like refreshments?' she asked.

Rothwilde flinched, as if he'd been caught doing something he shouldn't have, but then he shrugged. 'Yes.'

After they were seated, Vivian could tell that Rothwilde and her father talked as if they were going to become family members. Her mother said almost nothing.

Then Rothwilde offered to show them the new carriage house he was having built and her mother forced a smile.

They were all examining timbers when the sound of another arrival reached their ears.

'Probably my son,' Rothwilde said, offhandedly to Darius. 'He might be in a foul mood. I wrote him that the expenses on the carriage house were running much higher than expected. I also told him another structure on the estate would be needed so I could have more visitors and the wagers would come to me. My own private gambling hell. I hoped his architect friends could be of assistance.'

He spoke to Vivian and her mother. 'Let's go inside and see how he is faring.'

Everleigh walked into the house, reached for the top button on his coat and slipped the fastenings open.

His father was punishing him in the only way available to him, or so he believed. The man would try to beggar Everleigh. Well, it would not happen. He would make certain of that.

The grey mouse of a housekeeper stepped into the room. His father's mistress.

'I'll take your coat,' she said.

He slipped the garment from his shoulders, not acknowledging her by name.

'Rothwilde has visitors.'

His movements froze, his hand still grasping the wool. His father rarely entertained. 'Who?'

'The Baron, his wife…'

Everleigh waited.

'And their daughter.' She took the coat. 'I thought you should know.'

He paced into the drawing room. Plans for the carriage house were sprawled across the sofa. His jaw tensed. Apparently Rothwilde had been showing them to Darius. He lifted the papers, shuffling through them. Nothing had changed. No scribbles on the side, or mention of any other structure.

Everleigh lifted the pages and rolled them into place, the paper rustling as he twisted it into a roll. He propped them in the corner.

His father had sent him an invitation that he'd known Everleigh could not refuse. He'd walked into it as easily as he might have walked into a spider's web on a dark night. His father was the only person who could gauge Everleigh so easily.

Voices alerted him.

'Rothwilde,' Everleigh greeted his father.

'Son.' He moved out of the way, leaning on his cane. 'How pleasant that you've arrived just when we have visitors.'

'How fortunate, indeed.' Everleigh watched as Darius walked into the room, followed by Lady Darius and, lastly, Vivian.

Anger at his father drained from his body. Anger at himself replaced it. He shouldn't be so happy to see Vivian.

Then she glanced at him and that anger faded as well. He'd been surrounded by machinations his whole life. One more wouldn't hurt. He would take care around Vivian. She had little choice in the matter, he was certain.

Besides, her cheeks were flushed with radiance and seeing her eased the irritations of his day.

But it wouldn't do to let the others be aware that he was pleased. He scowled at his father, who appeared oblivious to anything but the goodwill he and Darius shared.

So be it. He didn't want to make Vivian uncomfortable. 'It's always pleasant when Father invites guests to the estate.' That would mostly leave the last decade—all the years since his mother had died—out of the equation, but only he and his father knew that.

His father gripped the cane. 'I agree.'

Everleigh saw three expectant expressions and one tense one. He wanted to reassure her. 'I hope the carriage trip to the estate was less eventful than the previous journey.'

'Much,' she admitted.

Her father let out a deep sigh. 'I have to be thankful that Alexandria was not more daft than she was.'

'We all do,' Lady Darius said. 'What's important—*really* important—is that neither of our children was injured. My daughter is healthy and your son wasn't hurt.'

'True,' Rothwilde said. He thumped his son on the back. 'I'd not really thought of it that way before. My son seems invincible to me. I'd be lost without him.'

Everleigh stared at his father and tried to read beyond the façade. He wasn't sure this statement wasn't on the same level as putting in a gaming house, because his father had never said such a preposterous thing before.

The actual comments had run closer to suggesting Everleigh stay in London and they wouldn't ever have to speak again, and were peppered with oaths. Even the letters had to be burned on occasion as he'd not wanted anyone else to read what his father had written to him.

The maid arrived with tea. The ladies' dresses fluttered while everyone rearranged themselves to allow the servant enough space to enter.

The distraction gave Everleigh and Rothwilde a chance to speak.

'Truce,' his father muttered from the side of his mouth to Everleigh.

'Agreed,' Everleigh responded, teeth together.

'Cards.' His father brightened, raising his voice. 'Wouldn't a game of cards be an enjoyable way to spend the evening?'

The evening was as convivial as one could hope for. In fact, it had been years since he'd seen his father so at ease on the estate. His father was on his best behaviour and he suspected Vivian's father was the same.

Then he realised Vivian and her mother contributed only an audience to the conversation.

He stepped away from the group as a servant glided in with more refreshments and a tray of macarons.

As the maid moved from blocking his view of Vivian, he saw the glance between her and her mother. A second conversation was going on in his presence and he'd been totally unaware of it.

Joining the group again, he paid less attention to what was being said, than what wasn't being said.

Rothwilde and her father were indeed getting on well. In fact, better than he would have expected.

'Wait until you hear this...' Rothwilde shook his head, speaking to Darius. 'The cook had befriended a cat without my knowledge and it escaped into the main rooms. I sat on it and that infernal beast attached itself to me using all its claws and teeth. I was ready to send the cook packing, but I could not lose out on these macarons.'

Vivian and her mother were smiling at the right places, commenting pleasantly and enjoying their tea.

When the conversation slowed, Everleigh spoke to Vivian and her mother. 'I wish we had music tonight. The local blacksmith is an accomplished musician. He carries his flute with him more than he does his hammer. I'll send someone to see if he and his wife might slip away for a few moments. She has a beautiful voice and they often have a few songs prepared for events.'

'That isn't necessary.' Vivian's words brushed the idea away, but he saw the interest in her.

'You should not go to any trouble,' Darius added. 'Your father has been showing us around the estate and I must say we're impressed. He says all the recent renovations have been at your suggestion.'

'True. Did he mention a gaming house he has planned?'

Lord Darius shuffled his feet. 'No. He didn't.'

'Just in the planning stages,' Rothwilde inserted. 'The more I think about it, the less enthusiasm I have for it.' Rothwilde took a drink from his wineglass and spoke to Everleigh first, then directed his conversation to include the others. 'Now that I consider it closer, I'm discarding it. It would take away from the carriage house.'

Darius nodded. 'You do have a fine estate, Rothwilde. We'll take you up on your offer to see more of it tomorrow.'

'That would be wonderful,' Vivian's mother said, a *ton*-worthy smile on her lips. 'Of course, if the weather isn't too cool for Vivian.'

Everleigh knew then that neither woman cared about walking around the fields or seeing the size of the grounds.

Lady Darius patted her daughter's arm. 'I don't think I'm up to such an adventure. We might enjoy the indoors.'

Chapter Fifteen

~~~~~~~~

'If you and Vivian would like,' Everleigh said to her mother, 'I will be pleased to show you the library. You may even find a book you would like to read.'

'That's thoughtful of you,' her mother said, but her attention was diverted by a newspaper on the tabletop. 'But I've missed reading the latest news for the past few days. I'd rather catch up on that. Vivian might like a book, however.'

They walked into the library. Vivian noticed that the martyr book wasn't there, but now she saw about twenty books, including some novels. She stepped forward, reading the spines. Some of the books she would like.

'It appears that in honour of your visiting Father has added some from his collection in case you might wish to read while you're here.'

'Last time, all the books seemed in the vein of the martyrs and I'm pleased to see books with happier endings.'

'Has the scandal been a problem for you?' he asked. 'It concerns me—the thought of your reputation being sacrificed just as you have recovered.'

Putting her head down, she tried to hide her smile. 'Not at all. Some of my friends searched me out. They were pleased to find that I was well enough to be out of my home, and they wanted to know whether I was betrothed or not, as everyone was convinced, of course, that we had been courting.'

She moved away. 'It's given me notoriety. Alexandria had offended many families when she stole daughters' beaus and then abandoned them one after another. Everyone thinks her actions were shameful. She is ruined. I am a surviving victim. I have been asked many times if she shot at me. I have always said no, but I'm being seen as generous. The tale has been spread too many times that she pointed the gun at the carriage.' She patted her palms together. 'Everyone thinks Mavis was in the vehicle. After all, her hat fluttered out of the carriage and was left in the street when you and I were leaving. No one noticed she wasn't there. They were watching the gun and Alexandria.'

He moved his right foot behind him and rested his weight on it. His expression lightened. 'You've enjoyed it?'

'Most certainly, except for when my parents are near.' She angled her head. 'I don't want to cause them any grief at all. I really don't. But it has been enjoyable visiting with people who have been by to see that I am doing all right.

'One of my old friends married in her first season,' Vivian explained. 'I had hardly seen her since. She has been to my house to make certain I am well. She visited a second time to give me a note from her brother also wishing me well. I don't even remember him, but apparently he wants me to save a dance for him.'

Pausing, she glanced at him. 'You understand, I do have to think of my parents, first and foremost. I can't cause them any more embarrassment, so I do need to be extremely careful not to do that again. But my mother told the details to a few close friends. The news travelled from ear to ear. Everyone is enthralled about my promising to marry so I could get a lifesaving cure, and my concern for Mother's health. She's probably checking the newspaper now to see if there is mention of the story. She has hopes.'

She interlaced her fingers and clasped them at her chest. 'We've not told Father but the invitations have been pouring in. He refuses to talk about it and probably doesn't know Mavis was only there…in spirit.'

He stared at her. 'No one told me about this.'

'Your friends probably don't tittle tattle much. They would hardly think anything of it. After all, they're probably envious and see the story as two women fighting in the street over you. At least, that is what Mother has heard.'

'With my friends, I only talk politics.'

'That's important, too.'

Invitations?

He didn't want her to be ruined and was happy that everyone accepted the truth of the event, but he didn't want her flittering from dance to dance to man to man without a backwards glance for him.

His hand moved out, touching the small bit of her earlobe and resting on the pearl below. 'Lovely earrings.'

'Thank you.' But he barely heard the response. Instead, he perceived the reflection of emotion in her voice.

Holding the small of her back, feeling the silk under his palm and the swirl of her lavender soap plunging into him, he guided her to the doorway, fighting with all his strength to rid himself of his awareness of her.

At each of her steps, his hand moved slightly, feeling the change of the fabric, and her skin beneath it. He would have said he could have touched a hundred dresses, blindfolded, and been able to select the one which was now under his palm.

Without a single movement, his thoughts told him the feel of her entire back, down the swell of her bottom, and robbed him of any ability to do more than walk behind her. She moved apart from him as she glided away, each step lingering, prolonging his delicious agony.

He wondered how the pearls would feel if his cheek were against hers, resting against her skin. He imagined his teeth grazing the jewels and the softness of her lips against his.

Then he started thinking about more than her first kiss.

'Vivian, I'm not the person you might think.'

'What do you mean?'

'I'm pleased you aren't ruined.'

'I thought you would be happy.'

He took her hand and brought her knuckles to his lips, dropping a kiss on them. 'But I keep thinking about what it would be like to spend the night with you. To touch you. To hold you. To wake in the morning with you.'

'I told you. I don't want to talk about marriage.'

'I'm not.'

He put a fingertip against her lips. 'Don't answer.' He stepped back. 'Forget I said that. You deserve a life of dancing with a man who wishes to journey with you to Bath and do all the things you wish for.'

'I do.'

'I'll join the others.'

He left to find his father and Darius. He had to stay away from Vivian. She had narrowly escaped ruin before. He could not destroy her plans just when she was finally able to pursue her life as she wished.

Chapter Sixteen

Vivian lay in the bed, wide awake, reflecting on Everleigh. She couldn't be still. Too much energy resided in her, pent up from all the moments she'd been exhausted.

She jumped to the floor, slipped her corset half on and did a haphazard knot at the top of the back before tugging it into place. She wrenched the bottom strings close so they could be tied. Then she struggled into her dress, pulling it high in the back so she could reach over her shoulders to get the top two hooks, then sliding it into place and reaching behind to do up the lower hooks.

Leaving the bedroom, she pulled the door shut and tiptoed down the stairs and through the hall. Peering around the library entrance, she saw Everleigh, sitting at his desk and watching the doorway as if he'd heard every footfall. He held a pen above paper. The ink bottle sat at the side.

His waistcoat was open and his cravat was loosened. His dark hair, perfectly combed, fell lightly at the side of his face. His eyebrows arched in question. 'Couldn't sleep?' He rose, taking a step towards her. 'Neither could I.'

'You should leave the estate,' she said. 'You know what Father expects and I can tell your father does also.' She put out a hand towards his chair. 'You can. I can't without causing an upheaval in my parents' lives. If you go, they will not get their hopes up so high. It will be best for everyone.'

'I'm not certain I can leave either.' He put down the pen and pointed to the hard-backed chair, indicating she sit. 'There's this angelic vision in my home. So fetching. I've kissed her and I keep thinking about her.'

She walked over, lifting the chair and putting it in front of his desk, but to the side. Facing him completely seemed too precarious. 'That's a good reason to stay.'

He crooked his head and motioned to her as if challenging her to ask an amusing question. But she didn't speak. Instead, she examined a sheet of paper on his desk. A blank sheet.

'I was thinking,' he said. 'About you. Then I heard your footsteps.'

'I don't make much noise.'

'You don't even tiptoe quietly. You squeaked again.'

'I did not,' she muttered.

'Perhaps,' he agreed. 'But your door did snap when it closed and you took thirty-four steps.'

Her lips parted. She examined him. 'You could not hear my steps.' She'd crept down the stairs.

'Maybe not all thirty-four, but you did hesitate just before you stopped in my doorway.'

She stared at him, wondering how well he could hear.

'I'm glad I didn't write a letter,' she grumbled. 'The pen scratching against the paper might have deafened you.'

He laughed softly, the sound almost turning him into

someone different. Someone she didn't know. 'I learned from my grandfather, Vivian. Tell people words confidently and, if they are the least unsure, they will believe you. Especially if they do not know you well and you bluster better than them.'

Unease flickered inside her. 'What else did you learn from him?'

'To play with the finances and property as a game. I must realise, and accept, losses, but still play to win. Always play to win. I must anticipate all the movements and counter what I can when needed.'

'You didn't even check to see what my dowry might be. Mother asked Father.'

'So this has been a topic of conversation between your parents and you?'

'It is as if we are in the past, considering whether the Magna Carta is to be shared or not.'

'The decision?'

'Father has his. Mother is trying to remain impartial.'

Her mother did appear impartial, but was dead set that Vivian not be pushed into a marriage she didn't want. She said she could never be happy if Vivian wasn't, so she wanted Vivian to tread lightly.

'I had thought your mother might be aligned with your father.'

Vivian smiled. 'Mother hardly lifts her own spoon and says a wife should be subservient to her husband. But when Father was drinking, she would take the glass out of his hand on Saturday night. She made sure he was aware on Sunday and was at Sunday Services, and he was still a member of the family. She would have got two footmen to drag him from the drink if she had needed to for events. He knew it. Father leads the household, even if Mother is behind him pushing him in the direction she wants, and convincing him to change his mind when she disagrees with him.'

'So, what does she wish for you?'

'She is not so impartial that she doesn't see my perspective.' Vivian frowned.

'Do you know the particulars of your dowry?' he asked, straightening the pen he'd put on the desk. 'I don't need to know. I just wondered if you do.'

'I'm unfamiliar with the details, just that Mother says it will be tied up in such a way that a husband will see none of it. After the first time, she decided that would be best. An allowance for me, should I wish it. Bequests for any children. Mother says mathematicals make her brain hurt.'

'Finances are rather like a confectionery to me.'

'They are very confusing to Mother and me. When Father was foxed, Mother read his man-of-affairs's ledgers. She said they were jumbled. So jumbled that she talked Father into replacing the man. She says she hates financial matters and we are not to concern ourselves with them. That is what a man-of-affairs is for, so we must hire good ones. If Father is unable to read the ledgers, then she must do so for him.'

'Are you the same?'

'I have never given them much attention, but suppose I could if I had to. Mother believes she shouldn't have to worry about such things. She would prefer not to, but she has had no choice. She has always said I will have a home and that there will be enough to take care of the expenses for the rest of my life should anything happen to either of them.'

'It's fortunate you do not have to make a decision that's financially based.'

Vivian straightened her skirt. 'Mother says I am not to concern myself with her future. Only my own. She talks to me as if I were a son. She said she would not force a son into marriage. During the time Father wasn't paying close attention, our finances did diminish until the man-of-affairs was replaced, but Mother reassured me many times that we would manage just fine.'

Vivian straightened her sleeve, staring off into the distance, reconsidering her mother's actions.

'Mother said she didn't particularly care for the size of their house. So, Father rented it to someone else. She selected a smaller town house that she loves as it is right in the middle of London society. She thought it would be better for my marriage prospects. I did receive a proposal rather quickly.' She grimaced. 'Too quickly. He was more concerned about my finances than my health.'

Everleigh stretched back in his chair and contemplated her. 'I would half-expect household costs to diminish with your mother taking charge.'

'They might have. She has told me there is no reason to toss funds into the sky and expect them to grow there.'

'Your mother is making sure you are provided for.'

'Of course. That is just being practical and considering the future. A future that I almost lost hope of having, but is now at my fingertips.'

She hesitated, and rose. She moved to the doorway. Then paced back to stand at his side. 'I would like to… perhaps ask a favour.'

Chapter Seventeen

He remembered the first favour she had asked of him. He remembered it as well as if it were happening in that instant.

She stopped beside him, her hair tumbling from her knot after a day of travel.

His brow quirked up. His concentration increased, raising his awareness to new heights.

He reached out, taking her hand. He must let her know his refusal of her body had nothing to do with lack of desire.

He braced himself, making sure he had the strength to deny her if she asked for more pleasures. Oh, he would give them to her so easily. So well. He could help her explore her passions and their bodies together. But he could not let her know that. He could not. She lured him without effort. Her smallest movement captured him.

'I wanted to speak with you again and thank you for the kindness you have shown me,' Vivian said.

She'd moved so close to him that the lavender scent of her enclosed them both.

He reached up to touch her chin and saw a change as her expression softened. So little space between them.

Their kisses remained in his memory. He moved closer, inhaling her femininity. Letting her essence surround him.

But he would retain control of himself. Well, the parts he hadn't already lost control of.

'Could you withdraw your proposal and let my father know?' She ended the silence. 'He keeps asking me about it.'

He released her chin. He could have imagined a thousand other questions he would have preferred her to ask. 'Certainly. If that's what you want.'

She touched his forearm and ran her hand down to his, took his fingertips and placed his hand back on her chin. 'Yes. It's what I want.'

Everleigh stopped the deluge of feelings that rampaged inside him. Mentally, he stepped aside, reining himself in.

Watching her, he came closer again, their breaths mingling. Featherlight, he brushed a kiss across her lips. 'Consider it done.'

Vivian watched as notions flickered in Everleigh. She could see the process, but could not fathom what he thought.

'Goodnight, Vivian.'

He left the library at a normal pace, seeming lost to her.

True, she didn't want the proposal, but that didn't mean she wanted him out of her life. They'd shared a kiss, a carriage ride and a gunshot together.

She paused. She had Mavis, her mother and her father for friendship. The same people she'd had all her life, with a few acquaintances scattered about. Talking with Everleigh had been different.

More like a friend to whom she could bare her soul.

Or maybe, not like a friend at all. More like a lover. An almost lover.

She walked from the room, seeing his back at the top of the stairs as she followed him up.

He paused at his bedroom door, awareness of her visible in his hesitation. She expected him to tell her to leave and she stopped.

He continued inside and didn't close the door.

She moved forward, each footstep careful, precise and out of her control.

He stood, head down, arm outstretched and hand on the bedpost. But when she stopped inside the threshold, he observed her with blue flickering desire.

She wavered, aware of the stark furnishings. This room—she examined the fixtures—didn't have a single bit of softness in it other than the bedcovers and they were so basic she wondered that the person sewing them hadn't shaken her head over the utter plainness of them. A white towel lay folded by his shaving supplies.

Nothing sat on the fireplace except a flint and a striker. He had a boot stand and that, with the shaving kit, constituted the adornment except for side tables and two chairs. The lack of decoration made the room feel large and cold.

The room was definitely spacious in its austerity. Quite spacious compared to hers. Larger even than the library.

In two swift strides, he had his hands on her shoulders, holding her gently. His eyes—the colour intensified—were like stones under reflecting water. 'You should not be here. Even you cannot put an innocent twist on being found in my room.'

His fingers left a burning trail as they moved to hold her face. 'Why are you in my bedroom?'

'I only meant for you to withdraw the marriage proposal. Not our acquaintance. I keep thinking about what you said. About teaching me. About how you would like to show me... I can't remember the words, but I remember the gist of it and I am not ill now.'

'That doesn't make the idea a better one. It might make it worse.'

'If I'm planning to remain a spinster...' she said.

'This is not the way to do it.'

He placed an arm around her and moved, intending to help her from the room.

She twirled out of his grasp. 'I understand. The kisses...'

He stilled. 'When I see you, Vivian, I always think of more than kisses.'

She grasped the doorknob and didn't release it when she closed the door, remaining inside with him. 'It always seems that I am the one approaching you.'

He caressed her shoulder, the fabric of her gown no barrier from the marvel of his fingers. He turned her, his lips hesitating at her cheek. His breath touched her. 'Because I know the truth of it.' His fingers tightened. 'You tempt me, Vivian.' He moved nearer.

Her emotions surged, relishing the contrast between her femininity and his masculinity.

He raised one hand, taking the side of her face, resting his thumb under her chin, and his lips descended.

She felt the kiss more than any touch she'd ever

known. Cascading through her body, it removed her from conscious thought. When her knees dipped, he took his hand from her cheek and slipped his arm around her, securing her, snuggling her close. His lips pulled away, the brush of his irregular breaths heating her skin more than any flames.

'I could not have just one taste of you and not want more.' Desire infused his words.

'But—'

'You can lock the door, or leave.'

She didn't move.

Slowly rotating away, he picked up the lamp from the bedside table. 'I'll see you to your room.'

She slid the bolt.

He remained near the bed. 'Your reputation could be totally destroyed. Your father will not accept your decision to be my mistress. It is unthinkable. We would have no avenue to see each other regularly without people noticing and drawing their own conclusions. You will be ruined and the ramifications will be lasting.'

'You're right. You wouldn't have to worry about harming your reputation. It would be overlooked with you, an earl's son.' She closed the distance between them. 'I see your point of view. Through the perspective of society.' Raising her gaze, she whispered, 'Then I see you through my own eyes. I don't want to leave. I can't leave.'

He rested his thumb behind her earlobe, giving the tiniest tap to her pearl earring.

She felt the vibration run the length of her body to her toes.

'I've been wanting to do that all night. For an eternity. They shine like starlight.' He moved the lamp, causing the shadows in the room to dance when he sat it on the table.

'There really is no true light in this house.' She heard the strained sound of her words.

'I would argue with that... You.'

'Yet you do not want to make love to me.'

'I don't recall saying that.' He contemplated her. 'If I did, I shouldn't have said such a ridiculous thing. I only am concerned for you.'

'A few more seconds together, then?'

'Vivian. In only a second, it could become too late to turn back.'

'For me, that happened a long time ago.'

He pulled her tight, resting his forehead against hers.

She felt the scent of him touch her, all wool, and starch, and male. 'I feel so desolate when I stand near you and you're not holding me.'

'Then I would like to nuzzle away that desolation, because it's in me, also.'

'I had no idea how alone I was. How cold I felt inside.' She hadn't, until he held her.

Everleigh's face dipped close to hers. 'I cannot bear the notion of your not being happy.' His lips rested at her mouth. 'I could warm you more... If you wish...'

'Yes. I want you to make love to me.'

He slid both hands over her shoulders. 'I want you. Of course I do. But...'

He loosened the knot of his cravat, moving ever so slightly, releasing the bond, letting the fabric glide across her fingertips as he removed it.

Taking one end of the material, he brushed it against her and the fibres didn't feel like cloth any more, in the way a rainstorm in a desert didn't feel like mere drops of liquid, but bursts of life. She caught it, gripping, and pulling him into a kiss.

He slipped his hands over her dress and his touch burned. She couldn't feel the gown—just the heat of his touch.

'A kiss isn't about lips meeting. It's about tasting.' Everleigh bent his lips to hers.

When he stopped, his breath brushed her. 'I want to touch you. But there is so much I cannot let you risk. I can't.'

She moved, just enough, to catch his mouth with hers, but he tightened his grasp on the cravat and she glided forward, pulled by his backward steps.

When the bed stopped him, she released the cravat and he tossed it behind him. The soft sound of it falling on the bed more silent than her heartbeats.

He pulled her up, against him, dipping his head and taking her mouth, trapping her close. She felt him and his tongue.

Her body responded, more than it had for their previous kisses. She savoured the feelings plunging into her, pushing her forward. Enveloping her in him.

He didn't taste like any food, or chocolate, or anything of normal nourishment. Instead he was all shimmering lights and male strength—a power stronger than she'd felt before.

She knew his hands could have crushed her against him. Instead of feeling confined by the strength wrapped around her, he made her feel more supple than she'd ever been. Every fibre swirled alive inside her. Her knees gave way. But it didn't matter. He was not letting her go.

His lips were the only soft thing about him, but they

were turning her body into something else—or some-one else—because she didn't have control of it any more. He did.

He pulled back. 'I can't make love to you because I don't want you hurt. We can't decide that now. I don't want you rushed into a decision that you might regret.'

She opened her mouth and he captured her bottom lip, tasting, closing out everything in the world but what her senses could touch.

His kiss captured her, and blotted all the rest of the world from her thoughts. He pulled away, but kept her in his clasp. The embrace tightened. Running his lips down her neck, he continued, lifting her closer as his mouth caressed down to the top of her garment, leaving a moist trail burning behind.

He released her, letting her feet touch the floor.

'The night has hardly started.' His words enveloped the room. He slipped a finger under the lace at the shoulder of her dress. 'Neither of us will be able to sleep easily if we part now. I will be thinking about your mouth. About my lips on your body, trailing along the softness of your skin. The curve of your… Beyond even that.' He rested a hand on her hip, sending more heat into her than any bolt of lightning.

He took her wrist and put her palm to his mouth, pulling it slowly upwards, letting her feel the textures of him. The soft and the rough.

He lifted her elbow higher, until it was level with her face, and then he kissed the V of her arm. He moved, his lips again caressing hers, and his tongue darting inside, weakening her. He pulled away, his teeth grazing the skin he had just kissed.

Then he stopped.

Everything seemed to stop. Everything in the world.

Except the hooks on the back of her gown. They opened so easily.

Gently, he released the cloth from her shoulders, letting it pool at her feet.

He stopped, standing back, gazing at her. 'You're beautiful.'

As he removed his boots, one upward glance engulfed her with passion.

Vivian watched as Everleigh stepped behind her and her body pulsed when he found the ties of her corset, loosening them, releasing them. The garment slid from over her chemise, dropping away.

Their kisses mingled, while he reached to the small ties at the top of her chemise. He loosened them and swept the fabric aside, feeling the breast beneath it. Caressing the tip.

The woven fabric slid the rest of the way down her body. The fibres brushed her like silk and fell to the floor.

With his left arm, he pulled her closer, then removed his waistcoat and dropped it to the side. Within a second, his shirt went over his head and he continued their kisses. He never released her waist while he checked her reaction as he removed his trousers.

She wasn't shocked, and let him know with her eyes.

He sat on the bed, pulling her astride him, but not moving into her, and running his fingers up her back. They melded together, her breasts pushed into his chest, and her body burned with intensity. She savoured his taste, essence and absorbed all of him with her senses.

Then he lifted her so that she lay on the bed.

Taking her mouth as if it were the last breath he would ever have, and the one that would sustain him for the rest of his life, he kissed her.

He caressed her breasts, her waist, tightened her hips against him and slid his fingers down to the V of her leg, caressing, while he intertwined one leg over hers.

For Vivian, the sensation of muscle, and the brush of the fine hairs on his leg, contrasted with the liquid feelings inside her.

When she found her pleasure, she gasped, a thousand rainbows alighting around her.

She became aware again as he whispered her name.

He bit the inside of his lip, forcing himself to lie still, surprised at how much her release had pleased him and satisfied him.

Almost.

But not quite.

Vivian lay beside him, silent, the gasps fading.

She rolled to him. He moved forward, one finger combing her hair so he could see her better, before he nestled her in the curve of his arm.

She locked herself around him. The bedcovers rustled as he extricated them enough to burrow them together.

'It's a quiet night,' she said.

The night was silent. His conscience wasn't smug, or congratulating him on his strength, but it wasn't flagellating him either.

A shared interlude. Little more than an instant in either of their lives and yet it wasn't. A man could not lay naked in Vivian's arms and not feel something had changed in him and he knew she could not sweep this away as if it never happened.

He shouldn't have touched her.

He realised his conscience hadn't been mute, it had been gathering strength for an onslaught.

'That... This is wonderful.' She cuddled, almost purring, her body rubbing against him as she hugged him.

His conscience faded, replaced by a tightening of his body.

He could not ask her to leave. She'd never understand.

With more delicacy than he'd ever mustered, he patted her.

'It was amazing,' she said.

'Yes. It was.' But it could be so much more. He dropped a kiss on her forehead, then ran a hand along the smoothness of her body.

His conscience flared again, warning him. Another second, another moment of tenderness from her, and the night would begin all over again. A gentle caress here, one there, and the gentle touches would lead them back together before she understood what was happening. Only this time, he would not have the strength to stop.

'In another few hours, it will be morning.' He hated to move. Hated to leave her, but he had to. 'You can take the lamp back to your room.'

She tensed.

'It's not that I don't want you to stay. I just don't want you hurt.'

'I'll be careful.'

The chill of her body moving away hit him.

He snuggled her close, risking another second. He had to reassure her. 'I don't want you to leave. I don't.'

But it was for her own good.

Then the little voice inside him reminded him that if he'd been so concerned about what was best for Vivian, she would be in her own room now.

He had to shut it up. To speak of something. Anything.

'The house feels differently with you and your family here. Not quite the same. I noticed it when you and Mavis first visited. The same as when my brother was here.'

'Where does he live?' She edged away slightly. Pulling the covers up to her chest, propping herself on her elbow. No longer intertwined with him.

'I don't know.'

'Your only brother? You don't write to him?' Her voice rose. 'I always wanted a brother or a sister and wished I had one.'

'We had a disagreement. He left and hasn't been back.' Probably like what was about to happen with Vivian.

'Why don't you try to find him?'

'It wouldn't be that hard. Father is aware of where he lives. They correspond.'

'Your only brother?'

He heard accusation in her words. Yes. She was getting a message from him. Perhaps that would make it all easier.

'What did you fight over?' she asked.

He shook his head. 'It wasn't important.'

The fight really hadn't been over anything significant, but their grandfather had died only a few months before. After the death, he and Daniel had seemed to argue over everything from the name of the constellations to how the clock should be set.

Their grandfather had been a peacemaker between his grandsons. Rothwilde always took Daniel's side, though. Grandfather and Everleigh tended to see things the same way, but his grandfather tried to bolster Daniel as well.

Even as their grandfather placated them both, Everleigh always knew his grandfather favoured him most. After all, he'd inherited his mother's crowning jewels, her eyes.

'What *was* the fight over?'

'A saddle.'

He and Daniel were saddling the horses when Everleigh noticed Daniel hadn't cinched his saddle firmly enough and as the older brother he'd mentioned it. Daniel had pulled the leather tighter, fury flourishing, and they'd both grown angrier. Louder. More emphatic.

They were fighting over a saddle that Daniel had corrected just as Everleigh had said, but then it became over who said what and how often Everleigh said it and how Daniel wasn't a child but how he acted like one and how Everleigh acted like a Roman Emperor and not one of the good ones.

Finally, he'd told Daniel to take the saddle and ride off to somewhere better if he could find it.

Everleigh was certain Rothwilde had seen Daniel in the interim, but Daniel had kept his distance from Everleigh.

'You haven't seen your brother because of a saddle.'

'I gave my father a letter to post for me. Daniel didn't answer.' He'd felt worse than when Daniel had punched him. That hadn't hurt. It didn't feel as deep as the crevasse he was digging for himself now. A nice, safe, deep crevasse with a lot of jagged, piercing sides.

'Perhaps you should try again.'

'Some rifts never mend.' He felt judged again. By her. Yes, he was the heir. The chosen one, if only by fate. But in return, he gave his life to others. As he should. As was expected and required.

'For me, there is no rift to mend,' he said.

'Tell me,' she said, 'what you're not telling me.'

She stared at him the same way Mrs Rush did when she didn't know he saw her watching him. Women—some of them—were strange creatures. Well, all he had ever met.

He gathered his thoughts, putting them into words for the first time.

'My grandfather was more a father to me. Ella Etta was more like a roguish grandmother or aunt your family would keep you away from as best they could. Mother was a painting on the wall to be admired. Daniel and Father were close and, for some unknown reason, Daniel and Mrs Trimble, the housekeeper, had a friendship. Probably because he didn't remember Mother as well as I did. Perhaps he didn't really understand she'd been Father's mistress…for a long time.'

He recalled his mother darting in and out of his life. 'I remember my mother kindly. But not lovingly. From what I hear, she was as driven as my grandfather. Mother married Rothwilde for the title just as much as he had married her for what finances he planned to get from Grandfather. His views were simple. Hers were better thought out. She planned to become a countess.

My father was the incidental part. He didn't like discovering that, although he had no choice but to live with it.'

Everleigh shook his head. 'She married Father for the title and found a mistress involved. Father married for funds and found a father-in-law holding tightly on to them and grasping at everything Father had ever had.'

He slid his legs over the side of the bed, and sat. The wall loomed dark in front of him. 'My grandfather. I could smile at him and ask if the dung he spouted would make the flowers grow better and he would pretend to strike out to hit the pest—me—buzzing in front of him, missing on purpose. I would always dodge.'

'Your mother produced two heirs. That should have made both men happy.'

'It upped the stakes. Grandfather hadn't expected that Rothwilde could control through keeping Daniel and me near him. Since they were so alike, Grandfather made sure that if anything happened to me or Daniel the funds could not possibly be diverted to Rothwilde. If I died, Daniel would have been in control. Without him, and without me, the funds were set to go to the church.'

His grandfather had had no affection for religion. He'd only wanted to be certain that his son-in-law never gained another pence of his fortune without the heirs.

'You must have hated the struggle between the two men.'

'I knew no other life. I was used to their outbursts at each other and their silent struggles for control.' He was the only chess piece in the game. Each player felt so much depended on him and that, on a whim, he could change course. He strode a careful line, keeping the two from each other's throats. When he wavered, he could see fury building and made peace.

'My family was the opposite.' The covers moved. He could tell by the sound of her voice that she lay back on the pillow.

'Not all families need to prop each other up for Sunday dinner. Some even try to knock each other over.' He remembered the hidden barbs, the surface sunshine and the feeling of putting out flames before they became an inferno.

She paused. 'And you considered a marriage not based on love?'

'It worked well enough.'

'Well, everyone kept their head, so to speak.'

'It wasn't all fights and flare-ups.'

'What enjoyment did you have?'

'The fields. Pretending to be a vagabond. Playing at being a proper gentleman when Grandfather took us to London. Grandfather wanted us placed exactly as we should be in society. He and Father both agreed on that. Only Daniel rebelled. He didn't like it. Said some of it was nonsense. Perhaps it was, but Grandfather knew how to roll the dice, which pair to pick up and how much to wager.'

He could see enough of her from the corner of his eye to know she studied him. She could only see his profile, he knew. He slowly turned his head, meeting her gaze, enjoying the fascination.

His thoughts lingered on her form, his mind taking a pleasant interlude to sketch the contours of her body. All of the curves dangerous…to both of them.

'I share things with you that I didn't ever feel necessary to speak of before. It's my life, simple enough.' He shrugged the words away.

'My life was simple,' she said.

'Yet you want to escape from it. To explore. To dance. To be frivolous. Much like my brother does.'

'If you put it that way, I suppose so. The world is harsh and I want it to be less so.'

She rolled from the bed and collected her chemise.

He waited, then, when she reached for the corset, he stood, moved to her and laced it loosely. 'Will you be able to get out of it by yourself?' he asked.

'I just twist it around when it's loose. Though it's not as easy as it used to be, thankfully.'

He helped her dress, enjoying the simplicity. The connection. Her femininity.

'I'll light a candle for you,' he said.

He caught himself slipping on his trousers and knew why he did. To prolong the moment.

Vivian felt the brush of his hand on her back as she stepped beyond him and into the hallway, leaving him to follow.

She reached to pull at the shoulder of her gown, when she saw shadows moving. Rothwilde halted at the end of the hall, studying her. He lifted a dim lamp.

'Vivian.' He gave a nod of his head. 'Do take care. The hallway can be treacherous in the dark.'

She reached up, wishing she'd done something with her hair before she'd left the room. The door opened wide behind her. She whirled around. Everleigh stood in the doorway, shirt off, moving towards her. The lamp his father held, and her candle, illuminated them.

She saw Everleigh's inner calculations, trying to outguess his father. His expression hardened. His eyes flashed and she could feel—actually *feel*—anger from his body.

Neither man moved or spoke, until Rothwilde gave a tight nod to his son, then walked away, leaving them in darkness.

She shivered.

'I really am ruined,' she said, after she was certain Rothwilde could not hear her.

'He'll not say a word. Not one word.' Everleigh clasped her elbow, irritation fading. 'You have nothing to concern yourself with on that account. It is as if he never saw you.'

'But he did see.' She stepped back. 'He knows.'

'It doesn't matter.'

'But it does to me.'

He took her arm. 'I'll see you to your room. I'm more familiar with this house than you are. I can navigate in the dark.'

She hesitated before moving.

He stopped. 'Vivian, I'm not an innocent. Neither is my father. Likely he was planning a visit to his mistress and was interrupted when he saw you.'

'I know you say that to make me feel better, but it doesn't help. Not at all.'

He took the candle and pulled her close. His cheek touched hers. 'I'm not going to live the same life as he did. He has had a mistress since before he married my mother. When she found out, he spirited his lover away in the night and he brought her back when my mother died. She didn't have to come far as he'd put her in a house on the estate.'

'Why didn't he just marry her in the first place?'

'An earl can't marry his housekeeper, particularly an earl strapped for finances. He had no choice but to marry my mother. It really was an arrangement that suited everyone, more or less. Do not concern yourself, Vivian. It's the past. It's over.' The words had too much emotion. It wasn't over for him.

She took a step back, feeling a confusion she couldn't understand.

'This is only one night, Vivian. One night. Nothing happened between us that a sunrise cannot erase.'

'A sunrise can erase everything that happened between us?' she repeated softly.

'Yes.'

'You will withdraw the proposal?'

'I will,' he answered. 'Today.'

Chapter Eighteen

The knock on her door brought Vivian upright in her bed.

Her mother walked in. 'Dear, you're going to be late for breakfast. I came to help you get dressed.' She walked to Vivian's bedside. 'But what I really wanted to know is whether you and Everleigh have discussed marriage again?'

'We have,' Vivian said.

'Then we might extend our stay a little longer. It'll make you appreciate the way I've furnished our house more. If someone died, there aren't any mirrors in this room to drape with black.' She assessed the dark furnishings. 'It does give the sense of a room dressed for mourning, when no one cared enough to return it to normal.'

'This house is just dreary because of the weather.'

'It's dreary because it's hard to make dark furniture add a splash of brightness to brown walls.' She looked at the room again. 'Would it be a crime to put a few gilt pieces around to reflect the light? Open the curtains wider? Add mirrors?'

'I think we should leave, today,' Vivian said. 'As soon as Everleigh talks with Father. Everleigh is going to withdraw the proposal.'

Her mother took in a slow breath. 'Is it what you want?'

'Yes.' She had to want it. She'd been in bed with him and melted into him, and he'd kissed her on top of her head and moved away.

He'd turned a special moment into something darker and more painful. He'd told her of the rift between his family and the inability to mend it. He'd told her of the distance he'd felt from his mother.

'I can see things better now. More clearly.' She flicked her eyes around the room. 'The house reflects the owners.'

'You'll have to wait until later in the day for Everleigh to speak with your father,' her mother said. 'Rothwilde has taken your father off on some wild goose chase. With the weather this dreary, and for them to be out exploring the countryside, it can only mean that they both want the same thing.' Her mother stared heavenwards. 'Since I don't think your father is finding a tavern, it is a case of matchmaking papas. They're likely staying away to give you and Everleigh a chance to see things their way.'

Her mother helped her dress and took extra care with Vivian's hair.

'There,' she said, finishing. 'Everleigh is waiting at the breakfast table. I suspect he doesn't usually take this long to eat. I told him I would get you.'

'Et tu, Brute?' Vivian said.

Her mother smiled, then chuckled. 'Not really. If I were matchmaking, you'd already be married. Make your own choice. Either way, I'm fine with it. But I think you should have breakfast with him, as he is rather determined to have a meal with you.'

'You said you're not matchmaking.'

'I'm not. You're old enough to know your own mind, if that is an age any of us ever obtains.'

Everleigh had finished his meal, but he stood in the breakfast room, staring at the sole plate remaining. Waiting.

He'd expected to feel as if he'd done the right thing when Vivian had left his room. Not like a cad.

He owed her an apology, but if he gave her one, she might misunderstand.

He didn't want to tell her goodbye. He didn't want to see her walk out of his life, yet he didn't want her to remain with one foot in and one foot out, and him the same. They could not stay together without the whole world knowing. She'd be ruined. Vivian could hardly handle stumbling over someone in the hallway.

He wondered if the servants would be disappointed that Vivian wasn't to become mistress of the house, but he knew that the housekeeper would not welcome his wife easily.

Mrs Trimble would smile and say all the right words, but in a way that showed she was pained. That was as far as she would dare to go.

He had let her stay once after an infraction, but he would not do so again.

One could not throw an earl out of his own house, but his father knew where the funds for the salaries came from. Rothwilde had made certain Mrs Trimble kept out of Everleigh's sight when Everleigh visited. Not that the estate was his favourite place to be.

But it was home. Not a home that he preferred, but the place he'd spent his childhood. The place his grandfather had visited him and where he and Daniel had rushed outside to listen to tales of bravery, and stories of cunning.

The unwelcoming façade never cheered him when he arrived, but still pulled him into it.

A skirt rustled and Vivian came into view.

'It appears our fathers are out, roaming over the estate and meeting tenants.'

'I'm not surprised. Father does that often. Although it doesn't seem to stop his...'

He paused, thinking of his father's gambling habit. His father had not asked for funds recently, nor had he been to the clubs.

'My grandfather used to give me all sorts of advice,' he said, as Vivian filled her plate from the sideboard. 'He said I should always keep my vision on what is behind me, beside me and in front of me. And not to be losing my direction.'

'Why would he tell you a ridiculous thing like that?'

'He would laugh afterwards. He wanted me to keep aware, but not to let what was going on be such a distraction that I lost my own direction. If he were here now, he would probably tell me I'm missing something.'

He took a sweet from the sideboard. Shortbread. He looked at the triangle shape and realised he had an answer to whether Cook was pleased to have the guests.

Taking two of the triangle-shaped biscuits, he sat across from her. He offered her the shortbread for later consumption, but she waved it away.

He could see he might have trouble keeping a secret about their togetherness as much as she would. 'Did you sleep well?'

She took a bit of bacon and nipped an end of it. 'Of course.'

He tasted the confection. 'I'll tell your father, when he returns, that I'm withdrawing the proposal. Rothwilde will be disappointed.'

'My father will probably be upset. He even wished for me to marry while I was ill. He seems to think he's failed if I don't marry.'

'You may some day. You still can, you know.'

She deliberated on the bacon, then raised her chin high. 'I have options in my future.'

He couldn't respond. He had a feeling something might break if he did and he wasn't sure if it would be the bacon or glassware.

Then she popped the last bite into her mouth and the tension in her lessened. She lifted her fork. 'It may take Father a while to absorb the news, but once he sees that both of us are in agreement he'll accept it.'

'He'll have no choice.'

Everleigh rose and moved around the table. Her fork was poised in mid-air. He made sure no one was aware and brushed a kiss on her cheek before leaving.

Chapter Nineteen

Vivian watched and listened to the dinner conversation. The two fathers spoke as brothers. Her mother was silent except for a quiet word of assent when needed.

Everleigh seemed as convivial as the others, yet she suspected they all were seeing only his façade. His ever-so-proper society motions. The ones his grandfather had taught him.

Just as his father got up to move them into the drawing room, her mother put a hand to her temple. 'I'm so very tired. I must beg off for the evening. Please forgive me.'

Everleigh rose as well.

'Before you leave,' he said. 'I wanted to discuss the proposal of marriage I made to Vivian earlier.'

The fathers' heads swivelled to him.

Vivian's mother pursed her lips.

Everleigh gave a nod to Vivian. Then he informed everyone, 'I withdraw my marriage proposal, as I don't feel Vivian and I would suit. We have discussed it.'

Her father jumped up, throwing down his napkin. 'Breach of promise.'

'Absolutely unthinkable.' Rothwilde spoke with precision. He clenched his napkin, his hand fisted. 'Breach of promise.'

'I can do it and I have.' Everleigh spoke softly, without hesitation.

'What do you have to say about this?' Lord Darius scrutinised Vivian. He gulped when he saw her expression. 'You are behind this.'

'Father, I—'

'It is my decision to withdraw the proposal,' Everleigh said.

'But you need to get married,' Rothwilde inserted. 'Even your grandfather would have agreed with me on this. Both your grandfathers and your mother.'

'I'm not ruling out marriage,' Everleigh said. 'Just to Vivian. I don't feel we would suit. We were both forced into the proposal by Alexandria.'

'I'm sure Alexandria would still have you.' Rothwilde said, turning to leave. 'Although, in that case, we'd be better off letting your brother find a wife and produce an heir.' He groaned. 'You're doing this to spite me.' He turned to Vivian. 'I assure you if I had disliked you, he would have wooed you so thoroughly that you wouldn't have questioned his proposal. You will never convince me after—'

Everleigh took one step towards his father and the man stopped speaking.

Then Rothwilde swallowed. He addressed Darius. 'My apologies. For this. For all of it. His grandfather is turning over in his grave. His mother, too. My wife understood negotiations and a profitable marriage.' He stomped out of the room, his cane crashing with his steps. 'But my son does not.'

'Are you behind this, Vivian? Because if you aren't, I'm going to slap him with a breach of promise when I get back to London.' Her father's voice trembled in rage.

Her mother touched her father's arm. 'Rupert.'

'I am.' Vivian stood firm. 'It's not breach of promise. It's my refusal.'

Her father informed her mother, 'You need to talk some sense into her.' He tossed his chin. 'I'm going to get a drink.'

'No, Rupert,' her mother called out, moving to her husband. 'You have been doing so well.'

He shrugged her away.

Everleigh walked around the table, blocking the exit. 'Lord Darius. Might you have a smoke with me?'

'No,' he said. 'I—I don't smoke. I drink.' He glared. 'A lot. There is a time to be born. A time to die. Everything in between is a time to imbibe.'

'Father,' Vivian said, splaying her hands, 'you can't do this. You can't undo the efforts you've made. And you can't put the blame for drinking on me.'

Rothwilde stepped back through the doorway, thumping his cane on the floor. 'Come with me, Darius,' he said. 'Everleigh will never listen to me. It sounds as though your daughter has made up her mind as well... It was too good to be true.'

Rothwilde gave a grunt towards Everleigh. 'He is just like his grandfather, except on this. Even his grandfather would have valued this marriage. Both his grandfathers. I didn't get on well with either of them.' He jerked his head in Everleigh's direction. 'He's wearisome. She's better off without him.'

Her father gave a quick snap to the hem of his jacket. 'Very well, Rothwilde. The one good thing out of this debacle is that my wife and I have had a chance to make your acquaintance.'

Rothwilde stepped into the hallway, speaking to someone hidden from the room. 'Tea. The blend with the rosehips and chamomile. Bring it to my sitting room. Darius and I will be playing cards.'

Darius grumbled at his wife, 'We'll try to do a better job in the future.'

Both the fathers left.

'Well…' Her mother gave a wavering smile. 'If he can survive this, then perhaps he will survive the birth of a child.'

'But, Mother, I'm not getting married.'

Her mother smiled. 'Not your child. Mavis is going to be a governess again. I was seventeen when I was married and you were already on the way. Then we just weren't blessed with any more children. Haven't you noticed how plump I've been getting? My illness in the morning? That's what's spurred your father's decision to take better care of himself. You're not going to be an only child any more.'

Vivian stared as her mother shrugged. 'I'm tired. I don't care what you do, Vivian. I have other things on my mind.'

Everleigh grasped Vivian's elbow and drew her to him. The world came into focus again.

'Worked out better than I expected, Vivian.' His gaze locked on hers. 'I understand your father much better now. He wanted you married as he realised that he would be having another child to guide.'

'I suppose.' She stumbled over the words, still shocked at her mother's news.

Everleigh bent towards her, the scent of his shaving soap surrounding her. 'You're getting the sibling you wanted.'

He touched her. 'It was pleasant, those few moments I thought we might marry. I needed a wife in order to have heirs. At first, I didn't like being asked to withdraw my proposal,' Everleigh said. 'I thought you would change your mind in the morning light. I took it as a censure of my heritage, and…all of me. I was used to having my own way. In everything. It's time I changed. I must in order to complete my duties better.'

He brushed her shoulder. 'You've shown me how selfish I was. You've made me a better man, Vivian.'

Then he strode out the door.

Her mother brushed a thumb over her forefinger, tending to a fingernail. 'Your father's funds won't stretch as well for two children as it did for one. Wouldn't it be interesting if, as recklessly as Everleigh considered a wife for heirs, that you might need a husband for a fortune?'

Everleigh left. Being a better man wasn't the route he would have preferred to take. Right now, he would have liked being the second son. He felt like one. Recklessly barging ahead. Not considering all the alternatives to his actions.

He should not have touched Vivian.

Why could she not have married him simply for… himself? Himself, and a fortune and a title? What more did she need? A tiara?

Well, he could understand that the title and the fortune might have been considered costly to her.

Then, that morning, he'd given her that kiss on the

cheek. He'd had to go back for one more touch. He always had to go back for one more touch of Vivian.

Blast it.

He went to get a cheroot. He needed to stop Vivian's body from controlling his thoughts.

He'd always crept out of the rear door when he was a child and saw no reason to add extra footsteps to his path now. He would see the stars twinkling overhead and imagine he could have them.

He stood just outside the door, studying the clear sky, remembering the nights he and Daniel had stayed out and watched the night sky slowly come alight with the stars. They'd even stolen cheroots from Rothwilde. He and Daniel had often tried to be first to view the earliest star. And then to spot the second, and the third.

Ella Etta had said he would have the sun and the stars, but she didn't say how long he would have them. So few words for what was Vivian. No one had warned him that they could evaporate in his hands.

The sun burned too bright to keep. The stars disappeared in the light of day.

He had the remnants of a heart buried deep inside him and the thought brought a bleakness.

In the night, Vivian stared at the ceiling. Everleigh's house felt like a tomb. Wood creaked. An owl hooted. The night roiled around her.

With the windows shut against the chill night air, even the moonlight seemed reluctant to breach the sombre house.

During the early part of the day, the underservants were like spirits, darting about to tend fireplaces or bring water when no one else stirred. They were perfectly trained in invisibility. She'd stumbled across one. The maid had been too intimidated to do more than nod, duck her head and dart away.

She knew the action was subservience, but in comparison to her own home, it felt more like disapproval.

She couldn't stay in her room and she couldn't see her parents.

The library had been restocked with those extra books. She wanted to get something to read.

Taking a lamp and leaving the room, she crept to select a volume.

In the library, she noticed the books were dishevelled, as if someone had searched through them in the night. Spaces indicated where books were taken. She stood, recalling the last visit, trying to remember the former details of the room. Yes, books were missing. She supposed her mother had borrowed some to read. Several were by the sofa.

She studied the walls and thought of her choices, but kept feeling the starkness that engulfed her when Everleigh had withdrawn the proposal. She hadn't imagined the words would stab into her so.

Vivian paused, understanding that she'd expected the conversation to occur when she wasn't in the room.

She gathered the books that had been taken from their location, reading the titles as she sorted them by height to return them to the shelf.

She and Rothwilde had books in common. When she was too ill to sit up, sometimes she had been able to escape the sickness by concentrating on a story.

Absently, she opened the volumes, leafing through pages. But her mind couldn't focus, even on the titles. Too much had happened.

Even the air in the room seemed different. Gone was the scent of tobacco—of Everleigh. Now it smelled of damp wood and embers.

She wouldn't stay long, changing her mind about the book. The room had changed, just as she had. Now she shivered from the coldness.

Rotating, she considered each wall of the room, taking enough time to truly examine the space.

An engraving of Doctors' Commons on one wall. A true likeness of a pair of colts, surrounded by smaller paintings of different horses. Sconces. She reached out to the last wall, testing the blades of the two crossed swords. Dull and with dust hidden in the filigree at the hilt. Ornamental.

A house decorated with no softness. Swords, horses, an engraving and necessary lighting.

She went to the window, touching a finger to the pane. A flickering light moved not far away. A cheroot. Her senses told her who it was. The deft movement wasn't Rothwilde.

She saw a man who'd lived his whole life in a man's world, a man's house, and with the responsibility of his family and his heritage squarely on his shoulders.

Everleigh was created by his circumstances, his motherly love sparse.

Vivian put the lamp on to the table and hurried to her room.

After donning her pelisse, she moved to the servants' stairs and darted down. With a few quick turns, she was at the back door of the house. She expected she'd have to get the butler or housekeeper to unlock the door, but when tested, the door opened.

The sharp sting of night air brought her senses fully

awake. The trees loomed over her, casting out the moon-light.

She stared across the courtyard to the shadowy shape, smelling tobacco, but seeing nothing.

He must have left.

Vivian walked carefully, then stopped.

She waited, listening.

A breeze brought the scent of tobacco across her and she found Everleigh, a cheroot in his hand, observing her. He appeared as another shadow by the walls of the house, illuminated only by an ember. He sat on a wooden bench, which had been pulled back against the outer wall, his hand absently flicking ash.

'You shouldn't be here.' His voice stirred her.

'I had to tell you goodbye.'

'Didn't we already make our goodbyes?' His words were almost lost in the air and a slow puff of smoke.

He wore a greatcoat, but no gloves or hat. She stepped closer.

The night had brought out the darkness of his face, but he put the cheroot to his lips. His beard shadowed his jaw and she couldn't see his expression. The dark-ness concealed too much.

'Do I pass inspection?' He inhaled, then flicked ash away again.

'Do you normally keep cheroots at hand?' she asked.

'Only at my father's house.'

Before she could answer, he continued. 'It's an ex-cuse to step outside. There are no soirées or dinners or theatre.' His lips turned up, rueful. 'Last night, I had you to hold. Tonight, I only have the memory of it.'

'I already miss you,' she confessed. 'The house is

so dreary. Even the library seems—well, unwelcoming. My room is pleasant, but again unwelcoming.'

'It's Rothwilde's house. I moved away as soon as I could. At my town house, Mrs Rush has a free hand except she is not to ask me any questions about furnishings. I will let her know if something displeases me. I've yet to do that.'

'What are the colours of the rooms?'

He shrugged. 'Mrs Rush takes care of that. I don't interfere. Do you remember the colours of the rooms in my house?'

He sounded as if he really wanted to know.

'I didn't notice. Not at all. I had other things on my mind.' She decided not to wait on an engraved invitation. She let out a breath, then found a place beside the dark man. 'But I'm sure they are cheerier than this house.'

He didn't say more while he smoked. He put the cheroot to his lips, then exhaled, and rested his arm on his knee, letting the ash fall to the ground.

She relaxed, the air freezing some of the tension from her body. Or maybe it was Everleigh's presence and silence. 'I said I miss you and you didn't respond to that.'

'You shouldn't be here,' he said. 'For us to be together tonight is pushing fate. Pushing fate to remind us how lovemaking feels.'

Their shoulders touched, two coats brushing, but the connection warmed her. 'I know.'

One of his boots was tilted at the heel and he rocked his foot. He beheld the puff of smoke that wafted into the air. 'The longer I sat here, the more I've thought about it. I'm not a better man.'

'You didn't think I could say no. To marriage. After the shooting episode.'

'I thought I'd compromised you.' He laughed wryly. 'Blast it. We were alone in a carriage in front of a whole congregation and no one noticed.'

'Mavis's hat is apparently well known. Before, when I courted, everyone knew how well I was chaperoned. No one realised that had changed. And everyone was distracted. Neither of my parents noticed Mavis wasn't with us until we arrived home.'

She'd not really wanted to say no either and yet, conversely, she had desperately wanted to say no to the proposal. It was true she wanted to dance, but even more than that, she wanted a marriage in which the wife called her husband by his first name when in private.

She didn't even know Everleigh's given name. 'You don't love me.'

'I've been in love before. Love fades. It's what's kept me from marriage. It's a passion that tries to pull you into a whirlwind of the other person, then you wake up and examine the world freshly and discover you might not even like them.'

'When you woke up this morning, did you like me?'

'I was angry that I had to withdraw the proposal. That doesn't mean that I don't like you. I do.' His words wisped into the air, mixing with the smoke, then fading. 'You would have been the only person I would have wanted to tell, if you'd not been the one involved. I would have said something along the lines of… Vivian and I won't be married. But we were almost betrothed, and now we're not. And we nearly made love and it felt right, but now that we aren't going to marry, it doesn't.'

Vivian discerned the night air around her, avoiding the most sombre shape of all—Everleigh.

She did not want to live in the starkness that infused the estate. She'd made a good decision, even if it hurt.

'When you suggested marriage...' She tried to move so that their shoulders didn't touch, but it seemed impossible to pull away. 'To bring me into your world... It's too bleak. You and your father cannot even share books.'

'I suppose he moves the books around to remind me that it is his house.'

'With all due respect, it is not a comfortable home. There is not one evidence I saw of happiness.'

He shook his head.

'What about when your mother was alive?'

He thought about it. 'I suppose it had more of her things about and the housekeeper has moved them away over the years because Mother was the competition for my father's favours.'

'You didn't want mementoes of her about?'

'The painting. That meant a lot to me. It truly did. And, then... Never mind. But, no, I don't care about fripperies. What man really does?'

'A wife? Another frippery for the house?'

'If that's how you see it.' He paused, thinking. 'But you would be a mighty soft frippery. Pleasurable, you could say.'

'Everleigh, my former beau, the fortune hunter— whom I never wish to see again and would like to avoid in any afterlife that might be—said pleasant things to me. While he could not talk openly in front of the chaperon, he wrote notes telling me how ravishing he found me. That I was the fascination of his day and that, without me, everything was dust by comparison. That kind of drivel.'

Everleigh stared into the darkness. 'You didn't marry him either.'

'Only because he was interested in my dowry. I was sick, scared, and then I was angry when I found out he was taking advantage of the situation.'

'Are you still angry?'

She considered his words. Yes, she was. Angry and happy. Happy to be alive. Happy to have her chance to dance and move about in the world. But angry that she had been slipping away and now she could see how the world had been prepared to go on without her.

Now everyone expected her to glide right back into the world that had mostly brushed her aside.

Everleigh had even noticed her as a potential wife.

He had not even considered a courtship necessary.

She shivered.

'You need to go inside where it's warm.' He extinguished the cheroot on a paving stone, stood and stretched.

'I've been to your library. It's not much different from out here.'

He scrutinised the gardens, the sky, anywhere but her, yet awareness jumped between them.

He reached for her hand and pulled her to her feet. 'Let's go inside.'

Instantly, the heat of his skin surrounded her.

Taking both her hands, he trapped them between his own. 'If you're there, it will be much warmer than the outside air.'

Then he stepped closer and pulled her hands up the

front of his waistcoat. Heated breath tickled her ears. 'Put your arms around my neck.'

His hands went to her waist, clasping, and she'd never, ever swooned, but she felt her body weaken. She could feel his grasp even through the cloak and she was pleased she didn't have to speak.

His stubble-roughened chin brushed against her cheek briefly. Tendrils of his hair, feeling cool, touched her and sent warm shivers into her body. The man smelled of smoke, yet he made her skin come alive, her muscles tense and knees weaken.

'You're silk softness.' His voice was whispery gruff. 'Silken kisses and silken skin. You make me forget about tomorrow. All I can see is the silken promise of your lips.' His breath feathered the air and he pulled her against him.

Every bit of her exploded with delicious sensations. Flashes of power invaded her, but they instantly evolved into something else, something which controlled her.

She didn't know she could feel another's spirit inside her own body.

With his mouth, on her lips alone, he took control of her. With no more than a kiss, he blended into her, swirling desires, pulling her closer.

She could hear him say her name, which was impossible, because his mouth was against hers and he could not be speaking. But he was. It was the softest thing she'd ever heard. She kept spinning and spinning and spinning into deeper desire.

She didn't even know when he stopped kissing her, but her thoughts returned and she was looking at him, his face above hers, and he watched her.

With the same care of moving fine porcelain from the edge of a table, he embraced her.

'Vivian,' he said and her body reacted to the emotions in the word. She could hear the tension, the desire and the longing he'd put into speaking her name. He would tell her he loved her.

He reached out, and brushed back a lock of hair from her cheek. 'I think—' He interrupted himself. 'I do care about you.'

She thought he wanted to tell her he loved her, but he couldn't get the words past his lips.

'You know—' He gave up.

'Yes. I do.' But she didn't blame him for not being able to love, she cherished that he cared for her and that he had told her the truth.

'We should go inside where it's warmer. Together.'

He could have led her straight to the end of the earth, but instead he guided her forward with a gentle hand at her back.

Vivian walked inside the house with Everleigh and she hesitated. He clasped her gently. 'We can part when you get to the top of the stairs.'

'It's too early.' Even if it were approaching daybreak, it would be too early.

She moved quickly up the stairs, keeping ahead of Everleigh's long legs, but he kept up with her effortlessly.

When she stepped on to the landing, she gasped in air. She hurried into the library.

His words were soft and they had the merest hint of humour behind them. 'You run beautifully even if I cannot see well through the darkness.'

His mouth didn't relax, but she glimpsed the softest shade of the sky she'd ever seen.

If she hadn't been ill before, she would have accepted a proposal and continued on, blissfully happy that her life was following along the path that she'd hoped for.

In fact, she would have probably fallen in love with the next man who'd shown her marked attention and she would have been more concerned about her hair being perfect on her wedding day and the furnishings she might wish to select for the house.

Now she perceived potential suitors differently.

It wasn't about how perfect her embroidery stitches were or whether the pattern on the plates was the one she'd preferred. To marry, she wanted someone who was devoted to her. Someone who wanted to be with her more than anyone else in the world, ever.

Everleigh watched her. He was the only man who had truly intrigued her.

'I might fall in love with you,' she said.

'Would that be so terrible?'

'It might. If I woke up and discovered that I needed more.'

She waited, questioning him with her silence and her gaze.

'It never lasts long. You wouldn't have to worry about it.'

She gasped. 'Do you think you are capable of a lasting affection?'

'I don't know.'

'Had you considered marriage before Alexandria stopped our carriage?'

'I've never proposed to anyone but you. I knew I could easily recover from the scandal of Alexandria creating a spectacle. I had considered proposing to her, but I suspected she might have that side of her we saw. I wanted no part of that in a wife.'

'I fit your criteria.'

Brushing fingertips across the back of her hand, he let his touch linger before moving away. 'My criteria included an acceptance of a proposal. So, I would have to say you have failed in that regard.'

She felt the need to apologise and angered at the same time. *Failed.* She didn't like that word. 'You would marry me without love?'

'I suppose I would have to.'

Vivian's heart fell.

'When you're leaving, I will make certain your father knows that it is a lost cause for him to expect me to marry you, if you'd like.' He took her hand. 'After I do that, it is unlikely our paths will cross many times. They didn't often in the past. Your father will be pushing you to marry. He'll ensure that suitable men will be at the soirées. He'll give you a chance to dance. It just won't be with me.'

He could remember the feel of her skin against his. The strands of her hair brushing across his lips. Her scent. An innocent's scent.

He shoved those thoughts aside, remembering he could not touch her.

To continue making love to her and to watch her walk away would be too much of a loss.

The innocent who had first asked him for the kiss might have remained a spinster, but the temptress who came to his room and who refused to marry him would not. She would not only dance to the tune she wanted, but would find someone to follow along willingly.

He bade her goodnight and left the room.

Vivian reminded him of a baby wren, always safely in the nest at first. But now she was a fledgling, moving into the world on her own.

He'd seen fledgling birds, though. They cheeped so the mother bird could continue to find them and give them morsels to help them along as they learned to manage on their own.

The only problem was that the predators listened. Hawks swooped down upon them.

He didn't want Vivian to be anyone's prey.

He didn't want anyone else to teach her what he could show her.

But she didn't want to marry him and he didn't want to watch her navigate into a world where raptors resided, stomachs empty, talons bared and prey a momentary meal.

Blast it. He circled, not stopping, and returned to the room Vivian was in.

'I miss you,' he said. 'Already.'

She ran to him and threw herself into his arms. 'Make love to me.'

Chapter Twenty

He took her to his room, shrugging the coat from his shoulders and placing the garment across the back of a chair, next to the lit lamp he'd brought from the library. He wanted to see her.

With one long stride he was again by her side.

Guilt clouded his mind. He could not make love to her. The repercussions for her could be tremendous.

But he couldn't tell her to leave either. He could pleasure her as he had before. As long as he did not let himself go past the moment when it would be too late to turn back.

Then he undid the closures of the pelisse and helped her from the sleeves. He took the coat and threw it over his own.

She stared up at him and he remembered that she wanted sweet words. He could give them to her. She put them inside him.

He held her gaze. 'When I see you, I know your skin is like nectar against my lips. Something created for pleasure.'

Her body, with the smallest turn, inspired his imagination to see all her feminine twists and curves.

She didn't even seem to come from the same world he did—she came from a place of frilly frocks and gentleness and sunshine even on the coldest of days.

He rested his hands on her hips, savouring the moment of being in her presence.

She touched his waistcoat and undid each button. Taking the fabric, she slid it over his shoulders. Stepping back, she moved to put the clothing neatly, but he captured her again, and gave the smallest shake of his head. The waistcoat fell to the floor.

'There's too little time to think of our clothing,' he said. 'We're together. That's all that matters.'

Before she could respond, he held her hands, pulling her into a clasp that lasted only seconds before she tugged away, raising her hands to his white shirt collar.

'I agree,' she whispered.

Without hesitation, she slipped away the knot of his cravat, unwound it, and let it fall to the side.

She undid the fastenings of the shirt. He gave a slight nod, lifted the fabric from his waistband and pulled upwards. He helped her move the shirt away and her vision remained locked on the chest in front of her revealing a trim expanse of maleness.

He clasped both her wrists and put them to his cheeks, letting her feel the roughening beard, then moved her hands to the softer skin of his neck, the light hair of his chest and the pebbled nipples.

Her fingers hadn't recovered from the touch of his chest. She wasn't sure she could manage another set of buttons, when he stepped back.

His voice roughened. 'Boots first, I suppose.' He moved away.

He sat in the chair, his observation never leaving her, and removed his boots. Then he stood, and in his stockinged feet he seemed even larger. She leaned closer, reaching out to thread her fingers through his hair. He was a muse to lovemaking; his thoughts seemed to guide her.

She touched the fall of his trousers, letting the buttons rest in her hands. 'I'm not as shy as I thought,' she said.

His lips quirked up briefly into a true smile and she basked in it, wishing his smiles were not so rare.

'I'm pleased.'

He reached behind her, so close she could feel him speaking against her skin, while he freed the hooks of her dress.

Her hands fell from his trousers while the dress slid down her body and moved between them, revealing her chemise, before falling to the floor.

'No corset?' he asked, not waiting for an answer, but instead dropping a kiss on her shoulder.

Their consciousness blended. She saw the knowledge in him that she wore nothing underneath the chemise and the awareness she imagined in his mind flared heated cravings in her own body.

He found the hollow of her neck and nuzzled against her, the moisture of his lips doing nothing to reduce the flames of passion his hands stoked as he caressed her back, pressing her so that the only way they could become closer was with movement, twisting and turning, so that their bodies could soak up the sensation of more touches and more of each other.

Her hand slipped down his side, leaving his skin and returning to the cloth of his trousers—now an unwanted barrier. Her fingertips tangled in his waistband and she discovered fine hairs on the heated skin of his stomach.

Taking one of her hands, he put it on his top trouser button and she undid the fall, finding the man beneath.

After a moment he stepped back, sliding his clothes away, and stood before her, no more self-conscious than if he were fully dressed.

He touched her chemise and did little more than give a twist of his wrist and a flick, and she blinked as the cloth moved over her head.

She took his hand, and pulled him closer to the bed. Then, they fell back on to the mattress.

When his head swooped down and his lips took hers it took too much strength to keep her eyes open. Her fingertips absorbed the feel of his skin, taking it in, and the whole of her body did the same.

His mouth swirled over her. Her lips, her neck, her shoulders and her breasts. He moved along her body, taking the taste of her skin, and, as if he could not merely experience her with his mouth, he had to taste her with his whole body. And his hands.

She knew he was intensely aroused. She could tell by his urgency, by the pressure of his hardness against her and the heated air around them.

She grasped him, as if he could keep her from going over a cliff, and she pushed against him, ready for the edge, the tumble and the pillow his arms made for her.

The only thing keeping her from fluttering from her body was his clasp. Stronger than she realised. His lips came back to graze at her neck, her shoulders.

Liquid desire overtook her and made her restless for his touch.

She didn't pull him closer—it wasn't possible. He breathed into her skin.

Even when she arched against him, he kept her hip pressed into his arousal.

'Ev...' she whispered, but his lips stopped her.

Her body—every part of it—felt alive, lush, absorbing his touch. Time altered. Worlds changed. She could have parted clouds and pulled the moon to a higher part of the sky.

While she didn't say his name fully even once, he said hers. He whispered it in her ear, prayer-like, and said it against her skin and against her hair, and her body responded to his call.

He explored her with the reverence of touching a miracle, his fingertips grazing the softness of her stomach, the gentle slope of her hips and the femininity hidden within her.

Then he gave her a pulsating completion which could have shattered the sun.

While she learned to breathe again, he held her close from above. She saw him, but it wasn't the same man she'd seen before.

'I need to go,' he said, his lips blending with hers. 'You're an innocent. After you've had time to consider if this is really what you want, then I will meet you.'

'I thought about the things you mentioned before I entered the room,' she said. 'No one else I have ever met or seen comes close to making me feel the way I feel about you. No matter what else happens, I've gone too far to walk away as innocent as I was and I've gone too far to walk away without knowing that you're the man I want to share my first time with.'

He waited, torn. 'But if you were to change your mind in the morning…?'

'I'd rather risk regrets, which I don't intend to have, than risk wishing for what I have missed. I want to always have this memory. Of you. Of making love.'

She was silent, waiting for another kiss, tracing his lips with her fingertips, running a hand over his chest, exploring the form she would never forget.

'If you do have regrets in the morning, I will feel them for you. You mustn't. You mustn't regret this. We may never have another opportunity to share so much of ourselves with each other. I want you happy,' he said.

'The only way I can have that,' she answered, 'is if you make love to me.'

He held her chin and tenderly silenced her with his lips. Holding her at his side, he let them explore each other, the distance between them lessening with each kiss and caress.

With the tip of his manhood against her, he positioned himself, rose over her and pulled her bottom towards him, controlling her movements and his descent, watching her, searching for her pleasure while he entered her.

Their bodies intertwined and he was affected more deeply than he'd ever been before. He had no control except for wanting to give her something she would cherish and he'd find his pleasure in that.

His skin reacted as if it touched lightning and she was the life force that kept him breathing and alive.

He concentrated his attention, turning inside, reaching some unknown place. He breathed primitive gasps as he released inside her.

They rocked together and she felt his shudder. She clasped his back and knew, *knew* the oneness that enveloped them as her release followed his.

When she regained the use of her body, she could still feel him inside her, above her, pressed close, a sheen of exertion on his shoulders and sounding as if his breaths used all his strength.

Then he moved and pulled her to his side, resting his face against her. They lay side by side, embracing while catching their breath.

The moment soothed her, but then he moved, just enough to jostle her back into reality.

This had been a pleasing interlude away from their lives, one she'd never forget or regret. But it had to end. And it must end soon, before someone discovered them.

When she'd rolled away she slid from the bed, but he clamped an arm about her waist.

'A little longer,' he said. 'We have more time together.'

'I know…' She hesitated, then slipped out of his grasp, continuing to move away, surprised that he could lounge so completely unclothed.

She pulled her chemise in front of her, covering herself, and knowing a humorous glint lit his expression.

She saw the mirror and touched the countenance that stared back at her. That person had changed so much in such a short period of time.

Then she observed her hair. Strands poked out in ways she'd never seen before. Half the pins were missing. She noted how long it took her to dress in the morning compared to the seconds it took him to turn her into total disarray.

His reflection showed in the mirror and she became self-conscious.

'Turn away. I need to dress.'

He grabbed a pillow and held it over his face. 'Satisfied?'

'Thank you,' she mumbled, donning the chemise and taking a few moments for composure.

'It doesn't matter, I can still imagine you.' His tone was muffled, soft and endearing.

She sat on the bed and picked up a hairpin she'd felt under her foot, absently tucking it in place.

The bed shifted and she knew he'd moved. His hand clasped her side, palm stationary and fingers moving. 'Vivian. Stay in bed a while longer. A few kisses, sweet words and caresses wouldn't be remiss.'

'I want time to think of this—to cherish it...' She paused. 'It's just so private. Last time I stumbled over your father. The servants may be awake soon. People will be waking...'

'I assure you if they work it out, it will make no difference. It can't be undone.'

'Oh, my.' She didn't want anyone to know and yet she almost yearned for their union to be written in the sky.

She bent forward, her hand touching his cheek, her contemplation riveted on him. She couldn't get enough of their closeness and feared it. Feared it might lodge in her consciousness and she would yearn for it all the hours of the day.

She brushed her hand across his unshaven jaw, another connection she could share, if only for a heartbeat.

'Those are sharp,' she said, dropping her hand away.

'I didn't imagine them so…razor-like. So different.' She reached out, brushing back the hair above his ear. 'Soft here and still like little daggers on your cheek.'

Her touch stopped him. Trapped him.

'Such opposing textures. So near each other.' She spoke quietly, more to herself than him.

Her fingers left his skin and she felt an ache in her heart.

'Vivian. I have a feeling you have some things you wonder about?'

'Is it only in bed that a man and woman can talk freely to each other? And then, only with their bodies?' she asked. 'Why do you feel at ease talking with me? Does that mean anything to you?'

He gave a grim smile. 'Our first meeting. Mavis injured. You dying. I was at a loss.'

When he blinked his regard rested on her in a way that almost made her believe he couldn't see her, but the past. 'You were so thin. So pale. I felt I could tell you anything. You were almost a spirit, not a person. Fragile. I knew I could trust you.'

He nodded and spoke without inflection. 'I talked to you and had no trouble with it. You did not appear to have the strength to spread tales. I felt concerned for you, yet I liked the feel of speaking to you. You listened with your whole body while we were in my town house. But I wish we were there now, instead of here. I hate this house, but yet it is my ancestral home.'

'It's melancholy.'

'It's never been the same since my mother died, although she wasn't particularly happy here. She preferred London. But her portrait has always been here.'

He regarded her. 'You noticed her portrait and I told

you the eyes had been repainted. Several days after Mother had died, Father and I were away seeing that her things were sorted through in the town house. While we were gone, Father's jealous sweetheart scratched over the eyes in Mother's picture with black. I was furious. I was for sending Mrs Trimble packing, but my father threw himself in front of me and said I would have to go through him. We didn't speak for months, but he hired an artist to fix the painting. The artist used my eyes as an example to copy.'

'I'm surprised your father would allow someone to stay who would do such a thing.'

He put a finger against his stubble, in the same place she had touched. 'I was as well. But the talebearers then told me that Father has always had an affection for her, yet there have never been any tales of her having his child.'

Realisation flashed in Vivian's mind.

'You didn't—you didn't try to make sure I could not have a child from this encounter?' Vivian heard her voice and knew she wouldn't have recognised it if she hadn't felt her own lips move.

'No.'

'Why?'

He didn't speak at first, holding her waist.

'I didn't think of it.'

'You would force me into marriage?'

He shook his head. 'No. But I would not want any child to be born without my name.' He clasped her hand, intertwining their fingers. 'For those moments…all I could think of was you. And now all I can think of is how I have to say goodbye.'

'I would think we could still visit…on occasion.'

'It will be too risky for us to see each other in London, though I would relish it. So many, many things could go wrong. You would never be able to travel back and forth easily from my town house without being seen. The regret I have with touching you, and having to let you go, is nothing to the pain I would feel if I damaged your reputation…your future.'

'I understand. I didn't expect anyone to see us before and a whole congregation did. Then, last time, your father surprised us in the hallway.'

The slight movement of his lips, up, then firm, indicated an eruption of thoughts.

'Will you remember me?' she asked.

'I don't even want to think about how much I will dwell on you.'

'If you don't wake up and dislike me.'

'We could marry and find out,' he said. 'We could do this every night.'

She heard the breath through his nostrils.

If he didn't open his eyes one morning and consider her just another addition to the estate. The woman needed for heirs. She pulled her hand from his.

'Think about the passion we could share.'

She couldn't help thinking about it. She thought about *it* every time she breathed. When she didn't think about him, then her body reminded her in subtle ways, flashing a memory of Everleigh's skin against hers or his breath on her cheek or the feel of his hair brushing her body.

His voice softened. 'You're very soothing, Vivian. I'm amazed at how differently I feel when I'm with you.'

'You want an heir. To please your grandfathers. Even though they are dead.'

He opened his mouth and a second passed before he spoke. 'Yes.' His words, controlled, slightly louder than his last ones. 'Of course. It is not abnormal to want to continue a legacy that has been gifted to me.'

Every muscle in his face tightened. His words became soft, but underlying strength rested within them. 'I cannot banish you from my head. Every interval of the day memories of you are stroking me, heightening my need for you. Work rid me of such recollections in the past. But it won't this time. Something inside you trapped me, Vivian.'

She didn't move. *Trapped?*

He smiled. Part of his face did anyway. Not all of it. He pulled back the length of an eyelash.

He let his hand trail down, one finger following just above the scoop of her neckline, tracing the last bit of exposed skin.

Everleigh kept her locked in place with his intensity. 'I won't forget you,' he said. 'I'll be gone before you wake in the morning. You can think of me as a dream you had.'

He got out of bed and pulled on his trousers.

His voice, sombre, whispered, 'Stay as long as you wish. I need to wake the coachman and let him know I'll be leaving at first light, or before if possible.'

'You don't have to leave,' she said.

'I do. This is the cleanest break. The softest one. If we stay near each other, your reputation will become what I fear you truly want. Unmarriageable. I don't want to be the one to do that to you. I cannot.'

'You don't feel we've already done that, in a sense?'

'You're blossoming with life now. You're vibrant. When you do decide to marry—and I believe you will eventually—you will sweep into a room and there will be a man at your elbow, or many, and they will understand that you have passed the years of naivety and believe that the man who took your innocence and didn't marry you was a cad.'

'I will tell the truth.'

'No,' he said. 'Don't. No one needs to know. Let this be our private moment. Our secret for the rest of our lives.'

Then he left, striding out of the room, shutting the door softly behind him. The light seemed to fade.

She picked up his cravat and balled it in her hand, but instead of throwing it at the wall she swept it to her cheek.

Chapter Twenty-One

Everleigh was not at breakfast. Rothwilde gave them his son's apologies, irritation hidden in his words. He explained Everleigh often had financial concerns that he had to attend to, and he seldom stayed at the estate long.

Everyone stole a glimpse at her and continued on as if nothing had been said.

Her father and Rothwilde spent a bit of time commiserating about the weather and, somehow, Vivian felt they weren't really talking about the clouds, but about their children.

By the time breakfast was over, her mother had suggested returning to London and her father agreed.

The carriage ride proceeded with almost no conversation, each occupant lost in their own world.

A day after Vivian arrived home everything returned to normal—and she wasn't sure she liked it. She no longer felt like dancing as she'd expected and her father feared her recovery had ended.

Her mother shook her head and said such things were expected for a woman navigating a life course away from marriage. That Vivian was merely finding her foothold in the world after being ill so long.

The older woman sat in her favourite chair for sewing—the one with a touch of rose colouring in the fabric which she thought went well with her favourite day dresses. Her mother put away her spectacles, pushed her needle into the linen and tapped the frame. A maid whisked it away.

'It will be nice to have a child around again. I'd planned on it being a grandchild. But I am too young to be a grandmother.'

Vivian sat in the nearest straight-backed chair. 'I suppose I'll have lots of time to get to know the little one.'

Even with the family increasing, loneliness surrounded Vivian.

'I shouldn't have insisted Everleigh withdraw the proposal. But I don't want to marry someone who thinks they might wake up one morning and dislike me.'

'Dear.' Her mother raised her brows. 'No one should. And no one could wake up one morning and dislike you. You shouldn't have needed a courtship longer than an introduction. But if your instincts tell you not to marry, then you mustn't. You'd have too many second thoughts, and they'd strangle you. Or, at least, they'd kill your marriage.'

Her mother wrinkled her nose. 'I do like the young man.' She blinked and shook her head. 'Can you imagine what it was like for me to hear a gunshot while I was in church, walk out and see the sight, and then realise you were in the carriage? Very dramatic.' She smiled. 'Your father was much like Everleigh in his younger days. Then he lost himself.'

'But now he's working to regain the man he used to be. He understands the trials he's given you.'

'Oh, of course he does.' Her mother's lips turned up. 'We both love each other tremendously. That doesn't mean we particularly want to disrupt each other's day. Don't expect much out of marriage, dear. You can't have everything and love is rather overrated. I would say it's better to have good servants—they make your life flow so smoothly. And I do have good servants.' She tilted her head towards the maid who stood at her side. 'The best,' she said.

Her mother turned to Vivian. 'Do you think Everleigh loves you?' she asked.

Vivian paused. 'No.'

'How do you know this?'

'He doesn't. He doesn't believe it lasts. He thinks it's always temporary.'

'Daughter.' Her mother stood, then walked over and cupped Vivian's cheeks. 'He should love you. Any man worth a pence should love you. Leaving him on his own is the best way to get him to realise he cares for you. But I'd say if he's not here in a week, you'd best consider it over.'

She sighed. 'If he can't figure himself out in a few days, then don't expect a lifetime to be enough time. You need to get on with that life you were so anxious to step into. There are invitations to accept. Do so.'

Everleigh walked into his town house and handed his hat to the butler before speaking. He glanced at the fresh beeswax candles. 'Mrs Rush has been working.'

'She's had us all decorating about.' The butler glanced around, making sure no one else was listening.

'She wanted the house festive. She sensed… Well, you know she's friends with Mrs Mavis and they spent the whole time you were gone speculating about whether you would… I mean, Mavis came over to help Mrs Rush tidy up and they did speak about the possibility of a bride.'

'No bride.'

'But we had heard of your private betrothal from Mavis and we wished to celebrate.'

Everleigh noted the butler's new cravat, a bright blue that contrasted with his usual black livery.

Nervously, the butler touched it. 'I allowed it, as it made Mrs Rush so happy, and she advocates this colour as appropriate for your house.'

'I will tell Mrs Rush how much I appreciate the effort, but there is to be no announcement.' Somehow, his words wouldn't stop. 'As I have been refused.'

Waincott took a stumble back, sucked in a deep breath and spoke quickly. 'Mrs Rush will not take that well.'

Everleigh's expression tightened.

Waincott straightened and his arm dropped to his side. 'You see, sir, she thinks… She thinks no one would dare refuse your proposal.'

'I like the concept, but it is flawed.'

'I will inform her.' He briefly bowed his head. 'I fear this will end the friendship between her and Mrs Mavis.'

'There is no need for that,' Everleigh said. 'It is a private matter between myself and Miss Darius.'

The butler nodded, observing Everleigh. 'I understand. But I fear Mrs Rush will not. She had new recipes planned for a wedding breakfast that she had gathered together with Mrs Mavis. It was to be grand, but they just did not know which house to have it at.'

'We can still eat,' Everleigh grumbled, moving up the stairs.

He walked into the main drawing room.

Mrs Rush had overstepped her boundaries. Ribbons were tied on the candleholders. The lamps sat on a new indigo scarf. A matching fabric decorated the fireplace mantel and tassels hung from it.

He stepped closer, taking the scarf in his hand. Silk. But not as soft as Vivian's skin.

'No.' He heard Mrs Rush's voice in the distance. A gasp. She'd been informed.

Hushed mumbles.

He could hardly reprimand her for the decoration, as she sounded to be having a tirade on his behalf.

Striding to the door, he called down the stairway. He couldn't see them, but knew the staff could hear him.

'It is a matter between myself and Miss Darius. It should not affect anyone else in this household.'

Mrs Rush's face scowled around the banister at him. 'It's all that Mavis's doing, getting us all excited about a wedding when there wasn't to be one. I will not forgive her. I learned so many new dishes to cook and had planned such a celebration.'

'We will still have a celebration. It's…for my father. I'm planning to invite him to dinner.'

'Is he marrying again?' Mrs Rush asked.

'I don't think so. You can ask him.'

He put his fingertips to his temples. It would be joyous—he would bribe his father to visit and thank Mrs Rush, and they would watch their temper and he would give his father the gift of a large sum to gamble with. And he would invite his father to bring Mrs Trimble along as well.

An olive branch as big as all England—even though he hated the housekeeper still for defacing his mother's portrait. His father would be unable to refuse.

Even without the bribe, his father would know better than to decline. Everleigh rarely asked for anything from his father and Rothwilde knew that the funds could vanish.

It would be a solemn event, little different from the ones they'd had since Daniel had left. He considered his brother. Daniel had brought a lot of laughter into their home. Everleigh had always considered his brother too frivolous, but perhaps enjoyment was as equally important as solemnity.

He reflected on seeing Vivian walk into his house and noticing the colours. It would have pleased her. The knowledge that she wouldn't be there crashed his thoughts to the ground.

He remembered the comments Darius had made about breach of promise.

That irked him. Darius irked him almost as much as Rothwilde irritated him.

Vivian's mother annoyed him for some reason that he couldn't quite understand…and then he realised why.

She'd encouraged her daughter to think for herself and let her make her own decisions. An example of bad mothering, in his opinion.

She should have put her daughter's interests first, instead of letting Vivian make up her own mind. But perhaps her mother was a bit under Vivian's spell as well.

When Vivian was near, he never wanted her to leave. He relaxed and she soothed his concerns, and the spirit

of her took over and the world faded. Finances didn't
matter and nothing else did. She was a balm that erased
all cares and worries. Made everything else insignifi-
cant, but he had to take care, that could be a dangerous crevasse. Too deep to ignore and treacherous to the
people who depended on him.

He'd seen beauties. But Vivian's beauty came from
within and then reached out, arresting him. It pulled all
of a man. He could not get trapped in her.

When she'd first asked him to kiss her, he'd been
entranced. He'd never, ever seen such innocence. He
didn't even think children were born with such. He'd
not even suspected it existed.

She shouldn't have requested a kiss. His whole body
had responded to just the one word from her lips. Kiss.
He'd never been given a gift such as that.

And he'd been hard for days.

Then, he'd thought of trying for an invitation to Vivian's house from Lord Darius. Everleigh had used all
his strength and told himself not to be foolish. He could
never have her. It would not be right to court her when
she was ill. It would put her at a disadvantage. And,
perhaps, hurt her health.

Because as much as she intrigued him, and as much
as he suspected he would desire her if he stayed in the
same room with her more than a few minutes, he truly
didn't have the kind of feelings she wanted.

He liked Vivian. He liked her tremendously. But
love—love was nonsense with the same kind of frills
Mrs Rush had used in the room.

Utter rot.

A humbug.

A lie from a person's insides that faded away quickly and life became routine again.

He couldn't understand why Vivian would want such nonsense.

That just proved she was correct and that they were not suited.

Taking the stairs to his room, he hoped he would find no more decorations.

Everleigh paused at the top, his hand still on the banister. Then he gave a push and moved into the silence of his sitting room. He had his wish. Nothing brightened the room.

He could feel his heartbeat sounding in his own ears.

This was the life he'd have for the rest of his days.

A life without Vivian, a woman who truly belonged in the world she inhabited.

He would make sure not to travel about when he might see her. He would make sure to keep his world closed and confined to business where she would not venture.

He imagined her hair lying on a pillow next to his. The glossy strands running through his fingertips, each strand brushing his skin and caressing his body.

He checked the furnishings in his bedroom. Nothing had changed. Exactly as it had been all the years he'd lived there. Except for the new pillows on his bed.

There were not enough swear words in the world...

He sat in the library, head bowed, holding the side of the empty brandy glass to his forehead, letting the coolness ease the warmth of his body. The night had moved with the speed of ice melting on a frigid midwinter day. Trying to keep himself from getting hard if the

house creaked because it reminded him of the first secret meeting when she'd walked the hallway with him.
The day they'd kissed.

She wasn't in his house. She was in her own home.

He gritted his teeth.

Vivian was exactly what he needed in a wife.

She had taken what could have been a scandal and
earned the praises of society. The *ton* wanted to see the
best in her because of her genuine nature.

Vivian had appeared so soon after Alexandria and,
for a moment, she'd seemed to be cut of the same cloth.

Yet, when she believed that her mother might suffer because of Vivian not fulfilling her promise to Ella
Etta, he'd unknowingly not co-operated and she'd decided she would take the consequences.

Like in the book about martyrs, Vivian had chosen
the path of sacrifice.

But his attraction to her went beyond that.

When he'd spoken with her in the darkness at his
father's estate, her presence had filled him with a
calmness—a peace he'd been unaware existed. He'd
been teased with an indication that his life could be
different. That illusion had settled in the recesses of
his mind, forming stronger and stronger until it over-
whelmed him.

He'd never imagined someone such as Vivian. She
stirred him so that he could think of nothing else.

He had once said he would savour showing her all a
woman needed to know about a man's body.

But that wasn't to be.

Could he live with the knowledge that she might fall
in love with someone else?

Stepping to his bedside, he reached to touch the miniature of his grandfather that he had brought to the town house. His hand stopped in mid-movement, resting over empty air. He scrutinised his grandfather's portrait.

The miniature had been given to his grandmother once. His grandfather had had it painted before he married, for his wife-to-be to have while he travelled. He'd wanted her to have a likeness of him to be the last thing she saw at night and the first object she viewed in the morning.

Everleigh had known about the miniature. After Everleigh's grandmother had died, his grandfather carried it and always slept with it at his bedside. He'd said it reminded him of his wife.

Everleigh had taken it from his grandfather's bedside when he died, both in respect for his grandparents' union and to keep as a reminder of his grandfather.

He stared at it. When his grandfather had had the painting done, he must have been about thirty.

Shoving the thoughts away, Everleigh prepared for bed.

As he lay down, his brain whispered the word *fool* to him.

He was alone, in his room, with a picture of his grandfather at his bedside.

Chapter Twenty-Two

Everleigh knew by the sound of the cane following along with the footsteps that his father had arrived in town.

Everleigh strode to the doorway of his drawing room. He put both palms high on the door frame.

'Had you already started out before the post arrived?' Everleigh asked, stepping aside to let his father enter the room.

'No.' His father clasped the handle of the cane in one hand and the other held a book. 'I'd been thinking about visiting, though…with or without your invitation.' He softly clouted Everleigh's shoulder with the book. 'Good to see you.'

Then he put the tome in Everleigh's hand. 'I found one of your books in my room. One you used to read a lot, but I wasn't sure if you still liked it.'

Everleigh looked at the volume. He'd suspected the novel had made its way to his father's collection, but he'd not minded enough to search it out.

'Thank you.'

His father walked closer and thumped him on the

back this time. 'It's—' His voice choked. 'But what really means a lot to me, Son, is your accepting Mrs Trimble.' He sniffed. 'Your housekeeper is finding her a room. She cried happy tears all the way here. I just kept patting her hand.'

Everleigh lowered his chin. 'Did you care a sixpence about my mother?'

'I know I didn't show it—' His father's voice broke. 'I was young. Foolish. But I did care for her. I really did. She was dazzling. Almost too stunning to be in my path. I was overpowered by the assuredness surrounding her.'

'You brought your mistress into the house so soon after Mother died.' Everleigh narrowed one eye. 'I suspected that you went to Mrs Trimble after Mother's funeral.'

His father examined the rug. 'I will only say it was very difficult for me to put your mother to rest. Your grandfather needed you and your brother at that time. I wept a long time that evening. I did not want you to see that.'

Everleigh grunted, but didn't argue with his father's perspective.

'Mrs Trimble was my first love. She wasn't in a position to marry me. There was a Mr Trimble. He'd just walked out of her life one day and no one knew if he lived or had died. Your mother became my wife. My father insisted that I marry someone suitable and I knew the family home could not remain without the funds.' He stopped speaking. 'I thought you'd forgiven me when you invited her here.'

Everleigh thought of the joy he'd heard in his father's

voice when he'd arrived. He pushed acceptance into his words. 'I have forgiven you. Now. I understand.'

He didn't feel the same forgiveness for his father's mistress, exactly, because she'd defaced the portrait, but if it made his father happy to have Mrs Trimble accepted, then he would act the part.

His father walked to the table and inspected all the frills in the room. 'It looks like a clown died in here.'

'We were to celebrate my betrothal. Mrs Rush wanted to surprise me.'

Rothwilde paused. 'Have you seen Miss Darius since you left the estate?'

'No.'

His father looked around the room. 'Would you mind if I invited her parents?' Rothwilde asked. 'Perhaps tomorrow or the day after. I could ask Darius if his wife would mind if Mrs Trimble shared tea with us. Lady Darius spoke kindly with Mrs Trimble when she visited. I think they might get on. It would mean the world to Mrs Trimble.'

'That does sound joyous,' Everleigh said. He put the book on a shelf.

Joyous.

Then he went to the small drawer where he kept the ink, and pulled out a pen, a page of paper, and put it on the table. 'If you write out the invitation, I can have it sent around. Perhaps they would be able to arrive tomorrow. I've another appointment, so I will not be able to make it.'

Rothwilde went to bed early, as he tended to do, and with a book from Everleigh's library tucked under his arm. Everleigh sat alone, twirling an empty glass in his hand.

He rose from the chair and went to the window. The darkened houses along the street showed no life.

The fire had died down and the temperature in the room was dropping.

But all he could think of was Vivian.

The kiss. The lovemaking.

He liked Vivian.

He didn't understand why she demanded love. Love was that drunken feeling that wrung out a person, then evaporated after they'd made a fool of themselves.

It was a nonsensical feeling.

That would make a man keep a miniature of himself at his bedside, as his grandfather had.

He wasn't waking up with a dislike for Vivian, he was waking with an entirely different problem.

Love.

He'd never experienced whatever he was feeling before. Never. It was consuming him from the inside out. That had to be love. It wasn't Vivian he was disliking. It was himself. For not going to her. For not begging her forgiveness for withdrawing the proposal. For not courting her. But he still didn't want to court her.

He wanted to wed her first, then court her the rest of his life.

Everleigh put down the glass.

Love. The type of feeling that would cause a man to make a fool of himself and not care who knew.

It really wasn't that late. He heard the clock chime. Twelve.

Perhaps she was still awake.

Chapter Twenty-Three

He knocked at the Darius household, ever so politely. No one answered. Then he gave it a thump.

Blast it.

Someone moved a curtain, peering into the darkness.

'It's Everleigh,' he shouted at the window pane, knowing it was unlikely the person on the other side could recognise him as he couldn't comprehend who they were. 'I'm here to see... Lord Darius.'

The curtain fell into place.

Everleigh retraced his steps to the front door and, at what he gauged to be a quarter-hour later, someone unlocked it.

A servant and Darius stood on the other side, Darius holding a lamp.

Darius shooed the servant away.

'Here for tea?' Darius said.

'Thank you for the offer.'

'We're all out.'

'In that case, I have a note from Rothwilde for you.' Everleigh held out the paper.

Darius snatched it away, crumpling the edge. 'I will

read it in the morning.' Darius shifted his slippers while he regarded Everleigh. 'I would have thought you had a servant you could trust to deliver a letter.'

'I do.' Everleigh planted his feet. 'It's late. I didn't want to disturb them.'

'Is that the only reason you're here?'

'No.'

Darius squinted. 'I still haven't got around to that breach-of-promise suit.'

'I'm more than willing to negotiate. With Vivian. I'd like to see her.'

'You'd have better luck with me.' His jaw firmed. 'Follow me. You can wait in the drawing room while I see if she is…' his footsteps stopped '…at home.'

Darius took Everleigh into the drawing room, where a few coals glowed in the fireplace.

'If she is "at home"…' he glared at Everleigh, the lamp thudding on to the tabletop '…you have a quarter of an hour. Or less. If what you wish to say can't be said quickly, then it doesn't need to be said.'

Vivian walked into the room, her hair haphazardly pinned. The dressing gown she wore covered her more than any high-necked, long-sleeved dress could. She tugged the tie close. His imagination feasted on her. He saw beyond her to the warmth of her skin. The scent of her. To her goodness.

'Can we talk about the future?' He barely heard his own words, he was so awash with the emotion of seeing her again. He moved closer, touching her upper arm.

She pushed the door shut. 'I've missed you.'

She slid her fingers up his sleeve, stopping at the base of his neck.

He placed his head in her hand, raised his shoulder, almost trapping her with his cheek. He rubbed the side of his jaw against her fingers.

When he lifted his head, his arm moved out and he pulled her into his grasp. He held her with one arm and, when her hands went to his chest, he was so close he could feel the tips of her eyelashes.

She wasn't the same wraith he'd touched the first time. This woman was bursting with life—vibrating with spirit.

He didn't know how he'd lived so long without her.

She didn't care if she never moved again as long as she stayed in Everleigh's arms and he kissed her.

The room was still, except for the bursts of impulses from inside her, wanting to be closer to him.

He pulled away. She couldn't find words for the loss of him against her and the nagging fear that he would soon leave.

He put his hand at her temple and brushed back the hair that had fallen forward.

'I could not have waited until morning. I would have expired before then.' He spoke against her hair. 'I had to see you tonight.'

She laughed. Strength flooded into her bones and surrounded her.

She pulled herself closer to him. 'Perhaps this is the secret to my good health. Your kisses. They make me feel so alive.' Then she studied him. 'Until you leave.'

'We'll travel. Together. Married or unmarried.'

'I'm not sure that is as important to me as it was.'

'*Vivian.*'

'I don't want a marriage—or a husband—without love. Husbands seem to have the most choices in life: whether to spend the night with a mistress or a bottle of brandy, or both. I don't ever want to be in that world.'

'My father was not first in my mother's life. Her initial consideration was her position in life caused by wealth and she wished to increase it. Second, her children. Third or fourth, Rothwilde.'

'I suspect there is something inside you that causes you to fear being close to someone. It's almost as if you refused to commit your heart to me, even with words that didn't matter to you. And if you don't, you will always find something else to put before me. Perhaps work or politics or warfare. I don't know that I want to always be behind something else in my husband's life. It is better to be unmarried.'

'I thought I had fallen in love before and it had always brought me closer to someone that schemed or wanted to use me for position in society. I'd seen that with my parents. I didn't want such a thing in my own house. I saw all women as…similar to Alexandria.'

'You see marriage as safer without love.'

'I don't want a wife who is merely reflecting my smiles back at me.'

'Smiles, Everleigh? When do you *smile*? Not often, I assure you.'

'When I am with you. That is when I smile.'

'It doesn't show on your face.'

'I will have to change that, then. When I see you and I smile, I want you to know that I'm not just smiling on the outside, I'm saying I love you on the inside.' Everleigh pulled her against him.

A knock slammed on to the door, then her father walked in.

Vivian stepped out of Everleigh's arms.

'Do I need to continue with the breach of promise?' Her father's irritation flared.

'Father. You know it is not any such thing. We had no contract. No announcement of any kind. I do not even think I ever agreed to marry him.'

He glanced at Everleigh. 'Tell Rothwilde that my wife and I accept his gracious invitation.'

Then he mumbled to Vivian, 'See, that is how easily it is done. You simply accept.'

Everleigh reached out, pulling Vivian into the shelter at his side. 'She is perfectly within her rights to refuse marriage.'

Lord Darius bit his bottom lip. 'Hope I wasn't interrupting anything.' He smirked before glaring at Everleigh. 'Except your departure. I wish you could stay longer, but it's getting ever later and I have an appointment with your father tomorrow. Want to be at my best. It's not every day I get invited by an *earl*.' He speared a glance at Vivian. 'Not that it wouldn't be pleasant to have one in the family.'

'You would never force me to wed if I didn't wish to,' Vivian said. 'I know it.'

'That's true. But I don't plan to stay up any later for you either.' He strode to the lamp and grabbed it.

He held the door open and waved the lamp to indicate the hallway. 'Off to bed, Vivian. And off to wherever, Everleigh. I don't care. Just go.'

Everleigh took Vivian's fingertips and gave them a squeeze before leaving.

Then he walked by Darius. 'You're going about this entirely the wrong way if you want me for a son-in-law.'

'Don't I know it,' Darius said. 'I'll see you to the door.'

Chapter Twenty-Four

Everleigh watched as Vivian's father's carriage arrived and Lord and Lady Darius descended. No Vivian.

He had his own carriage waiting. He ran down the back stairway and signalled to his coachman, instructing him to stop at the musical instructor's home.

After that, they continued to Vivian's.

Everleigh heard the driver call out 'All clear' as the carriage stopped. Everleigh pushed open the door and jumped to the ground.

The second man stepped from the carriage and Everleigh focused his attention on the front door of the town house. He didn't need a fortune teller to alert him to Vivian's being inside. Mavis peered out of the window.

She beamed and waved him forward. Mrs Rush was quite good with delivering notes.

Lowering his head, he strode to the door. The butler opened it, but blinked as if he simply could not see Everleigh or the visitor with him.

He dashed up the stairs, the man following.

At the top, Mavis stood by a doorway.

He asked, with just a tilt of his head, if Vivian was inside.

A nod and he knew.

Everleigh walked into the room, the violinist behind him. The man lifted his bow. Then the violinist spoke to Vivian. 'I have been hired to travel with Lord Everleigh to Scotland, France and Rome.'

'May I have this dance, Miss Darius?' Everleigh asked, bowing. 'I cannot live without a waltz with you.'

Vivian let out a deep breath as Everleigh took her hand and swirled her around the room.

The waltz continued, a whirling delight of perfection she'd not believed possible. When the clock chimed, he stopped. Then the violinist bowed to her and left.

'I said I had no tender feelings—but I do have some very strong feelings for you. One might say unspeakably strong,' Everleigh paused. 'I breathe for you. My life has no light in it, except for the brightness I see in you.'

He kissed the palm of her hand. 'I do love you, Vivian. More than anything. More than I could have believed possible for any human to feel for another. With all the love in my heart, I ask, will you marry me?'

He waited. Waited for her to say she'd changed her mind. That she wasn't sure. That she'd meant something else entirely different. 'If you say no, we can still take those trips. Mavis will have you packed and we can dash off before your parents arrive home. Just leave them a note.'

Instead she snuggled into him and put her arms around him, pulling herself closer.

The daggers in his stomach melted away.

'I don't know if you truly believe it,' she said.

He breathed again. 'I do love you.'

Love was not the helplessness he'd expected. He had more strength than he'd believed possible, but only with Vivian in his life.

He pulled her into a tight hug, his hands clasped around her. 'I love you, Vivian. How could I not?'

'I will marry you.'

'It would be wise to have our betrothal documented.' He spoke, tossing the words out as if they meant nothing. 'With a special licence.'

'That would be acceptable. I would not ask you to withdraw a special licence if you obtained it.'

'If we hurry, I have an appointment with the bishop. We can get the special licence and be married today, go to my town house, surprise both our parents and eat the wedding meal that your parents don't realise they're sharing with my father and Mrs Trimble, then we can set out for Bath.' He paused. 'I'd rather leave the violinist behind…if you don't mind.'

He moved closer and leaned to kiss the edge of her mouth. His hand travelled from her shoulder, up her neck, and then he moved back enough so his finger could trace the kiss he'd left behind.

She locked her knees, and forced her body not to move.

His voice vibrated inside her. 'When my mother died and I was upset because she'd never again get to spend her days shopping, Ella Etta said my mother would look down from the stars some day and give me a gift she'd selected just for me.'

He grasped her shoulders again, gently, and leaned forward, their foreheads touching. 'You're my gift.'

* * *

'Well, the marriage went smoothly,' he said, as the carriage took them past the same spot where Alexandria had stood.

'Oh, goodness,' Vivian mumbled as the driver braked and she caught her balance. 'Not again.'

Everleigh surveyed the road outside their window, searching for the reason the vehicle had reduced speed.

Ella Etta's donkey cart rolled at a crawl in front of them.

Everleigh thumped the roof and his driver pulled alongside her, stopping.

He opened the door and leaned out. 'What are you up to?' he asked.

'Same as always. Mischief.' She saw Vivian's face in the window. 'And you?'

'Marriage.'

She waved him on. 'Only surprise to me is that you waited so long.' She sniffed. 'Now, get on your way, you're causing the dust to get in my eyes.' She rubbed the edge of her sleeve over her face.

'I expect you to send a wedding meal to my camp.' She clucked to her donkey and the cart rolled away.

Everleigh shut the door and settled beside Vivian.

The driver spoke to the horses, and they increased speed.

Everleigh turned to Vivian. 'Second thoughts?'

'Why?' she asked. 'Are you having any?'

'It would be late for that.'

She brushed at her skirt.

Then he reached out, took her hand and kissed the back of each knuckle. 'One kiss for your second thoughts, your third, fourth and fifth.'

She held up her other hand. 'I'm not having second thoughts about the marriage. But I can pretend to.'

He laughed before touching his lips four times to her.

The carriage stopped in front of his town house. The driver called out, 'All clear.'

The door opened. Everleigh stepped out, then helped her down the steps and through his front door.

Mrs Rush, Mavis and the butler waited inside and all were beaming. They reassured her they were available to help in any way she needed, then faded into the background as he took her upstairs, showing her the rooms, but saving until last where he'd first kissed her. Then he kissed her again.

When Vivian walked into the dining room Rothwilde was sat at the side, joined by Mrs Trimble and Lord and Lady Darius.

'We're having a late wedding breakfast,' Mrs Rush called out.

Mavis followed along behind her, sniffling happy tears. 'I had to tell them. I couldn't help it. I'm so thrilled for us, Vivian.' Mavis dabbed her handkerchief to her eyes. 'Your mother has asked me to stay on as a governess to the new baby and you're married to a future earl.'

Rothwilde glared at her.

'Hopefully Everleigh will not inherit soon,' she stammered, clenching the handkerchief as she realised what she'd said. 'And doesn't that soup smell delicious?'

Vivian saw the abundance of food on the table. Mrs Rush had a welcoming feast prepared. Soup, venison or beef—she wasn't sure which—fish, fowl and vegetables.

Rothwilde held out one hand to Vivian and clasped hers, before reaching back to his cane.

'At my age, a man begins to think of grandchildren more and more. I had lost hope Everleigh would marry. I was putting all my dreams of a grandchild on my second son. You should be able to meet Daniel soon. He's on his way here now.'

He glanced down at his hands crossed over the top of his cane, then looked at Everleigh. 'Once I knew for certain that you'd forgiven...the portrait, I knew that the two of you would be brothers again.'

'Do you mind if we put off the trip to Bath until he gets here?' Everleigh asked Vivian. 'I'd like you to meet him.'

'Of course not,' Vivian said and they joined the family for the celebration meal.

After eating, Vivian and Everleigh lingered behind in the dining room, standing at the sideboard, sipping wine and planning their honeymoon trip, while the others moved to the drawing room.

Boot heels slammed up the stairs and Everleigh stepped back from Vivian, giving her the barest clasp at her back. 'You are about to meet my brother.'

Daniel stepped into the room, surveyed it, then his gaze stopped on Vivian. 'You must be responsible for the fripperies. And the smell of plum pudding. I came home at the right time.' He drew in a large breath. 'I'm hungry.'

He gave his brother a bow. 'Father did write me... that you...had forgiven Mrs Trimble. I just saw her in the hallway.'

'He couldn't have written to you that I'd married,

though. Let me introduce my bride, Vivian,' Everleigh said, unable to contain his happiness.

Daniel gave her a bow before turning back to his brother. 'One thing you need to know…er…just in case you might want me to leave. It wasn't the housekeeper who scratched out the eyes on Mother's portrait. I did. I was so angry that you had inherited everything, even Mother's eye colour.'

Everleigh started forward. He'd never suspected his brother. Seeing Daniel, he didn't blame him for the jealousy. He only wished he'd realised earlier how angry Daniel had been to try to destroy the portrait. 'I suppose I owe Mrs Trimble an apology.'

'I do,' Daniel said.

'Well, she'll get two, then.'

'I thought the paint would rub off. I didn't realise it would ruin the only portrait we had of Mother. I had trouble living with that,' Daniel said.

'Vivian knows another portrait painter who can copy the original and she believes he can do a much better job in making it right. We'll have the portrait back.'

'Do you mind if I see if I can find Father now?' Daniel asked. 'I've missed him as well, and I want to tell him how well things have progressed.'

Then he stopped and slapped Everleigh on the back. 'Thank you for all the funds. I've been investing in a ship and it made it into the docks. We did well.'

'What funds?'

'Father's gambling debts.' He grinned. 'He was gambling with me. The ship paid off.'

Everleigh waved him away, smiling. He could hardly believe Daniel had arrived, all animosity gone, and they were a family again.

Then he enclosed Vivian in his arms.

She burrowed against him. 'When I heard your name for the first time at the ceremony, I didn't know who I'd married.'

'You married me, Evan Aarons, styled as Viscount Everleigh, and I knew exactly who I was marrying. The one I will love for ever.'

Then he paused. 'Before the new portrait of my mother is started I must have two miniatures done. One of you and one of me. I want us always to be able to look into each other's eyes.'

'We always will. Even without the paintings.'

* * * * *

*If you enjoyed this book, why not
check out these other great reads by
Liz Tyner*

The Wallflower Duchess
Redeeming the Roguish Rake
Saying I Do to the Scoundrel
To Win a Wallflower
It's Marriage or Ruin